Edward Toman

was born and brought up in [...] school in Armagh and universi[...] founders of the civil rights mo[...] ....vince in the late sixties when he was a lecturer in further education in Belfast.

After two years in Zambia in the early seventies he moved to London to organize Open University and distance learning courses in Holloway Prison. He studied for a Master's degree at Oxford and spent a year in America teaching on the Fulbright scheme.

In 1994 Edward Toman received an Arts Council of Great Britain annual writer's award.

He lives in London with his wife and two children.

EDWARD TOMAN

Dancing in Limbo

Flamingo
An Imprint of HarperCollins*Publishers*

flamingo

ORIGINAL

The term 'Original' signifies publication direct into paperback with no preceding British hardback edition. The Flamingo Original series publishes fine writing at an affordable price at the point of first publication.

Flamingo
An Imprint of HarperCollins*Publishers*
77–85 Fulham Palace Road,
Hammersmith, London W6 8JB

First published in Great Britain by Flamingo 1995
9 8 7 6 5 4 3 2 1

Copyright © Edward Toman 1995

The Author asserts the moral right to
be identified as the author of this work

Author photograph by Annie Morrad

A catalogue record for this book is
available from the British Library

ISBN 0 00 647984 7

Photoset in Linotron Galliard by
Rowland Phototypesetting Ltd
Bury St Edmunds, Suffolk

Printed in Great Britain by
HarperCollinsManufacturing Glasgow

For Geraldine

tá an Teamhair 'na féar
is féach an Traoi mar tá

Tara is under grass
and what now remains of Troy?

Prologue

At the very moment that the Popemobile passed closest to him, Father Frank realized he was speaking in tongues. Though he had never been much of a one for the languages, it crossed his mind that he might be speaking in fluent Irish at last, and that fifteen years' effort by the priests and the Christian Brothers might be paying a dividend. But this was something different from the plodding '*tá mé go maith*' of his schooldays. Different too from the cursory acquaintance with Latin and Greek that his years in Derry and Maynooth had given him. There on the grass of the Phoenix Park the talk just flowed from him in great fluent gushes.

His first reaction was embarrassment. He looked round surreptitiously, but the great tumult that had gathered for the occasion had more to do than pay attention to one loquacious curate. Everyone was as bad as himself, gibbering away, each in his own tongue, their voices drowned out by the roaring and chanting and singing and praying that echoed from the four corners of the vast park. 'So far so good,' he thought to himself. He was beginning to enjoy his new talent when another strange sensation came creeping through his body. Frank knew he was sober, or at least as sober as was decent for Ireland's favourite priest to be on this great day. But an unaccustomed detachment was stealing over his limbs, a feeling of lightness creeping up from his feet to his head. He felt that he was leaving his body and floating above it. Then his limbs began to move involuntarily, and seconds later he found himself floating up into the air above the cheering crowds.

He wasn't the only one. The air was suddenly thick with flying bodies, cartwheeling, dive-bombing, looping the loop. In the compound directly below him, from which these aerobatics had originated, the ground was now alive with writhing and twitching limbs. Some foamed at the mouth, some declaimed loudly in incomprehensible tongues, others lay intertwined in lewd, unseemly rites. He didn't need telling that Canon Tom would be in the middle of them.

Experimentally flicking his left foot as a rudder, Frank found he could flip himself over like a helium balloon. The multitude filled the entire park and stretched as far as the eye could see, the whole of Ireland gathered in the one spot, cheering with one voice. His Holiness was now moving on to the next corral of flag-waving faithful, yet Frank could follow his progress with the same apparent ease as Chief Inspector O'Malley in the hired helicopter overhead. 'This beats Bannagher!' he told himself, going higher. Beyond the park the whole of Dublin city opened itself to him, lying strangely peaceful and deserted in the pale sunshine.

But as he looked north to the blue haze of the far off Ulster hills he was aware of something moving in the distance and he heard, above the cacophony below him, the faint jangling of discordant bells. Fighting back a sudden rush of terror and vertigo he fell like a stone to the ground.

One spectator alone stood aloof. Sister Maria Goretta was making a poor fist of hiding her disgust at the turn events were taking. Cynically she let her gaze wander over the hysterical crowd, now embarked on a bacchanalia of groping, French kissing, and wild, ecstatic, abandoned dancing. She noted the Canon in their midst. She noted too the wrinkled features of the native speaker, sweeled in plaid rugs and propped up in his bathchair, with Snotters MacBride dancing attendance on him. She lit a Sweet Afton and turned away from their obscenities. She would let events take their course, there would be no need for direct intervention this time, she decided reluctantly. The time to break heads would come later.

Then her eye lighted on the recumbent figure of Father F. X. Feely (Mister TV himself!) lying concussed on the ground with Noreen Moran kneeling solicitously over him, and her features hardened. Involuntarily her hand slipped under her habit and felt the reassuring contour of the semi-automatic pistol lying snugly against her thigh.

❖

A thin trickle of blood dripped from Frank's temple on to the crumpled grass. He was only half aware of the crowd milling around him, only dimly aware of Noreen bending over him. A hundred vignettes of his past flashed before him. He thought he was in service again, forced to skivvy in Schnozzle's kitchen for the scraps from the Archbishop's table. Then he was suddenly a schoolboy again, wincing from the blow to the head that Brother Murphy had dealt him and that had left him speechless for a decade. Another memory flickered into his mind's eye. He saw himself and Noreen kneeling in supplication at the feet of the Dancing Madonna. In his delirium he tried to reach out to her. She had cured him once, made him whole again, back in the days before she had disappeared. But as her features grew more distinct he began to tremble. He saw in her eyes, not pity, not compassion, but cold, remorseless anger.

As he groped into semi-consciousness, Frank became aware of the throbbing in his head, and with it he had new terrors to confront. Memories of the past which he had hoped were suppressed for ever began to crowd inexorably into his jangled brain, each more awful than the last. A catalogue of atrocities and betrayals rose before his eyes. Men and women slaughtered as casually as beasts in a shambles. Hypocrisy dressed up as piety, and brutality masquerading as love. Echoing and re-echoing through the recesses of his mind were the words of the poem his father was for ever quoting, shouting it to the empty hedgerows above the noise of the tractor. Some rough beast, its hour come at last, was slouching towards Bethlehem to be born.

His head began to clear. He stumbled to his knees and vomited, spewing out on the grass the gorge rising from deep within him. Noreen cradled his head between her breasts, staunching with her mantilla the flow of blood from his wound. But his mind was clearer now. He staggered to his feet and seized her by the hand.

11

He had detected a new restlessness sweeping through the crowd. Something unexpected, unplanned was happening. The massed choirs on the Tannoy faltered in their rendition of 'Deep in the Panting Heart of Rome'. The multitude was beginning to move with a new urgency, pushing towards the gates of the park where the top of the papal transporter was still visible, moving hesitantly in the direction of the exit. Frank heard the crack of wood splintering as the crush barriers that corralled them began to collapse. There were wild men with fanatical eyes running through the throng now, urging them onward with garbled snatches of news, screaming the name McCoy. The helicopter was low overhead, and above the clatter of the rotors he could hear O'Malley on the megaphone frantically ordering the Guards to shoot.

And then he heard again that most chilling of sounds from his childhood in the North. The discordant jangle of McCoy's bells. And he knew that what he had seen approaching over the Black Pig's Dyke had not been a mirage.

He and Noreen were clutching each other tightly now, struggling against the tide of the crowd, hunched against their thrust, trying desperately to stay upright against the stampede. He opened his mouth to shout to them, to warn them. Something malevolent had come among them, something more powerful and more ancient than their petty sectarianism or their puny religiosity. There had been a time when they might have listened. But Frank Feely had wasted those years, years when he had them in the palm of his hand, wasted his opportunity with jazz bands and futile chatter. Now he wanted to shout a warning to the great mass of humanity rolling past him. But no words would come to him. Again and again he tried to warn them. But his voice had deserted him as surely as it had in his youth, condemning him for ever to a silent scream of rage and impotence and despair.

ONE

One

Sammy Magee's sausages were never going to win any prizes from the true epicurean, but though fatty and flaccid they had one remarkable feature that brought him customers from as far away as Tandragee. They were faintly marbled throughout their full length – red, white and blue – the colours running through them like a stick of Portrush rock. 'I'll take a pound of thon Protestant sauce-dogs!' the farmers would demand in their mountain accents, sidling into the butcher's after conducting their bits of business in the town of a Saturday. And though the gristle content was enough to make even the farmyard dogs think twice before tackling them, Magee's sausages sold like hot cakes, especially coming up to the Twelfth of July.

The farmers sidling into the shop had another motive too, one they didn't dare remark on to the butcher's face. They wanted to get an eyeful of Lily. For it was a curious fact that, like the chameleon, Lily Magee never seemed to be the same colour two weeks running.

It was with the arrival of the Marching Season proper, when for a brief few weeks Portadown bedecked itself in patriotic livery, that the mystery was solved. Magee was spotted at midnight, trundling a handcart of bunting into the back of the Orange Hall and the cat was out of the bag. By morning the whole town knew that the butcher had a secret sideline supplying loyalist flags and favours, and the coloured sausages and the coloured wife were revealed as the side-effects of this cottage industry. Week in and week out, early on the Sabbath morning, he and Lily had been scouring the dustbins at the back of the linen mill for discarded remnants. They dragged these home through the silent streets and stored them in the shed behind the house.

During the weeks ahead Lily cut and snipped while Magee himself trundled away on the old Singer, seaming each triangle at the base to accommodate the twine on which he would later thread them. Once a month, on a Saturday night, he shut up the shop early. The rest of the town, by way of entertainment, would be out on the streets, busily preaching the word of the Risen Lord and prophesying His imminent return. But Magee and Lily would forgo the delights of the soap box, for there was work to do. He would hose out the big copper he used for boiling up the black puddings, drag it out into the backyard and begin to brew up the colour of the month. He had three large barrels of industrial strength dye, purloined from a factory in Antrim, which he kept in the coal-hole, the smell of them acting as deterrent enough to anyone who might be tempted to sample them in alcoholic desperation. He collected up the month's output and bundled it into the pot while Lily stirred with a stick.

As she walked to the Meeting House next morning, Lily's complexion reflected the labours of the night before. The dye permeated her hair, it clung to her clothes, it lurked in the cuticles of her fingernails, resistant to all exertions with the Sunlight soap. If it were a red month then Lily would glow with the deep red of the blood of martyrs spilt in the defence of her heritage, the red of the Red Hand of Ulster itself. 'Little Plum, your Redskin Chum,' a corner boy might quip as herself and the butcher passed on the street, but sotto voce, for you didn't get on the wrong side of Magee. Or a month later, seeing her approaching from the mill, her natural pallor bleached to a spectral white, the same corner boy might snigger about the ghost of Christmas Past. Or whistle 'Blue Moon', what he knew of it, if the colour of the month were blue. During the cheerless winter Lily's changing appearance provided a measure of much needed entertainment round the town.

But in the new year the people of Portadown, to their consternation, began to discern the colours of the republican tricolour running faintly through their breakfast offal, and noticed that Lily was now exuding a faint but unmistakable glow of papist infamy. It was clear that once more things were getting out of hand.

Though the Protestant, with his complex calendar of memorials

16

and marches, is a great consumer of red, white and blue bunting, Magee had realized long ago that he would never become Portadown's first millionaire by trading with his own side of the house alone. His kinsmen, for one thing, retrieved their bunting from the lampposts when the patriotic moment had passed, drying it and storing it carefully for another day. Furthermore, the Loyalist marching season lasted only for the summer months. They commemorated the Somme in the spring, and remembered 1690 in July. But after they had marched round Derry's walls and honoured the Apprentice Boys in August, they were ready to put away their banners and their trombones for another year. Magee faced six long fallow months till the lambeg drums summoned them to arms once more.

But with the Fenians it was a year-round business, and Magee wasn't long in spotting the market gap. He knew enough about the habits of the Romanists; if it wasn't the Ancient Order of Hibernians who were celebrating, it would be some Holy Day or other. What was more, they alternated their need for the green, white and gold of the Republic with the yellow and white of the Papal States. And what he'd seen round their side of the Shambles appalled him. Tattered and torn green and yellow banners, badly made from old vests and knickers, crudely stitched, the colours running in the rain. Home-made efforts, of uncertain size and design. The papists, it went without saying, showed nothing of the parsimony or foresight of the Protestant when it came to retrieving their bunting after the bands had passed, leaving theirs to rot in the rain till it fell down. If Magee could expand his enterprise and start selling bunting to the Fenians he knew he could be on to a winner. But it was a mad thought and he knew it! To turn out the green and yellow of papist treachery in the heart of loyalist Portadown! Through his butchering business he had occasional contact with the Fenians, bartering with them through the rituals of fair days, necessary if distasteful intercourse. He knew how untrustworthy they could be in financial matters. But that wasn't the only snag. Before he could even consider such a scheme he would have to obtain the blessing of the big boys. The 'GPs' as they liked to call themselves! Had he the nerve to approach them, offering them a percentage, come rain or shine, in exchange for their approval? Or was he mad altogether, getting himself mixed up with the men in black glasses? He was still wavering when McCoy's message arrived, summoning him to the Shambles.

❖

Every since the débâcle with the dancing statue, he had been giving the Reverend Oliver Cromwell McCoy a wide berth. McCoy might be a true blue bigot, but he had an uncanny knack of ballsing up everything he touched. And since his daughter's disappearance, Magee knew he had forsaken the preaching and was reduced to scrounging drink round the back of the Boyne bar. But when the boy appeared from Armagh with the news that Brother Murphy was in urgent need of papal flags, that he was buying only the best, and that (unheard of for a Christian Brother) he was paying cash on the nail, Magee swallowed his principles and set off for the town to check things out for himself.

'Where's that girl of yours now that we need her?' he demanded. 'I could have done with an extra pair of hands.'

'She'll be back in her own good time, never fret,' her father said. 'When she tires of the bright lights of London.'

Chastity McCoy, the preacher's daughter, had walked out on him on Christmas Eve, disappearing from the Martyrs Memorial Chapel like a thief in the night without as much as goodbye. Her desertion of him hadn't come as a total surprise to her father, for the pair of them had been fighting like cat and dog for the best part of a year. But she had packed her bags this time, taking with her what scanty possessions she could call her own, and it was beginning to look as if she had gone for good.

'London!' Magee spat on the hearth at the mention of the place. 'You should have married her off the day she turned fourteen. Many's a farmer would have been glad of her, and there'd have been less lip out of the same lady.'

'I'm only relieved she's safe,' McCoy said. Since she had flown the nest he had discovered a soft spot for Chastity. He regretted now that he hadn't treated her better. 'There was a card from her this morning. Old King George, no less.' He reached up to the mantelpiece and took down a tattered postcard. King George the Sixth, looking ill at ease, stared back at them, framed by his family and the household dogs. 'I swear I was having nightmares she'd been kidnapped and I'd have to fork out good money to rescue her.' He turned the card over and read once more the message on the back. 'She sends you her best at any rate,' he said. '"Greetings from the heart of the Empire. Give Mister Magee my regards." There you are! Mentioned in dispatches.'

'No doubt the same lady will be back when it suits her, eating you out of house and home.'

'And she'll be welcome. There is more joy in heaven over one who is lost . . .'

Magee cut him short. 'About these flags . . . ?'

'I heard it from that scut from Tyrone.'

'The bucko who's never out of the Patriot's across the way?'

'As tight as an arsehole, like the whole shooting gallery of them. But it appears half Tyrone has been cutting up sheets this past month and they still can't meet the demand.'

'The Fenians must have something special planned,' Magee said with suspicion.

'What concern is that of you or me, Mister Magee! Let the Romanists damn themselves in whatever way they want. You, Sir, are an entrepreneur.'

Magee pondered this news for a while. Then he came to a decision. If the Fenians needed flags badly enough to be paying for them he was their man!

'I'll need all the rags I can get my hands on,' he demanded.

'If you think I'm going round the doors collecting hand-me-down drawers . . .'

'Send McGuffin! What else is he good for?'

'Fuck all else and that's the truth,' McCoy said. 'But I can hardly have him put down after all the trouble he's put me to.'

Outside the window, cowering on his mattress under the ice-cream van, they could make out the shadow of the renegade. Patrick Pearse McGuffin cut a pathetic figure, a Belfast man, a native of the Falls Road, who had turned his back on his faith and his people, to embrace the dubious pleasures preached by McCoy. It had been the action of a desperate man to desert Father

19

Alphonsus on his pilgrimage to Lough Derg, an action that had left him friendless in a bitter land. It had been the action of an even more desperate man to convert to McCoy. If the truth were to be told, his conversion to the loyalist lifestyle had not been totally voluntary. But beggars can't be choosers and as a runaway his hopes for the good life were sorely curtailed. When he had taken the soup Patrick Pearse had dropped the Republican forenames in an effort to integrate into his new surroundings, but changing your name was an old McGuffin trick that fooled no one; and since the day he had embraced the Lord as his personal saviour, McGuffin had been lucky to eke out a precarious existence round the Martyrs Memorial.

'Did the girl leave on account of him? Was he bothering her?' Magee demanded.

McCoy shook his head. 'Chastity was always headstrong. Like her mother.'

'I'll wring that wee bitch's neck when I see her next!' Magee declared. 'Just when she could have been some use.' There was something about Chastity's disappearance that made him uneasy. He lifted the postcard down from the mantelpiece and scrutinized it again. The postmark was smudged. It could have been from anywhere. The lassie was giving nothing away either. No address, no details. Just a message in her neatest handwriting telling them not to worry. Inside Magee's gut an icy finger of doubt began to stir.

He outlined his scheme to meet the Fenians' demands to Lily that night as she was scrubbing herself down at the scullery sink.

'Do you want your head examined?' she asked.

'There's no harm in trying,' he insisted.

'And get the pair of us lynched! It's bad enough you have me walking round like a Union Jack! How in the name of God can I put my face out that door and me green, white and yellow!'

'If anybody's bothering you, you refer them to me.'

'They're already complaining about the black pudding.'

'I'll get it cleared at the highest level. I'll take a wee run over to the doctor's next week.'

'You'll do no such thing! Do you want us killed in our beds?'

'You're afraid of your own shadow! What harm is there in putting it to them as a business proposition!'

'Those are the same boys who'd drop you in the shite if anything goes wrong. Take my advice and stay well away from that crowd. I don't see your buddy McCoy getting too closely involved.'

'McCoy would only balls it up. Besides what use is he with the daughter gone?'

'I never liked that wee bitch,' Lily said with sudden vehemence. 'She had her mother's snotty looks. Too good for the Shambles. He's well rid of her.'

'She's run off before,' Magee said uneasily, 'but never for as long as this.'

'If the pair of you had taken my advice you'd have put her out to service years ago,' she grumbled. 'They were offering a fair price on the Antrim plateau for girls willing to work. Not that the bold Chastity was ever any use except for giving cheek and eating him out of house and home.'

'The same lady will be back, mark my words. To embarrass the lot of us unless I'm very wrong.'

'If McCoy had wanted a woman that bad,' she said, remembering the Señora, 'why couldn't he have stuck to his own sort instead of running after darkies? What was wrong with a decent Ulster Protestant?' She turned her rump towards Magee by way of invitation. Lily's was a solid arse, an arse bred of generations of Protestants, now faintly stained in variegated patriotic hues. It was an arse as solid, reliable and unexciting as the plains of Antrim or the farming land of North Armagh. Magee closed his eyes and conjured up a memory of the Mexican, her sultry looks, her voluptuous body, her dark hair cascading in wanton profusion. Señora McCoy was dead and buried a decade ago, but an old, guilty lust began to stir somewhere deep in him. He pulled Lily roughly towards him and began to fumble inexpertly at the strings of her pinny.

❖

Round Armagh there were other omens that springtime, foretelling imminent changes. The uneasy equilibrium of the town was about to tilt again. The tinkers with their gift of second sight were the first to grow suspicious. In old Cardinal Mac's day tinkers would be for ever round the back door of the Palace of Ara Coeli, squatting stoically in the lee of the limestone wall, knowing there'd be either a handout or a bollocking before the end of the day, for you took the old man as you found him. And even after Big Mac had taken to his bed, which he did in the last years, they could rely on Major-domo MacBride to see them right. But all that had suddenly changed. Those who trekked up the hill now from the Shambles to Ara Coeli, found Schnozzle Durante O'Shea in residence and every door and window bolted against them. The place was sealed as tight as a drum. Tighter than the Sistine Chapel during a contested consistory. Every window shuttered, every door fastened. Not a sign of Major-domo Mac-Bride nor the staff of skivvies who worked under him.

And strangest of all, not a sighting of Schnozzle himself since Christmas. Curious and mysterious behaviour for a party who had been, until his recent elevation to the Primacy, so keen to keep poking his nose in the public's business.

The tinkers cursed the new man on the hill when they returned to the Shambles, cursed him and his new ways more openly than any local would have dared, for tinkers are a law unto themselves, beyond even the reaches of the Sisters. There was a notice on the saloon door expressly barring travellers from the Patriot Arms, but Eugene served them through the window, letting them squabble and spit in the entry till their money was through. Tinkers were the prime source of information in the countryside; there was little they didn't know. He listened to their complaints and forebodings without a word. And when they had gone he sent next door for Peadar the vegetable man, ordered him to close up the stall forthwith, to proceed to the cathedral on the hill above, to recce the territory and to report on what was going on.

'The whole place is locked and barred,' Peadar told the company when he returned, pale and terrified that evening. 'There's definitely something up! No one allowed in or out, Schnozzle's orders.'

'Holy God! That sounds ominous.'

'You'd think he'd be out and about, making a name for himself, instead of closeted away,' the Tyrone man ventured. 'Now that you mention it, we haven't seen hilt nor hair of the major-domo.'

'Aren't I telling you, they're all confined to barracks,' Peadar said. 'The breadman is stopped at the gate. The milkman too. With the Little Sisters sniffing every bottle before they take it inside. The grounds are sealed off. The Sisters patrolling the gardens with walkie-talkies and some class of an Alsatian they've got their hands on. A fucker that would take the leg off you quick enough!' He had been forced to make an ignominious retreat in the face of the dog when he had stumbled on a posse of Sisters, their faces blackened, bivouacked near the tomb of old Cardinal Mac.

'A special retreat or something?' speculated the man from Tyrone. 'Praying for the soul of poor old Ireland? I'd have said myself it's a bit late for that.'

'I was wondering why young Frank hadn't shown his face. When he first got the job he'd be in here every morning,' Eugene said.

'The lad hasn't been home since Christmas,' the Tyrone man told him. 'He's cooped up with the rest of them. All leave cancelled till further notice. His poor mother's half out of her mind.'

'You're still interested in that quarter, I see,' said Peadar bitterly. 'Tell us, which gives you the bigger hard-on, dreaming about the widow or dreaming about her ten acres?'

'Fuck off with your dirty talk!' the Tyrone man told him. 'The farm is nothing but a liability.'

'The young pup left his bicycle in the passage. I'm never done tripping over it.'

'They're saying you can see strange lights playing round the tomb of Cardinal Mac at night. Great devotion is getting up already, and him hardly cold in the grave.'

'And now I hear there's a big order out for papal flags. Where's Snotters MacBride now that we need him to give us the lowdown?'

23

'Someone somewhere has a treat in store for us,' said Eugene dubiously, catching perfectly the mood of the occasion.

Mister MacBride, they all acknowledged, was a martyr to the lumbago. And though it was somewhat infra dig for a man in his position to be found drinking on the Shambles, hardly a night would pass that Snotters didn't slip down to the Patriot's for a medicinal rum and black. Though he wore the Pioneer Pin proudly, he would allow Eugene to urge a second or a third glass on him to ease the ache in his joints, and with his tongue thus loosened he could be pressed discreetly for details of the comings and goings on the hill.

'It's not like Snotters to desert us in our hour of need,' the Tyrone man said again. 'It must be a three line whip. If you ask me it's the thin end of the wedge. If somebody doesn't get a grip, the head-the-balls from Fermanagh will be up to their tricks again.' And at the mention of Fermanagh the bar fell silent. With the coming of the long nights they knew it could only be a matter of weeks before the Derrygonnelly Donatists started to feel the Spirit moving among them again. And without the Palace for protection, who could say how far things might deteriorate this time?

The GPs' surgery was a small room at the back of the lounge that Billy kept reserved for any passing member of the profession who might drop in to entertain colleagues and to discuss patients and their upcoming treatment. Though a hard man in anyone's books, even Billy felt uneasy till his guests had gone silently about their business. These were men you didn't mess with. Men you didn't question, men you didn't contradict. They arrived unexpectedly by taxi, flanked by their minders and personal assistants, looking relaxed and exuding bonhomie, but behind the dark glasses their eyes were cold. When there was company in the back room an unnatural quietness fell on the bar. There was no singing, no raucous ribaldry. A careless word could give offence. Billy's regulars kept their noses in their pints and their eyes to themselves; only the very drunk or the very foolhardy ever staggered in from the saloon to interrupt their conferences or regale them with unsolicited camaraderie. For the man who can pay a house call is one of a very special breed.

To give Billy his due, though he had done his share in the Loyalist cause, he had never made a house call. He lacked the bedside manner. But he recognized and admired the talent in others. The true GP is a professional, a member of a unique brotherhood, who can officiate at death and take it in his stride. Billy could picture how they went about their business. The playful chiming of the bells in the hall, tinkling the theme from *Z Cars*, announces to the excited children that there is a visitor at the front door. Soft voices, solicitously inquiring of the youngsters if Daddy by any chance is in? But Daddy will be in; the GP will have checked in advance. Into the hall and through to the kitchen, as casual and natural as a member of the family. Daddy is behind the table, eating his tea and watching the box. The GP, unruffled, opens his bag and delicately removes the tools of his trade. Daddy's brains splatter the chattering television and congeal on the fry, while the baby gurgles vacantly at the stranger and the children stand helpless and embarrassed at the foot of the stairs. The GP is in no hurry out, closing the door behind him quietly. There is no need for conversation. It is too late for speeches, for recriminations, for anger, for abuse. Only the new widow, running flushed to the banisters above will interrupt the banal normality of the scene with her sudden screaming.

The Boyne Lounge, already subdued by the presence of company in the surgery, fell silent when Magee entered. He wasn't a regular and like all Portadown men he was rarely welcome on licensed premises. But Magee needed no whiskey to fortify himself. He indicated to Billy that his business was in the back room. Billy slipped away and returned a moment later to inform him that they would see him now.

McCoy was scrutinizing the latest postcard from Chastity when Magee arrived next morning to tell him that they were in business. The boys in the dark glasses had given their grudging blessing to his interdenominational scheme. They had spelled out the exact percentage of his profits they would be expecting, and outlined to him the penalties that nonpayment would incur. He didn't need their reminder that any cock-ups, especially in a venture involving the papists, would not be appreciated. 'Put that away and get off your arse!' he ordered McCoy. 'It's all systems go! Lily'll need all the rags you can get your hands on.'

'Would you look at the weather they're enjoying in London,' McCoy said, ignoring his impatience. 'Couldn't we do with a bit of it here once in a while.' He held out for Magee's perusal the sepia portrait of the dowager Queen Mary at her most disapproving.

But Chastity McCoy was nowhere near Buckingham Palace. Unknown to McCoy and Magee on the one side of the Shambles, and to Eugene and the Patriot on the other (and certainly unsuspected by the boys in Billy's back room), unknown in fact to everyone but Archbishop Schnozzle O'Shea, Chastity was at that precise moment no more than a stone's throw away, locked in the attic at Ara Coeli. And though she could glimpse nothing through the skylight but the gilded cross atop one of the spires, she could recognize every muffled noise from the Shambles below and was sobbing with homesickness. But the door was locked. Nor would it would have done her much good had it been open, for the door beyond that was locked, and the great front door too. And Schnozzle had the keys in his pocket, where he checked them with obsessive regularity every five minutes.

Suddenly the window frame shook and the room vibrated as the bell from the north tower began to toll the Angelus. It was a sound that could be heard all over the county, a summons to the faithful to stop what they were doing and face the church on the hill, united in prayer. Chastity had heard the Angelus bell every day of her childhood, journeying with her father in the ice-cream van to the loyalist townlands, proclaiming the Crucified Jesus. She had seen the papist farmers in the fields cross themselves when it tolled. Her father had always cursed its intrusion on his preaching, cursed the papists for their superstition and blind adherence to the error of their ways, cursed their priests for whoremongers and parasites and their pontiff as the Antichrist himself. Now for the first time she understood the ritual of its summons. She crossed herself carefully and knelt to pray before the picture of the Dancing Madonna.

When she had first presented herself at his kitchen door asking for religious instruction, Archbishop Schnozzle's immediate reaction was suspicion. He smelled a rat. A childhood round the Shambles had tutored him well in the wiles of the other side. But closer inspection revealed that the girl with the battered suitcase standing in the snow was indeed Chastity McCoy. Was it a trick or was it God's work? He felt his heart racing. It was a miracle in itself that she had got past the guards, for the Sisters of the True Faith should have picked her up at the bottom of the Cathedral steps. He opened the door cautiously, checked that the coast was clear, and invited her to step inside.

'Did your father send you?' he demanded, still looking for the catch.

'I came on my own.'

'Does he know you're here?'

'He'd kill me if he knew!'

'Did anyone follow you?'

'I saw no one.'

'Did the Sisters not challenge you?'

'They were asleep.'

'What age are you?'

'I'm fourteen.'

'Do you realize what you are doing?'

'I'm old enough to make my own decisions.'

'You know you can never go back?'

'I know that. Am I safe here?'

'You have my word on it!'

She would have his word indeed! A cast iron guarantee! For no one in Ireland had followed the story of Chastity McCoy more closely than Schnozzle. He knew every detail of her strange upbringing, a childhood steeped in the bigotry that was her father's hallmark. It had all started with the arrival of Ramirez, the apostate priest and his blasphemous circus, who travelled the roads at McCoy's bidding to shame and outrage the Catholic people. He remembered all too well her late mother, a one-time nun seduced away from the convent to join in this provocative charade. He could say with pride that he himself was the only man brave enough to confront them, to stalk them fearlessly from townland to townland, risking the wrath of Magee and his bully boys. Schnozzle foretold that it would end badly and when he heard that Ramirez had been murdered he knew he had been proved right. God was not mocked! But what was he to make of the corollary to this tale of shame? The Señora moving into the Shambles with McCoy, heavy with his child? For years it had troubled him, this enigma of the half-caste girl playing in the gutters on the Protestant side of the square. If God had a plan in all this, Schnozzle couldn't see it. He reluctantly accepted that the ways of the Almighty might not be ours. He prayed that the blood in her veins would one day prove unsuited to the cold Presbyterian ways of Armagh. And in time his patience was rewarded.

The rumours at first were will-o'-the-wisps, ephemeral whisperings, fading away to nothing when he tried to pin them down. Ireland had always been full of rumours, of visitations and apparitions and miracles, all promising deliverance from the horrors we had brought on ourselves. At first he dismissed them, but they persisted. There was something unsettling about them, something that marked them out from the ordinary run of superstition, these whispers from Donegal of a broken chapel at the end of the Yellow Meal Road, in a place they mockingly called Ballychondom. Whispers of a dancing Madonna, a mysterious icon, a statue of unrivalled potency. He began to hear of powerful cures for the sick and wonderful promises of the nation united under the leadership of the One True Church. Briefly Schnozzle dared to hope.

But the tale, so full of expectation, had ended suddenly in shame and humiliation. The rumours that reached the palace now spoke of dark and treacherous deeds. He heard how McCoy and the girl had ventured to the very end of the Yellow Meal Road and stolen the Dancing Madonna on the eve of Her Epiphany. Stolen it for an exhibit in a peepshow, to mock him and his people once more. Terror and bloodshed still ruled the land, tolerance remained as elusive as ever. Protestant and Catholic still slaughtered each other with ritual regularity.

Few now remembered, or cared to remember, the Madonna of Ballychondom. She had been consigned to the scrapheap of collective memory, along with a thousand other lost hopes and false dawns. But Schnozzle hadn't forgotten her. He still clung to a wisp of hope. For one rumour, stranger than all the others, had reached his ears. A sting in the tail so implausible that it could only be true. The Little Sisters had reported to him that on her trip to Donegal with her father the Madonna had danced for Chastity McCoy.

When the door was safely bolted he sat her down at the kitchen table and gave her the third degree for a bit, to allay any residual suspicions, but her answers measured up. What had given her confidence to cross the Shambles and turn her back on her father and his heresy? Shyly she hinted at the presence of Patrick Pearse McGuffin round the place, and Schnozzle, though his eyes never left her, offered up a pious ejaculation to the Sacred Heart for His mysterious ways. To be on the safe side, though, he'd have Immaculata give her a full gynaecological examination in a while to check if she was a virgin or not. Immaculata was a veteran among veterans of the never-ending abortion struggle; the foetus had yet to be conceived that could escape her stringent searches. Was McGuffin her boyfriend, Schnozzle asked, all smiles now? Maybe he was and maybe he wasn't was all she would concede. He pressed her further. Was she expecting? She blushed, denied it vehemently, began to cry and got up to leave. He put his hand firmly on her shoulder and let her cry; these were things he had a right to ask. If, with the help of God, she joined the Church, she would have to answer questions like these every week in the confessional.

He was on the point of questioning her about the Missing Madonna, but he bit his tongue. An inner voice counselled caution. This was something that could wait. He had gleaned enough already to know that these were deep waters. He knew that the three of them had seen Her dance and heard Her message. An unlikely trio they were too! Frank Feely, a simpleton from the hills above the town. Noreen Moran, gauche and unschooled, the

29

child of a spoiled priest forced to share her father's wretched exile. And Chastity McCoy, least likely of the threesome! A ragged half-breed from across the Shambles. He had the boy in service below stairs where he could keep an eye on him in person. Noreen was in the convent in Caherciveen out of harm's way. He had a monthly report from the Reverend Mother on her spiritual progress. And here was the third of them, landing on his doorstep without benefit of preliminaries. Subtlety and patience had never been virtues that Schnozzle admired, but for once he knew better than to go probing too deeply the will of the Almighty. All would be revealed in time. In the meantime there were a thousand practical details to attend to.

Already his mind was racing with the responsibility of the project. How much time had he got? How long would it be before McCoy sobered up and spotted that the bird had flown? Was there some way he could throw him off the scent till the job was done? Normally it would take a year's instruction to turn a Protestant, but given the girl's pedigree could the job be expedited? He had a month, two if he was lucky. It would have to be done by Easter. She would receive instruction under conditions of the greatest secrecy, and her conversion would only be announced when it was complete.

But then what was to become of her?

Anywhere in Ireland would be out of the question. She would have to be returned to Mexico. It was the only place she would be safe. Was there anyone he could rely on there? Mentally he ran through a list of those with experience in Latin America. Father Alphonsus was the man he needed! Father Alphonsus had connections in Tijuana, he remembered. When the time came, Chastity would return to the land of her forefathers, and the great sin of her mother would be expiated. He looked up in gratitude at the portrait that hung over the Adam fireplace. A hint of a smile was playing round the lips of old Cardinal Mac. Schnozzle dropped to his knees on the Persian rug, gave the girl his rosary beads, and showed her how to count them as he offered up the five decades of the joyful mysteries. Our Blessed Lady had answered his prayers! Saint Jude had intervened on his behalf! The old Cardinal's dream, of one, just one lost sheep returning to the true fold, had come spectacularly true! He had the genuine article on his hands at last.

On the mantelpiece beneath Big Mac's portrait, propping up the Peter's Pence inventory, stood three fading photographs in silver frames. He picked up the middle one and stroked his nose. Then with the air of a man making a momentous decision, he ripped the backing from the frame and removed the picture of King George.

The young Schnozzle O'Shea had grown up believing that the late king of England was the father he had never known. It was a strange fantasy for a boy from the slums of the Shambles. A dangerous fantasy too, for such an idea might be construed as a denial of the men of 1916 and could get you kneecapped, or worse. But Schnozzle's childish loyalty to the House of Windsor was based on the evidence before him. Throughout his youth, the face of the old King had stared down on him with bovine resignation from the dresser. His Majesty formed the central panel of a royal triptych, his picture flanked by sepia lithographs featuring the youthful princesses, his dumpy queen and his haughty mother. No other house on the Shambles would dare display the portrait of the British monarch, tempting as it did summary court martial at the hands of the forces of the Republic. But old Mrs O'Shea was acknowledged by one and all to be several coppers short of the full shilling. There were few visitors to her house, and fewer still who needed to be ushered into the parlour where these strange icons held pride of place.

The pictures were a memento, the only memento, of his real father, who had taken the mailboat to England the day before he was born and had never returned. They had arrived together in the post the morning of his birth, a concertina of perforated postcards, bearing no forwarding address. Where other children grew up believing in Santa Claus, Schnozzle O'Shea grew up believing that the man in the beard would one day arrive on the doorstep and claim him. He would have done better with Santa. Even round the Shambles, Santa was good for a Bramley apple, a tangerine, and a Roy Rogers sixshooter in the stocking. When George the Sixth died, shunning the Shambles to the end,

Schnozzle's hopes died too. When he had grown old enough to stand on tiptoe and see himself in the mirror he realized that not even the Battenbergs could have bequeathed him a nose like the one he saw reflected there. He set aside his dream and turned to the cultivation of his vocation, knowing now that he was on his own.

But our childhood dreams never fade completely. A resonance lingers. His mother died before he was ordained. When he cleared the house the only souvenirs he took back to Maynooth were the faded postcards from the dresser. And now it looked as if the hand of God had intervened, and that the old monarch had a purpose after all.

'Let's send your daddy a postcard,' he told the girl. 'To stop him worrying.'

'Mister Magee too,' she said. 'He's worse than my da!'

'You can set his mind at rest while you're at it. What could be more appropriate than one of His Majesty? The Christian Brothers will see that it's delivered first thing on Boxing Day.'

Then he rang for Immaculata McGillicuddy.

Frank Feely had been on his way home when he found the kitchen door bolted against him. He rattled it a few times, knowing it for a door that stuck easily in the damp weather. But when Sister Immaculata appeared at the noise, took him firmly by the ear and led him without another word back inside, he realized that something was up and knew better than to start asking questions. All day and all evening he sat in the scullery, listening to the muffled sounds of the house, the frantic scurrying of feet and the far-off ringing of the telephone. As it grew dark Major-domo MacBride appeared, looking flustered and ill at ease.

'My mother will be worried if I don't get home,' Frank told him.

'There's nothing to be done about it! She'll just have to fret like the rest of them.'

'Any idea what's up?'

Mister MacBride looked at him. 'Nobody tells the likes of us anything. But there's a three line whip out. No one in and no one out till his nibs gives the order. If you take my advice you'll lie low till whatever it is blows over.'

It was as well he got on with the major-domo for Snotters was a petulant wee man, inflated by notions of his own importance, who could have made his life a misery. He had served the old Cardinal and his humble needs for forty years, supervising the kitchen and the cellar, checking the linen when it returned from the convent laundry, cuffing the young servants into line. He liked the title 'Major-domo' and the quasi-clerical soutane that went with the job. The permanent candlestick of red eczema hanging from his nose and the hint of a hare lip had earned him the nickname Snotters round the Shambles, but they never used it to his face, for the major-domo was touchy to a fault. Frank always gave him his title, even in the Patriot's of an evening when he called to collect his bike and answer Eugene's gentle interrogation.

The major-domo had belted him round the ear often enough in the first months, when Frank was still cack-handed and awkward with the clumsy kitchen implements, cutting himself as he peeled the sprouts or scalding himself as he teemed the potatoes. But he learned fast, and in the slack periods after breakfast, the major-domo would sit him down and make him learn his declensions, over and over till he was word perfect. 'Do you want to be a skivvy all your life?' he would shout, if Frank hesitated over the dative or the ablative. 'Book learning is the only way a lad like you will ever make anything of yourself. Your father, God rest him, would have wanted more from you.'

He had begun to grow during his time in the kitchen. The food that came daily from the college farm was nothing but the best, floury red King Edwards, a churn of buttermilk for the soda farls, yellow butter and long root vegetables. They killed their pigs in the autumn and salted the carcases for the rest of the year. There were chickens and boiling fowl for holy days of obligation, salmon from the Blackwater and Warrenpoint herrings for Friday abstinence. But Schnozzle was a picky eater. He would turn up his nose at everything, pushing away his plate half-eaten, to the despair of the major-domo. 'You're a growing boy,' Mr MacBride said as yet another plate of bacon and cabbage returned untouched from the master's study. 'Waste not, want not,' he said, beckoning the boy to the kitchen table. Frank rarely needed a second invitation.

Not all his time was spent in the scullery. Sometimes, if Schnozzle rang for a sherry late at night, the major-domo would send him to the drawing-room with the fresh decanter, spitting on his hair and smoothing it down before he let him out of his sight, and reminding him every step of the way to mind his manners, not to speak till he was spoken to, and not for the love of the suffering Jesus to drop anything. In the corner of the study the machines kept up their endless chatter, ticker tape and telex and telephone, monitoring the moral pulse of the nation. From every parish in the land the information poured in round the clock. The Archbishop sat humped over the computer screen, a silent spider at the centre of a web of information. Frank would slip unobtrusively into the room, set the sherry down on the occasional table and try to slip out again. But Schnozzle would call to him to stop, order him to stand against the light, scrutinizing his profile for the features of his father Joe. He knew the details of Frank's upbringing. How as a boy he had been dragged through every parish in the land as Joe searched for a cure for his affliction. He knew too that his speech and his understanding had been miraculously restored by the intervention of the Silent Madonna herself. And though the boy was still gauche and ill at ease, Schnozzle could recognize in him a certain quality that made him both excited and uneasy.

'How old are you now, boy?'

'Fifteen, Your Grace.'

'Have you cultivated a special devotion to Our Blessed Lady?'

'Yes, Your Grace.'

'Do you practise the virtue of Holy Purity?'

'Yes, Your Grace.'

'You're attentive in your spiritual duties?'

'Yes, Your Grace.'

'Do you pray for the repose of the soul of your poor father, God rest him?'

'Every day, Your Grace.'

'You're not neglectful of your studies?'

34

'No, Your Grace.'

'And Mister MacBride looks after you well enough?'

'He does, Your Grace.'

But there were no further conversations after the mystery guest appeared. No further visits to the drawing-room. All areas were out of bounds. Frank found himself banned from everywhere but the kitchen, ordered to sleep in the scullery and wash at the cold tap. The Sisters were suddenly everywhere, at his elbow when he bent over the jawbox to scrub the carrots and among the pots and pans when he tried to cook them, checking and rechecking his every movement, censoring all idle speculation. Every door had its turnkey. A tense silence had fallen over the house. No phones rang. He knew better than to speak to the major-domo, or even to catch his eye.

But alone among the cockroaches, night after night, Frank could hear the faint faraway sound of a young girl weeping. It haunted his dreams. He knew that the crying came from the deserted attic at the top of the house. It was the crying of a tortured soul, a cry that echoed the accumulated terrors of his native land.

The path that leads to Truth is never an easy one. And for someone raised in bigotry it can prove particularly stony. Schnozzle knew that if he relaxed his vigilance she would be gone, running down the long steps that led to the Shambles, scurrying across the wide square to the Protestant quarter where her father would be waiting for her, belt in hand, to welcome her back into heresy. But with God's help, he told himself, that would never happen. Long days and longer nights followed, the Archbishop and the girl closeted together, going over and over again the mysteries of the true faith. She learned by rote the catechism and the creed; she recited the unfamiliar prayers till she had them word perfect; she practised her responses till they were automatic. He coached her in how to lead the rosary and how to comport herself during Mass. He explained patiently the true meaning of the miracles at Lourdes, Fatima and Knock. She was a keen pupil, with a ready grasp of the intricacies of the faith as he unfolded them to her. With the help of God, he told himself, she would make a lovely convert. By the beginning of Lent the girl knew enough about the Trinity and the mystery of Transubstantiation to pass muster and it was time to get down to what really mattered, what would make a real Catholic of her.

Sex!

As he prepared her for her first confession, he explained to her how she should examine her conscience. He probed her soul for sins. He winkled out her impure thoughts. Her innermost fantasies were exposed and analysed. He told her about hell and purgatory and the terrors that lie ahead for the unclean in spirit. He questioned her again and again about Patrick Pearse McGuffin, the gorge rising in his throat every time he pronounced the name. Had he interfered with her? Had he kissed her? Had he put his hands on her breasts? Up her skirt? How far? How often? Had she enjoyed it? What had she done in return? Chastity was as pure a virgin as any convent school girl, but she learned to answer these and other questions without tears and without embarrassment, in a spirit of thoughtful remorse.

They discussed sex in marriage, they discussed sex outside marriage. Every aspect of carnality was dissected and analysed. Like every member of his celibate profession, Schnozzle was an authority on sex. He knew with unerring certainty the Church's position on every aspect of the marriage bed. No man in Ireland could hold a candle to Schnozzle O'Shea when it came to knowing about women and their sexuality. From the confessional he had learned of their little ways and wiles. There was not an orifice of the female body that he had not explored and dissected with the aid of the Church Fathers. He knew the precise viscosity of the mucus on the vaginal walls at the time of ovulation, and the mean temperature of the urine in the week before ovulation. To within an hour, maybe less, he could instruct the women of Ireland on the exact time for coition to fall within the morally acceptable safe period. He could advise on the best moment for conception to occur, and the best position for it. He knew every pore of their bodies, their changing smells as the cycle of fertility waxed and waned with the passing month, their swelling bellies when they were pregnant, their emissions and discharges, shows and flushes, menstrual, pre-menstrual and postnatal. He hovered vicariously at the elbow of the gynaecologists in the Mater Hospital, advising them of their moral responsibilities, giving them permission to break the waters or forbidding them from inducing labour. In all matters of reproduction he stood above contradiction. He could tell to a centimetre, to a millimetre, how far penile penetration must go for it to be within the natural law. He could calculate the degree of guilt attached to each party when anal penetration had been attempted or even considered. He could spell out, for those contemplating matrimony, the four requirements of canon law, *erictio*, *introducio*, *penetratio*, *et ejaculatio*, and how they must take their appointed order before he could be certain that a pious consummation had taken place. He knew the difference between *praecox voluntare* and *involuntare* and the respective degrees of divine wrath attaching to each. Any attempt to frustrate the fullness of the sexual act he was wise to.

Chastity took notes and learned them thoroughly before each confrontation. They devoted a month to contraception alone, leaving no stone unturned till he was sure she fully grasped the difference between mortal and venial digressions. But it all seemed to come naturally to her. When she told him on Palm Sunday that she had awakened to find the picture of the Madonna smiling at her, the crude features in Sharkey's painting rearranged into a smile of beatific acknowledgement, he knew that her doubts and fears were behind her.

Old Cardinal Mac had his miracle! He was home and dry!

Brother Murphy appeared on the Shambles on Good Friday morning with a ladder, a cartload of flags and a dozen shivering orphans. He propped the ladder up against the Patriot's gable and without as much as a by-your-leave ordered one of the lads up to check if the gutter would hold. The other boys clambered on to the roofs of the low houses at the top of Irish Street, hauling coils of bunting behind them. The work went on all morning, and by the time they had bedecked the south side of the square

Brother Murphy had lathered himself into a right state. After the Angelus he retired to the Patriot's snug demanding free drink, running out occasionally to kick the backside of any orphan he found slacking off.

By nightfall the town was bedecked. The bunting fanned out from its epicentre in the Shambles down all the narrow streets of the Fenian quarter. The flags hung limply in the damp air the length of Thomas Street and Banbrook Hill; they doglegged into Dobbin Street, skirted one side of Callan Street and back over Windmill Hill. They faltered a little as they crossed into the mixed territory round Abbey Street, but when they took the left-hand bend into Irish Street again and ran its full length down to the Shambles they were a sight to behold. They fluttered and danced in the breeze, as numerous and promiscuous as the host of golden daffodils. A canopy of yellow and white arched over the entire street, transforming the familiar thoroughfare into something magical.

The people stood on their doorsteps and gazed in wonderment at the metamorphosis. No Fenian had ever seen flags like these. There was no denying it, Mister Magee had done them proud. 'Somebody's got a right treat in store for us and no mistake,' said Eugene, surveying the boys' handiwork through the window.

'There'd be no harm in inquiring what it's all in aid of?' asked Peadar, emboldened by drink. Brother Murphy began to turn red, the veins in his neck bulging like taut hawsers. As is often the way with the Christian Brothers, the drink had made him querulous and the sight of a past pupil had inflamed him with dim memories of unfinished business. He lurched across to Peadar, lifted him by the scruff of the neck and began to cuff him round the head. 'You were a pup then and you're still a pup! I see you've no more manners now than you had in Book Three!' Eugene didn't interfere. The bar was as good as empty anyway, even the Tyrone man having taken his custom elsewhere. A Christian Brother on the premises was always bad for business. He poured another rum, knowing the Brother would need it when he'd finished with the greengrocer. He made it a double. With God's help Brother Murphy would pass out on the floor before long. He could see the foundlings standing outside in the rain, waiting to wheel him home.

When he realized the extent of the Romanists' preparations McCoy grew worried. It was one thing to sell the Fenians flags for special occasions. It was another thing altogether to have them turn the Shambles into the Papal States. This was a challenge that could not go unanswered. He sent for Magee post haste.

'Suddenly we're on all fours with the papists,' Lily protested when she saw him parcelling up a jumbo-sized order of the red, white and blue. 'You expect me to run the shop singlehanded while you gallivant off at McCoy's beck and call!' But she knew him too well to say any more. The Portadown soul loves to show the flag. The only thing that brightens the drab grey streets of his environment are the primary colours of the polyester triangles. But even Magee was unprepared for the show of Fenian defiance that greeted him when he hit Armagh. He stood at the door of the Martyrs Memorial Chapel and gazed with anger and incredulity over at the papist quarter. The Brothers' boys had returned and were adding the finishing touches to their handiwork, fixing cardboard shields to the lampposts, portraying the emblems of the four provinces.

Magee spat into the gutter. 'A man of my age has more to do than running up and down ladders. Is there still no sign of that girl of yours?'

'Another postcard. The Little Princess, Margaret Rose.'

Magee turned his attention to the ice-cream van that was parked on the pavement behind them. Underneath it, up against the rusting exhaust pipe, Patrick Pearse McGuffin had fashioned a makeshift nest. Cardboard cartons had been torn in strips in an effort to keep the rain out, and there was a soggy mattress stuffed with discarded newspapers where the renegade now cowered. 'Why keep a dog and bark yourself?' Magee growled, striding towards the van.

Patrick Pearse McGuffin too had been looking out on the sea of papal splendour and dreaming of happier times. He had been dreaming of Saint Matt Talbot's, the parish on the Falls which he would never see again, and the people of the ghetto he could

39

never meet again. He knew in his heart of hearts that he belonged on the Falls, among the warmth of his own people squabbling in the ladder of backstreets that led down to the no man's land round the abandoned peace line. But there would be no going home for McGuffin. Not this year, not next, not ever! They had their own ways for dealing with touts and informers where he came from. And if they needed any reminding of his perfidy, Father Alphonsus was still there, still condemned to eke out his days in Matt Talbot's; and as long as Father Alphonsus was there, McGuffin would never see the Falls Road again.

But how much longer could he survive like this, away from his natural habitat? The Shambles was as foreign to him as Timbuctoo. It would never feel like home. These were not his streets. They had a different smell, a different sound. These were not his people either. Nor ever would be. He knew he was living on borrowed time, despite his insistence to any who would lend him an ear that he was now as good a Protestant as they, any day of the week. They could smell the Fenian on him still. He suffered daily ignominies, especially from the farmers when they had drink taken, or from the children in the gutters when he ventured out. He had learned to suffer their jibes and insults. He had learned too to live with his fear of the GPs who had left him alone so far. But he didn't need McCoy's reminder that they would eliminate him at the first hint of backsliding. The Protestants of Scotch Street might be accustomed to the sight of McGuffin running messages for McCoy, but one of these days he would be murdered before he'd reached the end of the road, and no one would raise a finger in his defence.

He was gazing at the riot of papal flags with tears in his eyes when his reverie was rudely interrupted by the butcher Magee's boot demolishing his cardboard home and ordering him to get off his arse and start earning his keep.

Though he had to work far into the night, by morning the job was done. The red, white and blue fluttered the full length of English Street, down to Scotch Street, round the Mall and back up by way of College Street. The entire town was now decorated. Like isobars on a weather map, the interweaving colours of the flags delineated precisely the political affiliations of every street.

In the Shambles itself the loyalist bunting zigzagged into the square, interfacing with the green and yellow over the latrine at the centre. Everything now stood in readiness for the epiphany of Chastity McCoy.

❖

Forty miles to the east, in Saint Matt's vestry at the foot of the Falls Road, Father Alphonsus McLoughlin knelt at the dying embers of the fire praying like a man condemned. You wouldn't have known it to look at him now, for he was a gaunt figure, wasted to skin and bone, but luck had once smiled on Alphonsus McLoughlin. He had won the most coveted prize a Belfast priest can hope for, the sabbatical to California, to spread the faith among the beautiful people. Alphonsus had briefly felt the sun on his back and the warm Pacific breeze playing through his hair. He had gambolled chastely with the gilded youth in the surf off Big Sur, and had ridden the ferryboat daily to Sausalito. But the sun and the surf and the laughter of innocent voices was now only a distant memory. His tan and his accent had faded and the pallor and the harshness of the ghetto had returned to his face and his voice.

He looked up at the stern features of the Sacred Heart on the wall and redoubled his efforts, screwing his knuckles into his eyesockets and howling aloud the words of the De Profundis. Alphonsus had been praying without a break since Ash Wednesday. He had persevered in his Lenten vigil, fasting for forty days and forty nights, not a morsel of food passing his lips, a hunger strike to draw heaven's attention to his plight. And now it was Holy Saturday night, the eve of Easter, the last day of Lent, and it was clear that the Sacred Heart was determined to let his suffering continue. In a few hours it would be dawn. There would be no reprieve, no escape. He rose from the lino, spat on the fire and cursed, as he did day and night, the name of Patrick Pearse McGuffin.

Alphonsus felt there was a jinx on him that no penance could lift. He was haunted by a guilt he could neither understand nor explain. What latent malignant force had he unwittingly unleashed that day he had gone into the mountains beyond Tijuana

41

and brought back the figurine of the little Virgin? Had he been seduced by a graven image of idolatry? Had he become a catalyst for the slow blight that was spreading over the land and its people? And how could he atone for what he had started?

A faded tricolour hung from the gable of Saint Matthew's vestry in deference to the season. But there was nothing but despair in Alphonsus's heart. He crossed himself one last time. The features of the Sacred Heart above the mantelpiece stayed as stern as ever. If only he could be given a sign, just one, no matter how small, that he would not have to see out his days in this dreadful place among the McGuffins and their bastards, scraping for a living among the fetid backstreets of the shanty town. But the Sacred Heart, as so often, was keeping the cards close to His chest. Alphonsus started his last, desperate rosary unaware that back in Ara Coeli, the powerhouse of the organization to which he had devoted his life, Schnozzle had called a meeting to brief his senior staff, and that his own name was prominent on the agenda.

Major-domo MacBride was run off his feet. In all his days he had never known anything like it. There were bishops and archbishops from the four provinces, the papal legate in person, monsignors and administrators, all crowded into the boardroom upstairs with their personal staff. The back parlour was overcrowded with lesser clergy and selected laity, awaiting their orders. Sam O'Dowd of the *Irish News* was there, waiting patiently on the stairs for Schnozzle to check his spelling before he gave him the Imprimatur. Sister Immaculata McGillicuddy guarded the front door, showing each of the guests to their places. And to cap it all, John Joe Sharkey, the new Taoiseach, was there, ordered up from Dublin, slipping unnoticed over the border with his minder O'Malley. John Joe, like everyone else who had arrived, would have his part to play in the momentous events of the morrow.

'There isn't time to stand about!' Immaculata shouted, bursting into the kitchen where the major-domo and Frank were having a well-earned smoke. 'Their Lordships need more whiskey; a cappuccino for the papal nuncio, and a brandy for the Taoiseach. Quickly!'

'Brandy if you please!' shouted MacBride when she was out of earshot. 'Whiskey is good enough for the cloth, but John Joe wants a brandy!' He rose unsteadily to his feet.

'Sit where you are,' Frank said. 'I'll see to John Joe.'

'You'll be lucky!' the major-domo declared, holding up the Napoleon Four Star. The lumbago had been playing him up all day and the bottle was as good as empty.

'He'll drink whiskey with the rest of them! What is he anyhow but a jumped-up gombeen man from Annagery,' Frank said with sudden vehemence.

'Spoken like a true man!' the major-domo concurred. 'Take it in to them while you're on your feet. You'll easy recognize the Taoiseach, he's the one in the morning suit, done up like a conjuror on the London Palladium. You'll find him in the corner with Schnozzle's hand up his ass, pulling his strings,'

'I'll recognize him all right,' Frank said. 'I remember the same boy from long ago.'

Frank carried the Waterford decanter carefully up the wide staircase. With each step the noise of male bonhomie grew louder, with each step the smell of cigars and aftershave grew stronger. Here was power, palpable power, a heady sensation. He paused at the door, steadied the tray and pushed it open carefully. The bulky shape of John Joe's bodyguard sprang forward, barring his way. O'Malley! He recognized at once the close-set eyes, the sweat-flecked jowls of the guard. It was not O'Malley's first trip across the border since John Joe had plucked him out from his contemporaries for special duties. But the North left him feeling uneasy. Amid all the splendour of Ara Coeli he stood out like a sore thumb. He wouldn't stop sweating till he'd delivered John Joe safely back to his fancy woman in Monaghan town. He took the decanter roughly from Frank and ordered him back below stairs. But not before the boy had caught a glimpse of the splendour within, of the red capes and purple robes of the hierarchy gathered round Schnozzle, vociferous in their congratulations. And a glimpse too of the man in the corner, John Joe Sharkey, whom he had last seen at the end of the Yellow Meal Road.

At the stroke of midnight, Schnozzle's limousine sped quietly down the drive, crossed the square and headed out towards

Belfast. Its siren was silent, its lights dimmed. Only the Patriot, the last defender of the purity of the national dream, keeping vigil at the window, witnessed its passing. *'Tá gluaistean ar an bhóthair,'* he called up to Eugene. There's a car on the road. There had been a procession of motorcars up to the Palace all that afternoon, but this was the first movement out.

'The Easter Bunny is off somewhere in a great hurry,' Eugene observed, staggering to the window in time to see it speeding away from the Shambles. He caught a glimpse of Immaculata McGilli-cuddy sitting at the wheel, and despite a lifetime rigorously devoted to the military cause, found himself wincing at the thought.

Major-domo MacBride, sobered up with a pot of black coffee and hastily dressed in his best soutane and surplice, marched the servants in through the back door of the cathedral while it was still dark and ushered them into a corner behind a pillar. They huddled there as slowly the great cathedral came to life. One by one the priests of the parish filed out of the sacristy to say their trinity of masses at the scattered side altars. At ten o'clock the organ began to play, great improvised voluntaries of joy. At eleven the choir scrambled into the loft and sang a glorious Te Deum of thanksgiving. The pews began to fill, and Frank was soon conscious of the vast, expectant congregation that was crushing into every nook and cranny. And though he could see nothing of the ceremonies that began at the stroke of noon, he wasn't long in realizing the true import of what was happening on the high altar. The clouds of incense that hung in the air told him that every clerical dignity in the land was in the church that day, and the voice of the organ and the sound of the choir underlined how momentous the occasion was.

The procession moved out from the Lady Chapel, ranks of dignitaries leading the swaying and buckling canopy. Under the cloth of gold, closely flanked by *Schnozzle* resplendent in Pascal robes, Frank caught a glimpse of a frail girl in a white dress, her face hidden under a veil. A shiver of terror ran through him for what it might presage.

She was baptized in the Lady Chapel by the Bishop of Derry as the choir sang 'Hosanna'. She was led to the confession box where the Bishop of Galway was waiting in the dark compartment; she confessed her sins and was shriven. At the High Mass that followed she made her first communion, receiving the melting host from the hands of the Bishop of Down and Connor. And then, as the carillon pealed out the news to the waiting city, she was led up to the great high altar and there formally confirmed in her new faith by Schnozzle himself.

On the grave of Big Mac the scarlet fuchsia round the Celtic cross burst forth miraculously into unseasonal blossom.

The congregation erupted from the cathedral and poured down the hundred steps into the Shambles, shouting and chanting and giving thanks for the miracle they had just witnessed. They swarmed into the Patriot's, regulars and teetotallers alike, filling the bar with their chatter. A group of them broke away, and emboldened by the occasion, crossed the square to taunt McCoy with the news of his daughter's perfidy. But McCoy didn't need to be told. The *Irish News*, a special colour edition, had already hit the streets, with the story on its front page, in capitals six inches high.

❖

'And to think I nearly missed it!' said Peadar for the tenth time, regaling the company with news of his good fortune in witnessing the conversion of Chastity McCoy.

'It was a great day for the town all right,' said a wee man from Drumarg who had been stranded in the bar since early evening. From somewhere further up the town there came the dull thud of another explosion.

'Not that I saw a thing with the crowds, and the leg killing me after kneeling so long on the cold marble.'

The Tyrone man was at the window, cautiously peering out at the riot through a crack in the plywood shutters. 'It's as good as over, I'd say,' he said.

'Go off home then!' Peadar shouted.

'I will like fuck! Magee and that crowd will be out and about and they won't rest till they've killed someone.'

'They'll be out searching high and low for her, no doubt about it,' said the wee man from Drumarg.

'The trouble's only starting, if you want my opinion,' Peadar said.

'Aren't we as safe as houses where we are,' the Tyrone man insisted, 'with Eugene on the roof.'

The Tyrone man had been right. The riot was as good as over, but Eugene stuck to his place. From the skylight in the attic he had control over most of the Shambles, a clear line of sight half-way down Irish Street in one direction and in the other, over the roof of the Martyrs Memorial the length of English Street. The Armalite felt good against his cheek again. Good too to smell the cordite and hear grenades once more at Easter. In the Shambles below him no one was moving. The square was littered with glass and cobblestones and strewn with coils of collapsed bunting. Beyond the concrete latrine he could make out the giant ice-cream cone on the roof of McCoy's Salvation Wagon. He took aim and gently squeezed off a round. The shot echoed round the square. The bakelite shattered into jagged fragments. He laughed at the thought of McGuffin's discomfort, lying like a dog under the van while some maniac took potshots at the ice-cream cone above. Eugene set the rifle down and groped for a cigarette. He'd loose off a round or two more and then call it a night.

There'd been wild rumours in the bar earlier that the Donatists were heading for the town looking for trouble, but there was no sign of them, thank God. Magee wouldn't be bothering them any more tonight either. He'd seen the butcher and his cronies, bad-looking bastards, heading out of town and into the hills earlier. They'd be ransacking the high ground, plundering isolated farms, as much to vent their anger as in any hope of finding the runaway. He lowered his head before striking the match. From the bar below came the muffled sounds of querulous drinking, but it was oddly peaceful in the attic. At his side the figure of the Dancing Madonna silently surveyed the rooftops with a vacant, enigmatic stare.

Only two people in the whole of Ireland, himself and the Patriot, knew of her hiding place. Muire na nGael, Mary of the Gael, the Patriot had called her. She had been there since the night Frank's father had returned with her from the Antrim plateau, the Patriot decreeing that she would never be subjected to such ignominy again. She would stay under his roof till her mission

46

became clear. Some day, if you believed the prophecy, she would call the people together, planter and dispossessed, and we would be a nation once again. It was the Patriot's last great hope, to be spared to see that day.

She was a small statue, crudely carved from weather-beaten timber, yet with a hauteur that distinguished her from the thousand other representations of the Virgin. It was hard to think sometimes that a thing so small, so insignificant, so patently man-made could be the cause of so much conflict. But it was ever so. The icon had long ago become what every man wanted her to become. To one side a symbol of the unbroken line of their faith, a repository for their aspirations. To the other side an object of fear and illicit fascination.

Eugene finished his smoke and carefully stubbed the butt out on the joists. There'd been enough fires in the town that night already, he didn't want to go starting another one. Carefully he eased open the skylight and scanned the town below. All was quiet. He fired once more, in the general direction of Scotch Street, and ducked down. He waited five minutes. There was no return fire. The sniper who had pinned down the head of the town must have been disposed of all right. He fired once more and waited. All was quiet. He lifted the one-legged statue and slid it under the skylight. 'Be a good girl and keep an eye on things for us for a while,' he said, 'while I oil, strip and grease the rod.'

Frank pedalled homeward through the darkness, sticking as best he could to the back lanes that wound up into the hills. He hadn't dared leave till the rioting had died down. Even then there was no way through the Shambles, for there were snipers in Scotch Street covering every corner. Rumours of the unrest had been reaching the palace all afternoon, of three or four dead and others injured. He had heard it on authority that Magee had led a crowd into Irish Street, further up than they had gone in years, burning the Catholics out before them. Marooned on the hilltop he heard the sporadic crack of the Armalites, and saw the dull glow where the houses were ablaze. At midnight he decided to risk it.

He would take a detour out by Blackwatertown and bypass the town through the maze of lanes his father had taught him, heading for the safety of the hills.

It was a dark night, the moon only a sliver, obscured behind angry clouds, but he didn't dare risk even the flickering light of the dynamo. For an hour he had wandered through the Dark Lonen, unsure of his bearings, terrified of rousing the brutes of dogs that lurked behind each gateway, petrified of God knows what might be waiting for him around each corner. In the distance he could still make out the sounds of battle, the rattle of hailstones that he knew was automatic fire, the dull thud of grenades and incendiaries.

The scream of a gearbox! Dogs frantically giving chase! A sudden commotion on the narrow road a mile behind him! A car was coming through the darkness! More than one, at speed! Frank threw himself into the ditch and pulled the bicycle on top of him. In the nick of time, for round the corner raced a cavalcade of dark motors, one, two, three of them, at full speed, kicking up gravel and dirt, the tyres squealing on the narrow bends, rasping on the ditches and the overhanging bushes in the darkness. They roared past him. He lay without moving, listening till the noise of the engines had faded on the night air. When he was sure they were gone he quietly picked himself up. The bike was buckled but there were no bones broken. He threw it into the field and with a prayer to the Sacred Heart for protection, started to make his way on foot over the treacherous fields towards home.

In the darkened interior of the car, Father Alphonsus also said a prayer to the Sacred Heart, his protector and benefactor. Dear Heart of Jesus, don't let this prize, so unexpectedly bestowed, be plucked away from me at the eleventh hour! The driver was gunning the limousine like a maniac, tearing through the countryside in the dark, trying to keep up with the bodyguards in front. Dear Jesus don't let him crash! Don't let him put us over the side of the ditch, where we'll be easy pickings for the loyalist gangs who are everywhere this night!

Alphonsus couldn't believe his luck. Five years earlier, when Schnozzle had recalled him from the sunshine in California to the horrors of the ghetto, he had thought his days in the sun were over for ever. And here was a second chance! Twenty-four hours ago he was dying on hunger strike, sunk in despair of ever escaping. And now, like a man in a dream, he was hurtling through South Armagh, dressed in civvies by command of the boss, a wad of dollar bills in his pocket, guarded by a dozen armed Sisters of the True Faith, with a pair of one-way tickets in his hand and Chastity McCoy sobbing beside him. He crossed himself and shouted out His praise, shouted it loud above the screaming of the engine on the mountain road. Alphonsus McLoughlin would never doubt the goodness of God again! He tried to calm himself, to recall what they had told him. All arrangements had been taken care of. Inspector O'Malley of the Garda Síochána would meet him as soon as he cleared the border and escort him to the plane. Fidelma Sharkey, the Taoiseach's wife, would be waiting on the tarmac to see them off. The red carpet would be laid on; there would be no hitches. The authorities on the other side had been squared too. There would be no trouble with entry visas or residence requirements. Alphonsus started another decade of the rosary, and the girl, through her sobs, joined in. If only he could survive the next hour he would be home and dry. Magee and his lot would never follow them beyond the borderlands. If he were spared he would carry out his orders. He would deliver Chastity to the land of her ancestors, back to the Indians in the mountains of the new world. See her safely ensconced in the convent where she would spend the rest of her days.

And then what? Return to Armagh? Report back to Schnozzle that the mission was accomplished? Return to the grim despair of the ghetto, to live day after day among the unwashed?

The car was still climbing, up through the foothills and into the mountains that separated Ulster from the rest of the country. Alphonsus gingerly opened the window a crack and sniffed the mountain air. He lit a cigarette and started to relax. Chastity was crying now, openly weeping as she left the land of her birth. He put his hand on her knee and squeezed conspiratorially. All the same, he didn't put the beads away completely, nor reach for the Jameson, till they had crossed the Black Pig's Dyke and had started to descend again, down into the great dark central plain, and he was sure that the province of Ulster was firmly, and he hoped irrevocably, behind them.

Two

The *Irish News*, with its blurred pictures of His Grace, all nose and teeth, posing with the cruet poised over Chastity's forehead, wasn't long in reaching the four corners of the province. No one doubted that serious trouble could be far behind. The shopkeepers boarded up their windows, the farmers locked their barns, the women ordered their broods of children in from the streets. Before the day was done the vengeance squads would be scouring the roads for random victims. But in one corner of Fermanagh, that strangest of counties, the news that Schnozzle had set the cat among the pigeons was greeted not with foreboding, but with unalloyed joy.

For the villagers of Derrygonnelly, any opportunity for mayhem was a God-sent opportunity not to be missed.

The people of Derrygonelly were the last remnant of the Summer of Love, that brief season a decade before, when Canon Tom had unwittingly opened the floodgates of unorthodoxy. The Canon had been searching for the elusive gnomic formula that would reconcile the modernist aspirations of his flock with the traditional teaching of the Church. For a fleeting moment he thought he had found it, the philosopher's stone that would square the circle. But the movement that Canon Tom had unleashed in his *folie de grandeur* on Adam and Eve's, the top people's parish nestling in the hills above Dublin, was to spread rapidly out of control. Sects and heresies had mushroomed. Charismatics and New Age followers, Moonies, Loonies, Hippies and Screamers, Revisionists and Freethinkers, babbling in a thousand strange tongues, demanding the freedom to be themselves, to judge for themselves, interpret the world for themselves, threatening with their antics the very authority of the hierarchy. And of all the sects that had flourished at that time, none was more esoteric than the Derrygonnelly Donatists.

The Summer of Love was a thing of the past, a fading folk memory of headier times. There were very few now who dared mention it openly, for the walls had ears and in Ireland you never know who you can trust. Its brief promise had been strangled at birth. The Sisters had girded their loins and waded into battle to rescue the country for the True Church. Canon Tom was long in exile, a non-person, banished beyond the mountains where he could do no further harm. The Charismatics had been crushed. Adam and Eve's was under permanent occupation. The unswerving attention of Schnozzle had seen to it that things never got out of hand again. And yet . . . ! Despite the most stringent efforts to maintain orthodoxy, there were still outbreaks of strange behaviour from time to time that caused the Guards to intervene. And in Fermanagh, a wild and watery fastness where even Immaculata thought twice about venturing, one stubborn pocket remained.

The Donatists of Derrygonnelly were a self-destructive but self-perpetuating cult that not even the combined efforts of the Sisters and the Christian Brothers could totally eradicate. They enjoyed widespread popularity on the remoter islands and round the lakeshore village from which they took their name. Not for them the agapes and lovefeasts of the early church once favoured by Canon Tom; their road back to the catacombs took a different direction. They modelled themselves on a fundamentalist sect of the first century whose sole aim was to reach their eternal reward as quickly as possible. With a determination that characterizes the people of the lakeland, they set about things in the most direct fashion. The founder of the group had been a wizened little man called Donat Maguire, famed in the area as a dancer, raconteur and wit. For sixty and more years Donat's peculiar name had never bothered him; all his contemporaries had odd names of one sort or another, as was the local custom, to distinguish one Maguire from another. Donat Maguire believed himself to be called after a baseball player in the States, for his grandfather had once been Stateside, in the days after the famine, and returned with tales of oddly dressed men with odd names playing a strange ballgame. Quite what unhinged Donat's mind during the Summer of Love was never clear; sceptics in the townland put it down to years of soft shoe shuffle finally affecting the cerebral cortex. But his followers told a more edifying tale. Retiring to his bed one night after a particularly hectic session, Donat was visited by his eponymous patron saint who ordered him to stop farting around and expeditiously claim his eternal reward. He awoke a new man.

There was a snag with the new philosophy. Though convinced of their own righteousness, convinced enough to put it to the test, it was hardly *de rigueur* to top yourself and turn up at the Judgement Seat as bold as brass, demanding special status. While accidental death might do at a pinch, the only sure-fire method was slaughter at the hands of an unbeliever. Luckily Fermanagh offered considerable scope in both areas.

Donat was still struggling with this conundrum when his grateful followers decided to surprise him. He hadn't been long in gathering round him a group of disciples, for even in less troubled times Fermanagh didn't lack for eejits. A treat was arranged. The top room above Maguire's Licensed Premises was packed to the doors for a session. At the *fear a' tí*'s command the floor was cleared and Donat had the lino to himself. As he shuffled round and round, dancing in his inimitable fashion the ancient slithering two-step peculiar to the region, they accompanied him with *sean-nós* keening, the gentle, nasal music much esteemed in those parts. He was on his third round when, with an apocalyptic groan, the floorboards gave way. Donat Maguire dropped through the rubble to the bar below, impaling himself on the porter pump. Ecstatic at the success of their handiwork his acolytes prayed with him as he stoically expired.

Yet even in the moment of their triumph, doubts set in. Had they gone too far, pre-empting the Almighty's prerogative? Had they sinned against the commandment forbidding killing, maybe robbing themselves of their rightful reward? Henceforth, it was agreed, a different route to Paradise would have to be found.

Natural causes, farmyard accidents and the attentions of the Little Sisters saw off a few of their members over the next six months, but the rest remained firmly rooted to terra firma. There was only one thing for it. They would have to provoke their

Protestant neighbours. Under normal circumstances this would have presented no problem. The Protestant neighbours would have been happy to rise to the occasion. But the times were not normal. Those Protestants who had not been burned out were suspicious. There is no such thing as a free lunch, they told themselves. A few old scores were paid off, of course, but on the whole they remained distinctly lukewarm about the whole project. Having run up against this unexpected obduracy, the Donatists had taken to wandering the countryside, far and wide, especially at weekends, seeking natural hazards or man-made ambushes that would provide them with the release they so desperately craved.

Hardly surprising then that when news reached them of events in the city, and when they read in the paper of McCoy's wrath, they should set out at the double for the Shambles hoping for a share of the action.

Dawn was breaking by the time Frank reached the hill above the house. There was no smoke from the chimney and the hens were running in the yard unfed. He slithered down through the gorse bushes, fearing the worst. His mother was in the kitchen, talking to herself at the top of her voice. He rapped on the window; she turned to him with vacant eyes, turned away and continued her lonely obsession. He pushed open the back door and ran to her, trying to embrace her, but she remained unaware of his presence. He pulled her round to face him, forcing her to look at him, a cold stab of fear twisting in his heart with every unintelligible word she uttered. His eyes were filled with tears. 'Don't you recognize me!' he pleaded. But he found only vacancy in her face and foolishness in her words.

'Let me light a fire,' he said, fighting back the tears. 'You're blue with the cold.' She slumped into the rocking chair while he struggled with the range. He tried to clean up the kitchen, throwing the blue-moulded bread to the chickens at the door and searching for what would make a cup of tea. Anything to stop the full reality of his mother's craziness sinking in.

He was shocked at the change in her. Only a few years earlier she had been a hard and determined woman. But the death of his father had upended her world, left her with nowhere to turn for comfort. A madwoman going the roads was nothing new in Ulster. The troubles had unhinged the minds of many. Frank knew every Mad Meg between here and Armagh. And he knew too how they were treated. Shunned for fear of the evil eye and tricked by the gombeen man out of what little they had.

He made her drink the tea and she calmed down a bit, sighing to herself from time to time. He sat with her, speaking soothing words, waiting anxiously for the first flicker of recognition in her empty eyes. The old dog had appeared at his return, drawn into the kitchen by the warmth of the fire. It lay farting at their feet. Suddenly it pricked its ears and uttered a low growl. Frank strained his ears. The dog growled again. Frank could hear nothing but the moaning of the wind in the trees. But his mother had heard what the dog had heard. She flung the teacup across the room, jumped to her feet and began to shout.

She ran to the half door. The dog was barking now. 'It's only the wind you're hearing,' he pleaded. 'There's no one on the road below!' But she pushed him away from her roughly and ran to the mantelpiece above the range where the pledge to the Sacred Heart had hung since her wedding day. It was her personal pledge, her guarantee of a place in heaven. She reached up and tore it roughly from the nail. Then clutching it in one hand, and Frank in the other, and with the mongrel at their heels, she dragged him out through the door, leaving the house open to the four winds.

Magee and his henchmen were cold, wet, hungry and lost. He had gathered them up at short notice, half a dozen members of the Temperance Lodge Band, and led them into the mountains above Armagh. It was an act of desperation, but Magee didn't intend to be caught hanging round the town when the boys in the back room opened a post mortem into the débâcle. With each passing hour his frustration increased. Ignorant of the wild and treacherous terrain, they had clambered above the tree line round

Slieve Gullion. The land was deserted, as lonely and alien as the back side of the moon. The very sheep seemed threatening. A mist had come down and they had lost their bearings; they had squelched through moorland, slithered among the crags, wandered deeper and deeper into the wilderness with each step. The trombone player had caught the side of his face on a rock and his cheek sagged bloodily open. He muttered mutiny and when Magee rested he kept the Stanley knife to hand. They had run out of food and whiskey, and the cigarettes were long since finished. Had they stumbled on a homestead they could have plundered it for victuals and drink and sat it out till the cloud lifted, when they could risk the descent. But there were no farms here, only the ruins of long-abandoned settlements. All night long they tramped in circles, Magee watching his companions growing gaunt and murderous. They would all die if they didn't get back among their own people soon.

A forced march over the jagged rocks of a dried river bed finally brought them below the clouds. They headed for the valley below, stumbling all night among the boulders, afraid to sleep lest the cloud come down again. As dawn broke they came upon some tracks, and an hour later, dispirited, empty-handed, but at least alive, they found themselves on the crag overlooking the Feely house.

They saw that it had been hastily abandoned; its doors stood open, but a fire still smouldered in the hearth. The bass drummer kicked open the press in search of food; it yielded little but a few ends of hard bread and a scrape of margarine. Magee found a packet of Gold Leaf on the floor with half a cigarette still inside. He straightened it out and lit it from the fire. He had never set foot in a papist house before. He looked round the kitchen with fascination. A line of popish icons stood on a crude shelf, statues of the Virgin, the Child of Prague and John Bosco. There was a lithograph of the Holy Family with a prayer for peace in the home. But riveted as he was by these manifestations of idolatry, it was the framed photograph that caught his attention, a photograph of Frank's first communion. Magee recognized the man in the picture, even with the hat pulled down over his eyes. The late Joe Feely! With one swipe he scattered the lot on the floor. The red nightlight before the Sacred Heart still glowed. He ripped it from the wall, unbuttoned his flies and pissed on the lot.

His activities were interrupted by a sound in the distance. It was the sound of a crowd, a great crowd on the move. The sound of wailing and praying, and discordant music, and laughter and chanting. They were far away as yet, over the next hills, but they were approaching fast. His colleagues heard it too. All their bravado had been left behind on the mountains. They stood in the kitchen transfixed. They were in dangerous, unknown, unpredictable territory and the sooner they found their way out of it the better. The noise was growing louder by the minute. And then above the wails and entreaties of the Donatists they heard the bagpipes of a Hibernian band.

It had been many a long year since the Hibs had dared put their snouts out in decent company, but with the birth of this strange new sect a handful of old survivors from the lakeshore had emerged blinking into the sunlight to don their green regalia, dust off their banners and take to the roads. To a true blue Loyal Son of William like Magee, the raucous sound of a Hib band was like a red rag to a bull. He crept to the door and looked up the road. And as the main body of the march came into view his heart started to pound with anticipation. He was beginning to appreciate the meaning of their incessant demand. What was more he was in a position and in the mood to do something about it.

The serious Donatists were recognizable from their garb – an attempt at the sackcloth and ashes of the desert hermits of the early church – and from the weals on their bodies caused by the lashes of purification they rained down on their flesh. Their eyes were raised in supplication to heaven; there was no doubting their desire to join their heavenly master as soon as it could be arranged. Their lips moved constantly, pleading with the Almighty to grant them an early release from this vale of tears and a glimpse of the treasures in store for them. Their numbers had been swollen by a great crowd of hangers-on, the sort of character any diversion in a country district will attract. At the prospect of a bit of crack, especially at the expense of others, the lower elements of a dozen parishes were egging the pilgrims on.

56

Some of the young lads had cut switches from the hedges, and ran up and down the column of penitents whacking at their legs and backs to mortify the flesh. Others had grown weary of this sport and trudged dourly alongside, swigging from bottles. A few older women hobbled behind the crowd, carrying picnic bags and folding chairs. Bringing up the rear, an ad hoc colour party had raised a tricolour, on the grounds that any outing could be an occasion for showing the national flag.

Magee saw his opportunity. There was a narrow bridge on the road about a mile below the house. He directed the bandsmen into the fields on either side of the road beyond the river, ordering them to lie low till he gave the signal. His heart began to pound. Years ago himself and McCoy had employed a similar tactic at the ambush at Burntollet, when they had weighed into a crowd of students marching for civil rights. They still sang songs of that famous rout. With God's help today would see an even bloodier victory.

He kept to the lee of the hedgerows till he had reached the bridge and crouched below the parapet till the head of the march was nearly level with him. Then sure at last that he had not got the wrong end of the stick and was not making a ghastly mistake, he stepped into the road in front of them and held up his hand. In the other he clutched a meat cleaver. The pleas of the Donatists would fall on deaf ears no longer.

At the sight of the Portadown men the hangers-on took to the fields, scattering their flasks and sandwiches on the road. Some of them were not quick enough for the Loyal Defenders of William; their appeals for special status went unheeded. It began to rain and the road and the river ran red with the blood of the grateful dead. For an hour they stuck to their task. This was the sort of battle that coursed through the blood of Portadown men. It was another Dolly's Brae, another rebel rout. Then at last, the business taken care of, the sons of William shouldered their cudgels and pocketed their knives. They helped themselves to cold tea and sausage rolls which had been discarded round the killing ground. Their good spirits and sense of camaraderie restored, they set out on the road for home. They would have to keep moving, for not all the natives would be as obliging as those they had just dealt with. They would keep to the fields and ditches till they were sure they were out of hostile terrain. But once home there would be some serious drinking to be done. The whole business had given them a terrible thirst.

❖

Magee got to the Shambles and dismissed his companions. The square was littered with cobblestones. The door to the Martyrs Chapel gaped open. He didn't need to be told where he'd find McCoy.

'You didn't find her then?' shouted the preacher when he saw Magee, still bloody from the battle, in the doorway of the bar. 'She gave you the slip!'

'What the fuck is going on?' asked Magee, ignoring the taunt. 'Where did all this money come from?'

'It's the price of a Protestant soul!' McCoy said, turning away.

'Murphy the so-called Christian Brother paid in full for your flags,' Billy said. 'Sent it over with a simpleton to give to McGuffin. Rubbing salt in the wound.'

'And he's been drinking it ever since? That's money's that's owed!'

'Seventy-six trombones led the big parade,' McCoy shouted, 'but not one of them could rescue my wee girl from the clutches of the mother of all harlots.' Magee felt the blood drain from his face. It was bad enough to be mixed up with McCoy at a time like this, but to watch him squandering the bunting money might be more than his life was worth. Magee lifted a porter bottle and broke it with one gentle blow on the edge of the counter. It brought him the attention he required. There was no need for him to raise his voice now, for the bar had fallen quiet, each drinker lapsing into uneasy anticipation of what was coming. 'I asked what the fuck was going on?' he repeated. The money for the bunting, what was left of it, lay like thirty pieces of silver on the counter.

'You're a bollocks! It was you who scared her away in the first place!'

'Call me a bollocks one more time . . .' Magee said softly.

58

'I'll call you a bollocks for that's all you are. A useless, good-for-nothing bollocks. Supposed to be a hard man.'

'I've been tramping through fucking mountains all night,' Magee replied. 'I get back to find you and your cronies drinking the last of my money. So I'm asking for the last time, what the fuck is going on?'

'"What the fuck is going on? What the fuck is going on?" Put on another record. Isn't it obvious what the fuck is going on? We're washed up! Finished! Over and out!' He turned his back on Magee and called for whiskey.

Billy the barman didn't move, sensing the approaching denouement. The rest of the drinkers hung on every word, every syllable. Normally they enjoyed a good saloon bar brawl, all the niceties duly observed, all the formalities adhered to. They appreciated the slow build-up, the measured tones of sweet reason, the petulant hint of outraged complaint in Magee's persistent questioning and the way he could build on the one motif. But even as they watched developments they looked cautiously round for the best escape route for when the fur began to fly in earnest.

'The Lord giveth and the Lord taketh away,' said the man of God. 'Blessed be the name of the Lord.' He climbed off the stool and, swaying slightly, came over to his partner and put one arm round his shoulder. Magee let it lie there. 'A drink for my buddy, here, barman,' ordered McCoy. 'Mister Magee is a decent man. He'll have a drink with me before we discuss our little business arrangement. In fact we'll have a drink all around, Billy boy, and have one yourself, to welcome home the prodigal son from the far hills.'

He lurched towards the bar, scattering some of the coins lying there on to the floor. No one moved. Billy quietly locked the till and pocketed the key without moving from where he stood. Magee turned to the rest of the company. 'How long has he been like this?' he demanded. 'How long have youse been drinking my money?'

They looked away uneasily. This was a turn of events they had not bargained for, typical of a Portadown man.

'He's been like this all day, Mister Magee. He's wild upset. You'll get no sense out of him.' The voice from the doorway was

59

that of Patrick Pearse McGuffin. He had crept silently into the bar during the altercation to scour the ashtrays for dogends and the glasses for dregs of stout. His appearance was more than Magee could take. 'Get out of here you renegade! This is no place for you!' He lifted a chair and threw it at the turncoat. McGuffin snatched up the copy of the *Irish News* lying incongruously on the bar, ripped out the back page with its news of Easter Week dogs running at Celtic Park, and made good his escape before the butcher's boot connected with his backside.

But when Magee turned again to face McCoy, the menace had gone from his voice. The presence of the turncoat in a loyalist domain had unnerved him, taken the wind from his sails. A few of the men sitting closest to the door risked an unobtrusive sip of their pints, sensing with relief tinged with disappointment that the entertainment was over.

'You're nothing but a fucking liability,' Magee said. He dropped the broken bottle on the floor and grabbed McCoy by the lapels.

'As vinegar to the teeth and as smoke to the eyes, so is a sluggard to them that send him,' McCoy said. He located the stub of a roll-up and tried to bring a match into contact with it.

'If you ever cross my path again, so help me Jesus I'll personally brain you,' Magee said softly. He lifted McCoy off his feet and brought him close, so close that their faces were nearly touching. Then he head-butted him, suddenly and savagely between the eyes. The crunch of bone on bone could be heard across the room. McCoy fell against the counter, the blood already spurting from his nose. Magee turned defiantly to the rest of the company, inviting by gesture anyone who wanted trouble to step forward. There were no takers. He surveyed the silent tableau for a moment, spat on the floor, turned on his heel and walked out. Through the frosted glass of the window they could see his silhouette swinging a last kick at the battered chassis of the Salvation Wagon before heading off up English Street.

Though careful not to get too involved, the drinkers in the bar sensed that McCoy would want to restore his dignity by standing a few more rounds. As long as the hard man had really gone there would be no harm in humouring him. It wasn't every day that the Reverend was in the chair. They winked their approval of the way he had handled himself and allowed Billy to refill their glasses.

'Sing me a wee song about Portadown,' shouted McCoy. 'Does anyone know a Portadown song, for if they do they're a better man than myself!' His voice was nasal, for the blood had congealed beneath his swollen nose.

'That's a good one all right,' said Billy the barman, helping himself to a double scotch and most of the change.

'Portadown!' shouted McCoy above them in his best pulpit voice. He spat blood across the floor. Already he was feeling a lot better. 'Do you know what the trouble with Portadown boys is? They're always trying to be more Protestant than the rest of us. The meanest crowd of shites on the face of the earth . . .' he was warming to his topic now as the crowd quietly urged him on '. . . I've seen me and the wee girl reduced to begging round the doors, but do you think the hoors would give you as much as a cup of water? They wouldn't give you the smell of their fart if they could help it! But I've turned my back on Portadown, I'll tell you straight. I shall wipe Jerusalem as a man wipeth a dish, wiping it and turning it upside down . . .'

But at the memory of his daughter the tears sprang into his eyes. His hand had begun to tremble, and the whiskey he was clutching spilled over the bar. He turned grey. A glazed look came stealing over his face. Billy leaped across the counter, cursing, but he was too late to stop McCoy collapsing on the floor. He writhed in the sawdust in the throes of a fit, turning up the whites of his eyes and gasping for breath. Billy hauled him roughly to his feet and dragged him towards the door. McCoy put up no resistance, allowing himself to be thrown without further ceremony into the alley outside. A few of the drinkers peered out after him, staying well back in case Billy took umbrage and began barring wholesale. They saw his convulsions in the gutter, and saw that the turncoat McGuffin had crept out from under the van and was coming to his aid. Leave well enough alone, they thought, stealing back from the window to finish their pints.

But the evening's entertainment was over. Billy was in truculent mood. Any day now the GPs would reappear, taking over his back room, doling out their unique form of justice. He didn't want to be too closely associated with McCoy when questions were asked. He swept what was left of the bunting money off the bar and into his pocket, and began roaring at the company to finish their glasses and go home to fuck.

❖

The groans of the dying faded as the day wore on. One by one their souls shuffled off their withered bodies and, free at last, sped upwards to the throne of mercy. Frank lay silent at his mother's side as her life blood trickled away. His temple gaped open and his legs were twisted grotesquely beneath him. Night came slowly and the cold settled over the dead. A slow dawn broke. Night fell again. For three days he lay among the dead, drifting occasionally into fitful consciousness before lapsing into coma. Once he woke and the moon was out; he thought there was someone moving silently among the corpses. He wanted to call out to whoever or whatever it was but he drifted away again into troubled sleep. On the morning of the third day he cried out for water. Again he thought he heard someone nearby, someone hovering above him. He heard voices. He forced himself into awareness. He opened his eyes and raised himself up on one elbow, calling for help. A face bent down towards him, blotting out the light. He tried to speak but no words would come. He concentrated again on the grotesque yet familiar face that hung above him. Slowly his head began to clear, he began to focus, to remember, to recognize. He found himself staring into the cold grey eyes of his employer, Schnozzle O'Shea.

The Sisters had dug a shallow grave by the side of the road and were burying the dead. Though a Special Operations Unit, the élite of the Order under the command of Sister Concepta, they were edgy and nervous, eager to be on their way, fearful that a renewed attack might happen at any moment. Two of them crouched in the ditch beside the jeeps, their faces blackened, their rifles pointing up the road. Another had taken up position on the roof of the nearest farmhouse, her eyes anxiously scanning the misty hills above. Schnozzle pulled Frank clear of the corpses and beckoned one of the Sisters over. 'There's one more here,' he shouted, 'half dead, but with God's help he'll make it.' Frank could see his stole of authority under the flak jacket and saluted automatically. The Archbishop turned to Frank and studied him for a few seconds. Then the penny dropped. 'My God! It's Master Feely! Francis Xavier Pacelli Feely.'

'Yes, Your Grace.'

'I must say you have an uncanny knack of finding trouble. I hardly recognized you in that state. Is your poor mother among this crowd?'

'Yes, Your Grace.'

'God have mercy on her soul. You have no brothers or sisters?'

'No, Your Grace.'

Schnozzle reached into an inner pocket and produced a large handkerchief, stained with the evidence of repeated and copious use. 'Wrap that round the boy's head,' he ordered his aide de camp. 'Can't you see he's been bleeding like a stuck pig?'

As the tourniquet tightened on his temple, his brain began to clear. He remembered now the horror of the crossroads, the men with the knives and clubs, doggedly passing through the crowd; the screams of one half of them for their services, the screams of the others for mercy. 'No!' he wailed. 'No! No! No!' He was chanting the word, over and over, trying to fend off the memories that were crowding in on him. 'It's not true!' he started to tell them, denying the evidence that lay all round. 'Show me it's not true! It can't have happened,' he pleaded with them, softly at first, then louder as the terrible truth of the massacre sank home, then screaming it till it reverberated from the surrounding hills. 'It's not true! Tell me it never happened!' he pleaded, clutching at the unyielding figure by his side. Sister Concepta pushed him roughly away from her. He felt himself fainting, falling again on to the corpse of his mother. In his head he could hear the screaming of the multitude of victims. He saw the face of Chastity. He saw her face, the way he had glimpsed it in the cathedral, under the white veil. But they were leading her to an altar on top of a pyramid of stone where a priest with a butcher's knife awaited her. Suddenly she was Chastity no more, but it was the face of the Madonna herself, and he started to laugh, for he knew it would be all right; and then in his delirium the features changed again and it was the face of an Aztec virgin, screaming in terror as they led her to her sacrifice before the God of the Sun.

Sister Concepta slapped him hard and he stopped screaming. His mother's corpse was stiff; he saw them lift it and hurriedly throw it into the common grave. He wanted to go to her one last time, but Concepta held him firmly by the shoulder. 'Get into the bus, boy,' she ordered. 'Don't stand there. Move!' A battered charabanc had been drawn up across the road, loud with the wailings of orphans. Their confused, tear-stained faces crowded every window and as the engine revved they began to scream. 'That's the lot, Your Grace!' shouted the Sister with the shovel. 'We're sitting ducks here. Could I suggest with respect that we get our skates on!' Concepta gave a signal to the lookout and she scrambled down from the roof and climbed on top of the coach, automatic rifle at the ready. Schnozzle looked icily at the scene for a moment, then raised his hand in perfunctory blessing over the mass grave. 'Eternal rest grant unto them O Lord, and may perpetual light shine upon them.'

'May their souls and the souls of all the faithful departed, through the mercy of God, rest in peace.'

'Amen,' he said.

Sister Concepta was reaching the end of her tether. 'Get in the bus, boy, like I told you to,' she yelled from across the bridge. But Schnozzle had other plans. He took Frank by the collar and led him across to one of the jeeps. 'I'll take care of this lad myself, Sister, if it's all the same to you,' he told her. He pulled open the door and pushed Frank inside. They settled themselves on the hard seats and he gave the order to move out. 'I think we may safely assume that that's the last we'll hear from the Donatists,' he said.

'Until the next crowd of head-the-balls get some similar idea into their heads,' Concepta added bitterly.

'At least their prayers were answered,' scolded Schnozzle gently. 'And perhaps something good has come out of it after all. I don't blame you not recognizing this young man and the state he's in. But look closer and you'll see that under all the grime is Master Francis Feely. Master Frank works in the scullery, under the eye of the major-domo, and has done since the death of his father.'

'So he's an orphan now?'

'I'm afraid so. Alone in the cruel world.'

Concepta gave him a caustic look but said nothing.

'Maybe not quite alone, however. Master Frank,' Schnozzle whispered by way of explanation, 'is one of the children of the Dancing Madonna. One of the privileged few to whom Our Lady has spoken personally, if we are to believe what we've been told. It'll take more than a rabble of Portadown louts to kill Master Frank. That's why he has been spared the slaughter in which all the others have perished. Our Blessed Lady is saving Master Frank for something greater.' He took another handkerchief from his pocket, spat on it and wiped the caked blood from Frank's face. 'His father was a decent enough man in his way, but he failed in his mission. Somehow I don't think Master Frank is going to fail us! Are you, Master Frank?'

'No, sir.'

'I think the time has come for this lad to move out of the kitchen and on to something better. Mr MacBride has done all he can for him.'

Sister Concepta grunted. 'What had you in mind?'

'Something tells me that this poor lad here might have the makings of a great wee priest. He's got the perfect pedigree for it.'

'A few real priests are sorely needed at the moment, that's for sure,' Concepta muttered with ill-concealed distaste.

'Never doubt the wisdom of God. He never closes one door but He opens another.' He settled the travelling rug round his knees and produced his rosary beads. 'He'll make a great priest, mark my words. One that will lead the Irish people out of the dark ages and back to the true church. I feel it in my bones. A year or two under the unique services of the good men in Derry, in their bracing northern climate, will make a man of him.'

'You might be right.' She sounded doubtful.

'Of course I'm right,' he snapped, closing the conversation. 'I've never been wrong yet.'

The outriders hung on grimly as the charabanc swung round in the road, righted itself and the convoy moved off through the lanes. Frank was wedged between Schnozzle and Concepta, unable to move a muscle. A lethargy beyond tiredness, beyond hunger, was stealing over him. The conversation of the Archbishop and his bodyguard seemed to be coming to him from across an echoing chasm. Their words reverberated in his head, fighting for his attention with other noises that he was powerless to control. He could feel the enormity of what had happened welling up inside his brain. He fought the images away, forcing himself to stare at the scenery, to concentrate on the words of the rosary he was chanting automatically.

And yet the voices kept returning, screaming in his head, mocking him and tormenting him. He knew he was going mad. Again and again he banished them, refusing to let himself dwell on what he had witnessed. His mother's face, grotesque in its death throes, swam before his mind's eye, crying to him to join her. He refused to listen to her entreaties. He heard, welling up above the noise of the engine, the screams of the pogrom on the bridge. He fought them back. He knew that in the months and years to come these memories would give him no peace, but would live with him all his life.

Through the perspex panel in the canvas hood he could see the deserted fields of the borderlands racing past. They reached the outskirts of Aughnacloy an hour later and everyone began to relax. Schnozzle produced a hip flask and took a slow drink before putting it back into his pocket. The Sisters put aside their weapons and produced their beads. They had prayed their way through the five joyful mysteries and halfway through the five sorrowful when they arrived at the crossroads outside the town of Omagh. A fingerpost pointed north to Derry. With a squeal of its tyres the charabanc slewed to the left and without further formalities headed off unsteadily westwards, off into the badlands, its pitiful cargo still wailing. 'They'll bother us no longer,' announced Concepta with satisfaction.

'Hard work never hurt anyone,' Schnozzle answered tetchily.

No further reference was ever made to the orphans or their fate.

They picked up the river here and followed it north. The Strule was a modest stream at this point, bubbling over weirs and waterfalls where the salmon could be seen leaping. By Sion Mills it

66

had widened and by the time they had reached Strabane it had broadened to form the uneasy frontier between Derry and Donegal. Renamed the Foyle, its waters flowed deep, silent and menacing. They drove on in silence, except for the droning from the front seat where the Sisters still told their beads. An hour later they rounded a bend in the river, and below them there opened out on every side a panorama of the Maiden City in all its splendour.

Some sights have the power to thrill even the most jaded soul, and the first view of Derry from the hill at Prehen is one such sight. And though the daemons still haunted his thoughts, Frank couldn't suppress a gasp of amazement. The city rose dramatically from both banks of a broad meander in the river. On the Waterside the houses climbed steeply, clinging to the sides of the braes, each a different pastel shade. On the west bank it rose less steeply, a majestic progression from the masts of the hulks lying at anchor below the Customs House, upwards to the gables and towers and campanile, taking the eye higher still to a pair of spires that dominated the skyline. Even from afar the unbroken line of the city walls could be discerned, guarding the old quarter huddled round the Diamond at the top of the hill. Below them, stretching out across the twinkling water, ran the thin blue bridge, a two-tiered conduit between the opposing riverbanks and their peoples.

They crossed the bridge by the lower deck, skimming close to the waves, and sped up into the maze of streets on the west bank. But the mirage had suddenly evaporated. The enchanted city of a few moments before was but a trick of the light upon the water. From a distance what had appeared as imposing public buildings were now shown to be the gutted shells of abandoned warehouses. What had seemed rows of fairy dwellings were now revealed as alleyways of slums. All round were the palpable signs and smells of decay and despair. The streets were potholed and barricaded, though no one came forward to challenge the Archbishop's bodyguard as they drove unmolested past the towering tenements and the decaying monuments of symbolic defiance. 'They call it lovely Derry, on the banks of the Foyle,' Schnozzle said, echoing ironically the words of the song.

'It's the way they like it,' Concepta told him. 'They'd have it no other way.'

When they had been going the roads together, Frank and his father, they had avoided the populous cities, taking a detour round any place bigger than a village. His father had viewed all city dwellers with distrust. Up till now the Shambles had been all Frank knew. But here was something different! A sprawling town of steep streets, a place of smells and sounds and movement. He turned his curiosity from the blighted townscape to the people, who were now swarming on every side, oblivious of the siren and the screams of the Sisters. He had often heard his father, God rest him, joking about the Derry people. 'Derry wans,' he would say in the Patriot's, mocking their odd dialect, and the very expression was enough to elicit mirth without further elaboration. Now he could understand why. The town was inhabited by a race of pygmies! Unlike the tall tribes of the hills where he had grown up, these were a stunted people, yellow-skinned and short-arsed. The men, even the young ones, were prematurely old and wizened, with the pallor of early death on them.

But if the men were strange to him, it was the women who fascinated and terrified him. Derry women were the butt of many of the Tyrone man's jokes, jokes he had been too young to understand. Now suddenly he found himself surrounded by them, for the jeep had stopped and the driver and her helper had grabbed their blackthorns and leapt down to sort out an argument which had flared in the roadway in front of them. Queues had formed outside different doorways – he took them to be shops of a sort – and short, stocky women were haggling over the price of a few worm-eaten vegetables and some old clothing. As they rummaged and poked, they kept up a barrage of abuse, banter, complaint and invective, apparently oblivious to whether anyone was heeding them or not. The older women were stooped and haggard, but there were younger ones too. He caught the eyes of one of them, and received in return a look of insolence, curiosity and (though he could not have put a name to it) lustful enticement. Hastily he looked away, afraid she might be bold enough to approach the jeep. He had heard his father and his cronies joke about these people many a time, and even as a boy had recognized the hint of fear behind their sniggering.

At that minute the jeep lurched forward and the women scattered before it. They careered across an open space where the flea market was in full swing, overturning stalls as they went. Oriental merchants in turbans and palliaments haggled and cursed noisily over shoddy wares piled high on the backs of carts; gypsies squatted under the city walls lethargically soliciting alms. Then they were in a street again, a narrow winding street that rose up steeply through one of the gates of the city, where yellow young men scratched their backsides against the doors of derelict betting shops, muttering to each other from the corners of their mouths while the women fought each other for bargains among the rejects of the street barrows, crying to each other all the while in a strange gammon.

They climbed steeply out of the ghetto, up through the walls and past the ruined monuments to previous occupiers, then came to the gatehouse of the seminary. There was a flurry of activity; he heard bolts drawn back, orders barked, the clatter of boots on cobbled cloisters within. They drove into the forecourt and the massive gates clanged firmly shut behind them.

Three

In the small hours of the night, when the whiskey had worn off, McCoy would toss in bed halfway between troubled sleep and restless awakening, praying for another royal postcard landing on the mat that would tell him it had all been a bad dream. But with the breaking of each grey dawn he knew it would never be. His daughter was gone and he was disgraced. He would never see Chastity again. Even in death they would remain unreconciled, for what hell is hot enough for one who has turned her back on the word of the living Christ to embrace the obscenity of Rome? Night after night he called out to his God in his despair, echoing the words of Job, finding no comfort.

Till one night when his tortured soul, overcome at last with fatigue, let him sleep and in his sleep he dreamed of Chastity. He saw her, a small figure standing at the edge of the Shambles corner. He wanted to call out to her, for the place seemed suddenly filled with dangers, but his mouth was dry and no words would come. She was carrying a battered suitcase and looking strangely old. Slowly she walked past him across the Shambles and stopped at the door of the Temperance Tea Rooms. He could see that she was smiling. He wanted to run to her, to embrace her or to strike her he knew not which, but his feet were set in concrete and he was powerless to move. The dream faded and he slept like a baby till the raucous papist bells woke him to a new day.

McCoy knew that he had been given a sign. And that one day his daughter would return to him.

A letter clattered unexpectedly through the letterbox. A letter with an American postmark and all kinds of glorious messages on its envelope. He sank to his knees and gave praise to the Lord for this sign of hope. He opened it with trembling hands. Though it wasn't from his daughter and though his eyes could barely focus on the print, he read it through twice and knew it was a message from God.

Since the collapse of the bunting business, Lily was slowly returning to the insipid pallor that was her natural hue and Portadown had lost its one and only source of excitement. Magee was sitting in the bedroom above the butcher's shop staring down at the main street; shabby shopfronts alternating with the mean dwellings of the business classes, a scattering of churches without a decent spire among them, and beyond in the hollow through the tunnel, on the far side of the River Bann, the huddled houses of the papist poor. Portadown was a town noted for the industry of its people, the treachery of its fighting men and the God-fearing exclusiveness of its churchgoers. It was a dry town too, and the Citizen's Committee had their spies everywhere. Over everything there hung a pall of parsimony and righteousness. But these attributes profited it little, for the town had one great shame, one shared stigma that marked it off from all the others.

It was the only town in Ulster without a song to call its own. No sad émigré's lament extolled the fading memories of its environs, no lovers ever used it as a backdrop to their romance, no raunchy ballad praised the derring-do of its sons on the field of battle, or the labours of its girls in the mills. The surrounding countryside warbled to the strains of hundreds of ditties, some belonging to one side of the house, some to the other, a few shared by both with only subtle differences of intonation or emphasis to hint at the persuasion of the singer. The verses listed every brook or brae or hilltop, each famous for some exploit that had been immortalized in song. These songlines ran to the very boundary of the town, but there they stopped. Portadown stood unhonoured, a black hole against the surrounding white noise.

It was a serious matter, a matter of no small embarrassment, especially for a man like Sammy Magee who liked to travel away from town. People expect you to sing the songs of your fathers.

How else could you be known? They expect you to stand up for your native hearth, be it ever so humble. When your turn was called you would be obliged to give a verse or two, no exceptions. You might stumble over the words, you might be a corncrake, but honour would be satisfied. Who could say when such an occasion might arise? A night out with the Buffaloes or the Black Preceptory could easily end in an after-hours session. The self-appointed master of ceremonies would call on each brother in turn to do his bit, shouting at the others meantime to give their best order all round. Woe then to the Portadown man caught up in such innocent entertainment. Pity him as he tries to escape to the bogs, sensing his turn drawing near! See him led roughly back to his seat and forced to rejoin the company, for the baiting of the outcast is always bittersweet when the entertainment is homespun. In his time Magee had lived through a thousand such embarrassments, and tried a thousand such ruses, but they had unmasked him every time.

Magee, however, had never given up hope. He was as sociable as his upbringing allowed, and he chaffed against the restricted home life that the town, and Lily, imposed on him; the early mornings and early nights, the daily visits round the corner to her mother's, the twice-weekly visit with his brother and wife for gospel study. There must be more to life than this, he thought to himself, but he kept such ideas quiet, for subversive talk would end in trouble.

He turned from the window and picked up the fife once more. He tried a few more bars of the tune that was in his head. He was a player of only modest achievement, his career having been curtailed by his conversion, but then the LOL Temperance Defenders Flute Band was only a modest ensemble. That it existed at all was largely due to his perseverance against local censure. Music making, even Orange music making, was frowned upon by the more severely saved elements who ruled the town. The band had been his own father's pride, and his greatest joy had been to lead it annually to the field on the Twelfth. A natural musician, his father could lift any instrument and futter with it till he coaxed a tune out of it. But the son had inherited little of the father's talent, and the music had died the day Sammy had merged his soul in Jesus. The Temperance Defenders had sunk into near oblivion. Portadown had paraded without benefit of a marching band, to the derision and delight of their fellow loyalists.

He could play 'The Sash' competently; he could almost play 'Dolly's Brae' and 'Lillibulero'. A few slow airs and old time waltzes exhausted his repertoire. His one great, secret ambition still eluded him. It was a secret he had never breathed to another soul, not even Lily, for fear of the obloquy it would attract. He wanted to write a tune for Portadown, a song that would be for ever associated with the town, an anthem to the place that had reared him and made him what he was. And what better occasion to celebrate than the wholescale rout of the papist hordes at the bridge by Feely's farm. A handful of loyal brethren, undeterred, had stood firm against the odds and defended their heritage. He would try to find a tune that would recall that moment, then scribble a verse or two to fit the notes. He gazed down the windswept street and thought for a second that he felt an air coming into his head. He blew across the embouchure, letting his fingers follow their own pattern. The tune took shape for a few measures, till familiar snatches of other men's songs intruded.

He lifted the flute and tried again, a faster air; but within six bars it had turned into 'The Irish Washerwoman' and he quickly strangled its Fenian twittering. If they heard him playing jig music there could be ructions. The words of 'The Ould Orange Flute' were apt in the occasion:

For all he would whistle and finger and blow,
For to play papist music he found it no go;
'Kick the Pope', 'The Boyne Water' it freely would sound,
But one papist squeak in it couldn't be found.

His own flute was less noble, he noticed, and for some reason seemed reluctant to sing the praises of his home town and its citizens. Maybe Lily was right after all, maybe it had belonged to a Hibernian long ago, and was secretly itching to play jigs, reels and hornpipes? Bollocks, he told himself. It had been his father's

73

instrument, the one he used to play every evening when he came home from work. No papist mouth had ever blown a tune on it and never would. He put the instrument away; there was no point in going on. He'd sharpen the cleaver and cut chops for a few hours. Perhaps then he'd feel more inspired.

He was thus occupied when the turncoat arrived from Armagh with McCoy's note summoning him to the Shambles. Magee boxed McGuffin round the ears, for he had a reputation as a tough man to keep up in front of the neighbours, and sent him back with a message to tell McCoy to get stuffed. But as he continued chopping and mincing he was beginning to feel more cheerful. He'd let McCoy fret and sweat for a day or two, for he didn't want his services taken for granted. Then he'd take a trip over to Armagh to see what the fucker was up to this time.

As a younger man, McCoy had once purchased, for twenty dollars, the degree of Doctor of Divinity from Pastor Jeremiah Wallsteiner IV's Revivalist University of Kentucky. To this day the illuminated scroll testifying to this honour hung above the pulpit in the Martyrs Memorial. Since that shrewd investment, Reverend Oliver Cromwell McCoy BA MA DD had been on the Reverend Wallsteiner's mailing list. The letter causing all the excitement now, with its postmark 'Kentucky Loves Jesus', was one of these mailshots that still found their way to the derelict porch of the Martyrs Memorial Chapel.

Pastor Jeremiah had moved into television evangelism and was writing to all his alumni in great confidence and excitement, offering to share his ideas and secrets in this highly successful venture. Souls were to be won for Jesus in their thousands!!! screamed the literature, and there were $$$$s to be gained by the minister foresighted enough to buy into a piece of the action without delay. How To Help Yourself and JESUS at the Same Time!! read one booklet. Do You Seriously want to SAVE THE WORLD???? demanded another. DO YOU SERIOUSLY WANT TO MAKE $$$ FOR YOUR CHURCH??? screamed a third. McCoy found himself at one with Jeremiah on this one. 'THEN READ ON . . .'

74

ordered the great evangelist and millionaire. McCoy read on and McCoy was hooked.

The Reverend Wallsteiner had thoughtfully included in the package a short trial cassette of his successful television formula, by way of a taster for the full package which could be the reader's for a mere FIVE HUNDRED DOLLARS TAX DEDUCTIBLE (Send Cash Or Check Today!!). McCoy scrounged round English Street till he got his hands on a Walkman. Even before he retreated into the van to study it, he was aware of a clear inner voice assuring him that this was the new direction his revivalism should take.

Forget old tyme preaching in draughty gospel tents! Forget handling snakes in Hicksville! Forget cold open-air-style Baptism! The confidential voice of the American explained how the CHURCH OF TODAY did its business from the air-conditioned comfort of the studio. The big bucks for Jesus lay in selling air time. Hallelujah! The Reverend Wallsteiner illustrated his hypothesis with extracts from his own show, currently franchised coast to coast. In the background the celestial choirs hummed and wailed in perfect harmony, punctuated by hollers of aye-mens and 'Praise the Lord' from what sounded like a vast congregation. Then came the voice of the Preacher, strong and husky and confident, charged with emotion and close at times to tears, reaching out through this great new medium directly into the hearts and pockets of the folks at home. McCoy listened to it a dozen times without a pause, and knew that Magee would soon be putty in his hands.

'The perfect priest is born, not made!' the Dean of Studies announced. He paused. Among the new postulants a few heads nodded respectful agreement. The Dean repeated the aphorism quietly, inviting the boys before him to think about it and let its self-evident truth sink home. And then (he loved this bit!) he drew himself up to his full height, filled his lungs, brought the flat of his hand down with a crash on the lectern and shouted 'Bollocks!'

Dean Doherty opened the seminary year in the same way every Easter, and the effect had never disappointed him yet. 'Bollocks!' he roared again. And then to ram home the point, and because he was reluctant to abandon a word that had riveted the class so spectacularly, he spelled it out on the blackboard in letters a foot high. B.O.L.L.O.C.K.S. 'Learning to be a priest is the same as learning anything else. It takes work, hard work. It takes single-mindedness. You've got to be ready to put your backs into it. Learn, observe, study. You'll have to know your job inside out before you can be let loose on the streets in a dog collar. And one thing I can guarantee you, gentlemen, before any man jack of you is let loose you will know this job inside out. If anyone wants out, there's the door!'

He strode across the silent room and dramatically flung it open. He waited. Somewhere in the corridor a clock ticked slowly. No one moved. 'This is your last chance. Let it never be said that I forced any boy into the priesthood against his will. If any of you have any doubts, any scruples, any better ideas for your life than dedicating it to God Almighty, let him speak now or for ever after hold his peace.' The boys sat in silence, their eyes never leaving the Dean. He closed the door gently and walked back to the podium. For the first time they saw him smile. 'A wise choice, gentlemen, if I may say so. Welcome, then, to the greatest profession in the world. And together, with the help of God and a lot of hard work, we're going to keep it that way. I can make you one promise this morning; you will never live to regret that you took this step today, that you dedicated your lives to Our Blessed Lord and His Holy Mother, that you threw in your lot with the Church. You'll never regret that decision. Now let's all kneel down and say three Hail Marys and after that we'll get right down to business.'

Frank sat at the back of the cold classroom, hearing nothing, feeling nothing, understanding nothing. Since he had arrived in this place he had cried day and night. The image of his mother, running demented down the lane, was fresh in his mind's eye and would give him no peace. He wept too for his father, butchered on the Shambles. And he wept at other memories that came to haunt him, seeing over and over again the pale features of Chastity

McCoy led like a sacrificial victim under the swaying canopy. And he wept for Noreen, the only friend he had ever known, remembering his last memory of her innocent face pressed up against the window looking out at the bleakness of Ballychondom. They had been briefly happy once, if only he had known it at the time, happy with the innocence of childhood. Here in this alien place, surrounded by the harsh manners of adolescence, he felt more alone and more vulnerable than he had ever felt before. He began to dread sleep more than he dreaded wakening; for though the days were an ordeal, the night time held the real terror. He would wake in a fever, hearing once more the darkened car speeding through the countryside and imagining a face at the window pleading for his help. He would relapse and dream of her again, whisked off into obscurity, immured behind some foreign convent wall. Or dream of Noreen. Hear her calling to him, the lonely little girl with whom he had shared his childish secrets, marooned for ever in the wilderness at the end of the Yellow Meal Road, the secret shame of her parents dooming her to a lifetime of drudgery. And while the other boys groaned and tossed, he would cry himself back to sleep, and the face before him would be the Dancing Madonna, now lost for ever.

Dean Doherty watched his new charge with mounting apprehension. If it had been any other boy he would have taken the strap to him and beaten the devil out of him. But Frank was no ordinary boy. This was Schnozzle's pet project. The Archbishop had made that much crystal clear. There had to be something special about him. Dean Doherty decided to try a Holy Hour, said each evening at dusk, instead of the strap. But the terrors persisted. Frank had taken to wetting the bed and walking in his sleep. He had begun to pray, constantly, obsessively, filling all his waking moments with pleas to the saints for their intervention. It was unhealthy behaviour for a boy and the Dean knew it. He watched in horror as day after day Frank haunted the dark, musty chapel, going on his knees to each of the plaster saints in turn, beating his breast before the altar and prostrating himself before the tabernacle, trapped in a compulsive treadmill of ritual behaviour.

His dreams grew darker and more hideous. When the rest of

his companions had fallen into fitful sleep, Frank lay motionless on his narrow bed as the now familiar images of terror crept back to haunt him. He saw again the gaunt face of the renegade Patrick Pearse McGuffin, on the run from the Sacred Heart, desperately seeking asylum in a hostile land. McGuffin would be dead by now, he told himself as he forced the nightmare from his mind. Yet nightly, in the penumbra between sleep and wakefulness, he seemed to hear the forlorn voice of the Belfast man. Other, more dreadful alarms stalked him too. The river under the bridge running red with blood. The Madonna weeping like a banshee in her banishment. The face of the Archbishop, towering over him, bartering for his soul, locking him in a bargain he could never rescind, never renege on. Night after night he woke screaming and sweating, bringing the orderly running up from his chapel vigil to check the uproar.

The Dean began to panic in earnest. Who could name the day or the hour when Schnozzle (God forgive him for calling His Grace that, but didn't everyone these days?) would come calling unannounced and see his blue-eyed boy in such a state? Worse still, he knew that behaviour of that sort could be contagious, and already he was hearing rumours from Father Doherty the Confessor that made him uneasy. A general novena was announced and every boy in the school ordered to take part. For nine days they prayed in the dank chapel, all other business suspended. The Dean sent out to Doherty's Religious Wholesalers in the town for a dozen gross of candles, and he burned them before the altar day and night. He had the buildings blessed and the dormitories rededicated to Saint Columba, and he appointed one of the older priests to sit with Frank, praying the Sacred Office silently at his bedside as the boy tried to sleep.

And gradually the nightly terrors receded. The memories of his mother screaming mad in the roadway for deliverance gave way eventually to happier dreams, of a time in Lough Derg with his father, and of nights in Ballychondom with Noreen before the coming of McCoy. Dean Doherty noted the improvement in the lad's appetite and permitted himself a cautious sigh of relief. As the weeks passed even these memories faded. Frank no longer cried himself to sleep at night with the faces of his family fresh in his mind. The time-honoured routine of the monastery and the endless schoolwork began to absorb him. He began to apply himself to his studies. Dean Doherty ordered another novena, this time of thanksgiving. On the ninth day he was gratified to see Frank emerge from the chapel with the beginnings of a smile on his face.

At Whitsun Schnozzle, newly returned from Rome with the red hat, came visiting to monitor the progress of his protégé. A buzz of excitement ran round the corridors when the limo was seen pulling into the yard, and the tall, spectral figure of the new Cardinal came striding towards the main hall. Though they feared him, his arrival represented one of the few diversions in the school year. He marched into the refectory, asking them their catechism, throwing questions at them about the Nicene Creed or the Council of Trent or the Beatific Virtues. In the classroom he sat stiffly before them, poring over their school books, grunting quietly at what he found there. He interrogated them about holy purity. Did they keep themselves pure? Had they cultivated a true devotion to Our Lady? Were they ever tempted? Did they have unchaste thoughts or desires? About girls or boys? Did they suffer from nocturnal emissions? While his classmates reddened and squirmed under his questioning, Frank, as yet untroubled by the desires of the flesh, could look his patron straight in the eye and give him the answers he wanted to hear.

But Schnozzle wasn't easily foxed. He had noticed the gaunt and troubled look that still lingered in the boy's face and in the privacy of the study he subjected the Dean to an inquisition on Frank's progress.

'He needs a little longer to settle in, Your Eminence,' the Dean assured him. 'The poor creature has had a rough time of it growing up.'

Schnozzle grunted.

'His essays can be a bit on the pedestrian side,' said the Dean with satisfaction.

'I'm glad to hear it,' Schnozzle retorted. 'Many's the smart ass has read himself out of the church.'

'And spent eternity regretting it,' concurred the Dean. 'God is infinitely merciful, but the sin of presumption is a particularly hard one to forgive.'

'Is he troubled at all by impure thoughts?' His Eminence wanted to know.

'I think I can say for sure that he's not. It's quite remarkable considering the age he is. I think he must have the special blessing of our Holy Mother.' He had heard the boy's confession twice a week and knew first hand of his innocence. He hoped the Cardinal would appreciate fully the good job they were doing with his protégé and give credit where credit was due. There was a vacant bishopric coming up in the far west which the Dean had his eye on. He'd had his fill of pubescent boys.

Schnozzle picked his nose but said nothing. The Dean decided to try a different tack. 'With those good looks and that sunny nature of his, he'll make a great priest. A real ladies' priest.'

'Keep the women happy and you keep the men happy,' said Schnozzle. 'Lose the women and you lose the men.'

'He'll make a fine confessor too, I'm sure of it. I must start giving him more of my time. There's so much a young postulant needs to know these days. There's never enough hours in the day.'

Schnozzle had heard enough of the Dean's fawning. He rose abruptly and strode to the door. Dean Doherty rushed ahead to open it for him.

'You're never leaving?' he pleaded. 'There's a grand game of gaelic organized in your honour, between the lads and the day boys.' But Schnozzle hadn't come to Derry to watch football. He had heard all he needed to know.

'Sure you know where to find us any time, Your Eminence,' Dean Doherty assured him in his most obsequious voice. 'Our door is always open.'

Life in the seminary was as regular as a well-oiled clock, the motions of the boys governed by the age-old rituals of the monastic life. They rose at six each morning, heard Mass and prayed till breakfast time. A doorstep of bread and a mug of tea kept them going through the morning's work; and a plate of bacon and boiled cabbage, or some days a mutton stew, kept them going till it was time for bed. Their day was punctuated at regular intervals by devotional practices, and between visits to the chapel they studied their books. On Wednesdays they fasted and on Fridays they abstained. On Sundays they served collectively at High Mass, intoning the responses under the watchful eye of Father Amadeus Doherty, their singing tutor. Nor was the physical side neglected. 'I like to see a young priest with a bit of brawn on him,' Father Flaherty used to say as he led them twice weekly down to the sloping pitch at the bottom of the hill. 'A priest these days needs to be able to handle himself in a rough-house, should the need ever arise. God preserve us all, it's terrible times we live in when not even the clergy can walk the streets without some eejit or other having a go at them.'

Though many of them were rough lads, as yet unschooled, or at best having only the benefits of the Brothers' education behind them, a year in the seminary would make men of them, men who could pass themselves on the sports field as well as in the examination hall. They would learn the rudiments of their vocation, how to rise before dawn to prepare the vestments and the altar; they would learn how to sing, songs sacred and secular, for a priest with a cloth ear is an affront to his parishioners. They would learn the basics of scholastic philosophy and the outlines of Church history from the Dean himself. From Father O'Brian they would learn Latin and Greek. Before a year was out, they would be able to parse and analyse each without hesitation. They would learn Irish from one of the laymen, and from the Bursar delve into the intricacies of ancient Gaelic poetry. In a year's time, the Dean assured them, they would go on to Maynooth, if they still showed promise and if God spared them. There, in that great finishing college of the Irish clergy, among its quiet cloisters and rococo chapels they would be turned into priests of the One True Church.

And of course, as befits those training for the Irish priesthood, there was another, greater mystery to unravel. The Dean took them aside in groups, walking with them through the hurling field of an evening, demonstrating to the boys the finer points of the church's teaching on matrimonial coition. He paused by the muddy goalposts and explained about natural and unnatural acts.

81

Circumstances that would frustrate the lawfulness of the sexual act and the place of annulments and separations where such circumstances could be proved. How a lack of *animus copulandi* might be grounds for annulment. They followed him through the hoar frost to the fifty yard line as he outlined to them some of the other problems of the marriage bed – *vaginismo definitur fortis constritio* or *membrum supra normum*, that could lead to problems of consummation. It all sounded complicated to Frank, an obstacle course through which only one path ran without problems. But he was becoming used to complications; they were the very stuff of his future calling. He and the Dean could discuss these matters without any trace of embarrassment. They interested them in the same way as any other conundrum of scholastic philosophy.

As the long winter evenings dragged on, they trudged together through the mud and talked about the problem of women in general. Unlike his classmates, who were easily flustered, Frank took it in his stride when the Dean explained the intricacies of the female cycle and the mechanisms of the safe period; he took it in his stride, too, when the Dean showed him how you could tell what a woman had been at the night before by the look in her eye or the feel of her hand. Slowly and lovingly, he imparted to the boys all his knowledge of women and their secret, musky underplaces, confirming in himself with every sentence his lifelong vow of chastity.

But no amount of freezing walks could tame the rampant turmoil of Frank's classmates. Every night, when the last rosary was said, the postulants wrestled with the devil for possession of their immortal souls. They writhed in their hard, narrow beds, trying to deflate their throbbing tumescences with pleas to Saint Martin de Porres or Saint Theresa, patron of holy purity. Even as they prayed for help, their heads would fill with immodest images of thighs and breasts and inviting lips, crowding out their fears of the terror of hell and their imminent damnation thence if they entertained these fantasies any longer.

All but Frank. Unbothered by their nightly battles with the flesh, he took to applying himself to his books. He was growing tall while still retaining the boyish looks of the tousle-headed lad he had always been. Already his height was tempered by early hints of later portliness. By contrast his fellows appeared gauche. They had started to shave. Some had faces raw with acne, some had lost teeth, some needed glasses, some displayed signs of premature baldness. They had all the roughness and awkwardness of adolescence. When Dean Doherty brought himself to look into their faces, he could detect in many of them the makings of parish priests, canons even; rough enough characters, but good men in their own way. A few years below in Maynooth would knock the corners off them, fill them out a bit, teach them confidence, show them how to address women without stammering and men with the authority of their calling. They would pass muster with a few more years of hard work.

But Frank, he thought to himself, was different. The boy seemed totally content with life behind the high walls. Daily he rose with a light heart to serve Mass and receive the sacrament. He was scrupulous in his religious observance and assiduous in his studies. To his tutors he was polite and deferential, and he avoided most of the thrashings that were the daily diet of boarder and daydog alike. At night, when it had grown too dark for further study, he would lie in bed, arms chastely folded above the rough blankets, telling his beads.

The window of the dormitory gave on to the chapel roof, and the city lay huddled but unseen below. If they stood on tiptoes they could make out the contours of Creggan and beyond that, through the gloaming, the outline of Grianan Aileach, the hill fort standing sentinel over the twin estuaries of the Foyle and the Swilly as it had done for three thousand years. On summer evenings, when the moon was overhead, the boys would gather at the open window listening to the sounds of the city. Laughter, sometimes, or cheering; other evenings strange screams and stranger silences. They could hear at times a woman's derisory jeer, or the collective hooting of the men. Other nights there would come floating up to them the noises of battle, stones rattling on armour plating, sporadic bursts of gunfire or the thud of distant bombs. Perhaps if the evening were calm and the town quiet, the sound of the Apprentice Boys band would float over to them, the high sweetness of the fifes above the unsynchronized rattle of the snare drums. But Frank had little time for such diversions. While the others sat in the fading light, their cheeks pressed against the bars, straining to make sense of the disparate sounds from the world beyond, he would leave them to their speculation and turn his attention once more to the lives of the saints.

The playing field was about the only place they met the daydogs. Once a week they played gaelic and hurley against the biggest of these boys, thrashing them roundly every time, taking delight in tramping those pale, frail bodies into the glar and snapping their stunted limbs. Contempt for the town boys was encouraged by the priests, fearful of the corrupting influences of the outside world. They had a strict rule against fraternization. But unlike his companions who bartered illicitly with the dayboys at half-time, Derry held no attractions for Frank and he rarely acknowledged their presence. The other postulants, bound by their preliminary vow of poverty, had no material possessions, but they had time on their hands and a certain native wit. They could write compositions, translate Latin, help with the intricacies of Irish spelling. They saved many a dayboy from the hideous hidings that the priests doled out at regular intervals and in return were rewarded with snippets of chocolate and small packets of cigarettes.

But the dayboys brought into the seminary something more important than the tawdry confectionery stolen from the hucksters' shops; they brought illicit tales of a fabulous life outside its walls. Fights and drinking, gossip and feuds, births, marriages and deaths. What the boarders wanted to hear above all were tales of women, and the daydogs alone could feed this appetite. The women of the town had a reputation that stretched as far as Scotland, and the emaciated dayboys would boast of their conquests on the disused railway lines or behind the empty gasworks. The novices would listen open-mouthed to boys of their own age, who barely reached to their shoulders, bragging of smoking forty a day and needing three women a night. In all these stories one woman figured above the rest. Dymph the Nymph! Whether real or chimera, the image of Dymph the Nymph became the focus of their waking fantasies and their nightly dreams.

Frank would listen to none of their smut. Though he was fast losing his Armagh accent, replacing it with the distinctive sacerdotal tones they taught in elocution class, there was still enough of the country boy in him to recognize bullshit when he heard it. These jack-the-lads talked like hard men now, but in a few years' time they would be Bogside corner boys, no-hopers, has-beens. They could keep their filth to themselves, and their stories of the city beyond; he would stick to his studies and carefully cultivate his vocation.

Where Portadown is songless, Derry by contrast is the heartland of song. The very blackbirds in the bushes by the Foyle seem to warble more sweetly than any in Ireland. The boys of the maiden city may well have no asses in their trousers, but they sing fit to charm the birds off the trees. Their days are passed in cut-throat singing competition, *feiseanna* and festivals. There are tawdry consumer goods to be won, or sometimes cash prizes. Rivalry is intense. Each parish has its contenders and in the major league no adjudicator is safe, for the outcome is often bloodily resolved. But the Feis of Sacred Song, held the weekend before Saint Patrick's Day, is a civilized affair with only book tokens for the victors, a showcase for the purest and loveliest voices. Of all the competitors entered that year none was more dulcet than Frank. 'He's as sweet as a nut,' the Dean whispered with pride, listening to Frank's rendition of the Panis Angelicus.

'A voice, God be praised, that would bring tears to your eyes,' the other priests agreed. On stage, Frank was taking an encore. The lovely strains of the Ave Maria rose confidently above the rippling accompaniment of Father Amadeus Doherty's well-tempered piano. He walked off with the laurel wreath that day. There wasn't a singer in the town who could hold a candle to him.

But the adjudicator, Professor O'Doherty (if his opinion had been canvassed), could have told the Dean that Frank was singing his last as a boy soprano. Professor O'Doherty knew how fickle an instrument a boy's voice can be. In the higher register he alone had heard the first hints of puberty.

Trouble of one sort or another wouldn't be too far behind.

Four

A television station had been beyond even Magee's ingenuity and though McCoy huffed for a while, he eventually acknowledged the difficulty. But all was not lost; Magee was not beaten. He drew up a contract with the preacher, guaranteeing him a fifty-fifty share in the profits and stood over McCoy till he signed it. A week later he returned to Armagh with a radio transmitter he had burgled from a defunct firm of black taxis on the Shankill Road. It was antiquated equipment, its dials opaque and its valves encrusted with dirt, but he persevered till he had it rigged up, covering the floor of the chapel with wires and extension leads, held together by insulation tape. It was soon obvious that the whole device had a tendency to overheat; Magee borrowed a hairdryer and screwed it on to a stand to keep cold air playing on the machinery when he switched it on. McCoy eyed the microphone hungrily and practised his opening remarks.

The Reverend Wallsteiner had stressed the need to give what he called 'regular updates of the ambient temperature within the area of the callsign'. This handy hint, he assured prospective franchise holders, gave the viewer a feeling of community togetherness, and was cheap to run. It was not a service McCoy's listeners were much in need of, for they only had to stick their heads out of the door to check if it was raining again. Even that wasn't strictly necessary, for if ever it stopped raining you could be sure that a neighbour woman would be in your back door telling you to put your washing out. All the same, he didn't like to deviate too much from the formula, the 'Sure Fire, 100% Tested Formula for $$$uccess!!!' as laid down by the successful Reverend Wallsteiner. And so it was that the first words broadcast on Born

Again Radio, coming to you from downtown Armagh in the heartland of Ulster, was the ambient temperature in the Shambles area, calculated by Magee at a seasonable thirty-nine degrees Fahrenheit. With that out of the way, McCoy knuckled down to the real business in hand.

He blew into the microphone a few times. Magee, positioned on the wall of the lavatory in the middle of the square with a transistor up against his ear, gave the thumbs up to McGuffin at the door of the chapel, who shouted in to the preacher that he was on the air. At this assurance McCoy began to bellow into the mike.

'This is an historic day for the people of Ulster. May the Lord be praised! Can youse hear me out there? This is the Reverend Doctor McCoy, speaking to you from the Martyrs Memorial in Armagh. Some of youse thought you would never live to see this day, when through the miracle of modern technology the word of the Lord could be fearlessly preached to every home in this beloved province of ours. Them that have ears to hear, let them hear. For lo! the blessed day is upon us, the day that sees the Lord's message on its way without interruption into the homes and the hearts of the Ulster people.'

Overcome at this point by the emotion of these sentiments, he pulled out a handkerchief from his pocket and blew his nose noisily, clearing his throat volubly while he was at it. Magee, sitting in the lavatory, was assaulted by a blast of feedback and thought he had lost the signal. But before he had time to fiddle with the receiver, McCoy, his toilet completed, came back on the air again, loud and clear.

His voice sobbed with emotion. 'But you know my dear people, my fellow Protestants, you can't run a radio station on fresh air. These things cost money. Many of you older people will remember the time I started up the Protestant Newsletter. You'll remember those days with affection, and our enemies will remember them with trepidation. It was the only Protestant paper of its kind in the world, and what did they do? They laughed at it! They said it couldn't be done! They said it would never catch on! That there was no need of it! They said that the ordinary gutter paper, with its lies and filth and half truths, with its lying fabrications against true Bible Protestantism, with its advertisements for foundation garments and its articles written by Romanists and their fellow travellers in the so-called World Council of Churches, and faint-hearted so-called Unionists only waiting their opportunity to sell the Ulster people out to Dublin and into the bondage of Rome for a mess of pottage, they all said sure what's wrong with the ordinary paper? It's good enough for us! What do we need a Protestant paper for, you'll only go stirring up trouble! And the people, my friends, the people gave them their answer! They supported that paper! They weren't afraid to read the truth! They weren't afraid to know the truth! They weren't afraid to publish the truth! For the truth shall set you free!' He paused and once more had recourse to the handkerchief.

'But just like that great newspaper, we can't run a radio station on thin air. We need your contributions. Every penny will go to keeping this Protestant radio on the air, twenty-four hours a day, preaching the Risen Lord, preaching Christ crucified, preaching the old time evangelism that the Ulster people thank God have never and will never forsake. No matter how devious the wiles of the harlot of the Tiber. You'll hear no popery on Born Again Radio! You'll hear no backsliding ecumenicalism. You'll hear no nancyboy vicars advertising jumble sales! You'll hear only the Word of the Lord! Hallelujah! The Lord be Praised! And they taught in Judah, and had the book of the law of the Lord with them, and went about through all the cities of Judah and taught the people. And some of them brought him presents, and tribute silver, and the Arabians brought him flocks, seven thousand and seven hundred rams, and seven thousand and seven hundred she goats, for the valley sheep are fatter but the mountain sheep are sweeter! Now I'm not asking for seven thousand and seven hundred she goats! There wouldn't be room in the Shambles for them, though I'm sure Mister Magee, our chief technician here at Born Again Radio would be only too happy to receive the odd beast, for I can tell you he's a dab hand at preparing a carcass, and if any of you people out there are over Portadown way you could do worse than call into Magee's Select Flesher and Victuallers for all your sausage and mincemeat needs; the best butchers in Ulster I'm reliably told. But if we are going to continue to teach the book of the law of the Lord throughout the cities of Judah, and that means Armagh through to Loughall and over as far as Aughnacloy, then you're going to have to support this radio station with your gifts of cash. And if any of you are parents and have young ones in the habit of listening to the wireless, and that's the way it is with young ones nowadays, you can be sure that your young people will be hearing only things that are wholesome on this channel, for there'll be no smut on here! No disco music. No jungle drums or crooning or suggestive lyrics. No jig music either, the Pope has enough radio stations as it is! It's time the Protestant people of this province had their say. And that glorious day has come. Then the eyes of the blind shall be opened and the ears of the deaf shall be unstopped. Then shall the lame man leap as a hart and the tongue of the dumb sing. For too long the Ulster Protestant has been dumb. But no longer! Send off your donation, large or small, this very day. Do it now! A little one shall become a thousand and a small one a strong nation. Every donation will be personally acknowledged by me or one of our helpful staff here; every penny you send will be used in the fight for God and Ulster. But remember, my Protestant friends, if we lose this fight, we may as well throw in the towel and let them take over. And we will lose this fight unless we have your contributions, your covenants, your support. The enemies of Ulster are at the door! There is no peace, saith the Lord, unto the wicked. And now we'll have some music, after this word from our sponsors.'

A forum of critics had gathered in the saloon bar of the Boyne Memorial Lounge and were listening to this historic opening on the bar radio. Magee made his way over to them, nodded to Big Billy that he'd take a pint, and began to do some market research. He was well pleased with the signal; McCoy's voice, though strangely distorted, had come through loud and clear. The reaction of the boys in the bar was less satisfactory. The references to disco dancing and crooning, straight from Reverend Wallsteiner, had caused some mystification, while the intermission for a word from our sponsor had elicited snorts of derision. One of the reasons he had made for the Boyne was to canvass Big Billy for a sub in return for a few plugs on the air, but the gleam in the proprietor's eye made him defer this particular transaction until a more auspicious time.

The lounge was now filled with the harsh music of a marching band. It came from one of the records that had been donated to the station after he had been round the doors in Scotch Street. Already they had almost a dozen – two copies of 'The Pride of Shankill Accordion Band Playing Your Marching Tunes', assorted copies of the 'Southern Baptist Tabernacle sings Olde Tyme Favorites', all three LPs of the Reverend McCrea (Ballymoney's very own Country 'n' Western pastor) and an album of light orchestral. The latter had been vetted carefully before finding a place in the station's repertoire; when he was satisfied that there wasn't a Fenian note in it, or anything that could give offence to a salvationist household, McCoy let it join the others, with the proviso that it was reserved for the wee small hours when most Protestants with delicate sensibilities would be safely abed. Magee had found the gramophone in Portadown, and after more rewiring and soldering he got it to work. Another hairdryer had been called into action to keep the turntable cool. It was a solidly built piece of machinery, old-fashioned but serviceable. It had an arm that could be loaded with all twelve of the station's records; they would fall automatically, one by one, on to the turntable, provided McCoy could remember not to knock against the table, in which case the lot of them jammed with a grating sound.

'I see you're enjoying the entertainment,' Magee said to the boys in the snug. 'I hope now you'll agree that it's worth paying a little extra. The office is open for donations, or if you're too busy I'll be only too pleased to run across with it myself.' The boys in the snug ignored him (for who pays any attention to a Portadown man?) and went on with their drinking. Above them, the radio was still blaring out its medley of marching tunes. Here and there a foot was tapping, but it was clear to Magee that no one was going to pay the piper. Typical Armagh shysters, he thought. He finished his pint and went back across the Shambles to the chapel.

McCoy watched the slowly revolving turntable with satisfaction. The door opened and Magee tiptoed over the wires, avoiding contact with the equipment. The look on his face told his partner that they hadn't exactly been throwing pound notes at him over in the Boyne Lounge. He went to speak but McCoy hushed him, for the Pride of Shankill had just brought 'Derry's Walls' to a coda, and in the interval before 'Lillibulero' he leaned across to the microphone, turned up the volume on the amplifier, blew twice (old habits die hard) and then began to bellow out a message for the boys in the bar: 'Naked came I out of my mother's womb, and naked shall I return thither; the Lord gave and the Lord hath taken away; blessed be the name of the Lord!'

'Amen,' shouted Magee behind him.

'I need not remind you all out there, that those words are taken from the Book of Job, Chapter One, Verse Twenty-One. And I need hardly go into detail about what is meant by those words. You can't take it with you! Not one penny of it! Naked shall I return thither. To meet your Maker. What are you holding on to it for? Do you think you can buy your way into that Paradise that is reserved for the Elect? Do you really think that you can take it with you? This Bible Service on this here radio station, needs your financial assistance. Don't hesitate! Send your money now! The Lord's work will not wait on the morrow. Do it now! Mister Magee will be back over for your subscriptions in a minute!' He lowered the microphone and brought the accordion music back on. The transition was a bit abrupt, for though he had been shown a dozen times how to effect a smooth lead-in from speech to music he was still clumsy with the equipment and ill at ease preaching into a void without the feedback of a live audience to keep him on his toes.

'The signal's okay,' said Magee. 'At least round the town. I couldn't say how far out it might be reaching.'

'Did you hear me giving it to them?' asked the preacher. 'How do you think I sounded?'

'You sounded all right.' Magee was noncommittal. 'A bit up-from-the-country, if you know what I mean.'

'You're a city slicker yourself, I suppose! All of a sudden Porty-down is the Home Counties!'

Magee spat on the floor to indicate his contempt for McCoy and his household. 'You wanted a station and you got one. Just don't balls it up, that's all. The lads in the back snug will be wanting their divvy, and I'll be looking for my money back. Remember I've sunk a lot of my capital into this venture.'

'Capital? A clapped-out old contraption like this?' He flung out his hand and the record player wobbled. 'Lillibulero' died in mid-phrase; there was a rasp of static and then the Reverend McCrea dropped on to the turntable and began an interminable ballad about finding meaning in the cards of a winning poker hand. 'If it's your money back you want, you'd better make sure this signal is carrying a bit further than the Shambles Yard! If I wanted to talk to the Shambles all that bad, I could always stand in the window and shout! Sure what use is the Shambles crowd? People round here wouldn't give you the time of day!'

'You'll need an aerial if you want to get further,' Magee grunted. 'And if you think I'm risking my arse rigging up an aerial you have another think coming. If you ask me this whole scheme of yours is nothing but a load of bollocks!'

No one took a keener interest in their goings-on than Pearse McGuffin. All his life McGuffin, in common with most of the males of the ghetto, had nursed two impossible ambitions. The first was to get his hands, even fleetingly, on a Protestant woman, preferably a nurse. Mitching school with his classmates from the Christian Brothers, he would spend the afternoon on the disused railway banks masturbating to lascivious daydreams of submissive Protestant flesh. He had boasted like the rest of them of the Orangewomen he had ridden and would ride again, but in his heart of hearts McGuffin knew that his fate lay with the scrawny, wall-eyed women of his own side.

His other ambition was to be, even temporarily, a disc jockey, playing the top ten and reading the weather and the traffic news in a mid-Atlantic accent. The Falls Road held few opportunities for realizing either dream. Little wonder then that he viewed the birth of Born Again Radio as an opportunity to kill two birds with the one stone.

His initial job was to stack the gramophone, for it was soon obvious that McCoy was cackhanded where even the simplest machinery was concerned. One afternoon, a few days after the opening, McGuffin found himself alone in the studio. McCoy had just delivered himself of a long peroration on the text: 'If you prick us, do we not bleed? If you poison us do we not die? And if you wrong us shall we not have revenge?' which he announced came from the Book of Obadiah. He had elaborated it to draw parallels between the Chosen People of old and the modern Protestant. The Ulsterman was as decent a man as you could meet in a month of Sundays, he declared, but let the Pope or the Pope's men in Dublin, or anywhere else for that matter, try to interfere with our historical rights and they'd see how quick we were to rise to revenge. And so on and so forth till, satisfied that he had put the Protestant position straight with the help of the Good Book, he had faded in the familiar strains of the Singin' Preacher (still finding inspiration in the Royal Flush that Jesus had dealt him) and hurried across the Shambles to check the reception once more in the Boyne Bar and Lounge. He was in the snug taking a little something for his throat, with the volume turned up full so that the strains of the Singin' Preacher flooded the premises, when the record stuck. One minute the Reverend McCrea was going great guns, his exegesis on the deck of cards almost complete; next minute he was stuck in a repetitive groove, vacillating between the Jack and the Queen.

It was a crisis. McCoy was on his feet, scattering the glasses from the table. If it wasn't stopped this minute he'd be a laughing-stock. He knew country wit; they'd be crooning the crackling phrase after him for the rest of his days. But Patrick Pearse was equal to the task. The preacher was hardly out the saloon door when they heard him lift the needle and put the Reverend McCrea out of his misery. There was a moment's silence, and then the voice of the renegade filled the room.

McGuffin's diphthongs were elongated into a tortured imitation of the voice of America, but there was no mistaking the accent's genesis on the Falls Road. 'That record's a bit scratched,' he said, 'so I'm just going to take it off and play you all another one.' The sound of a genuine taig on their airwaves, albeit one that had come home to Jesus and could show you the scars to prove it, sent a shudder of collective excitement round the

Shambles. They deserted their domestic chores, called for hush and turned up the volume. 'Anyway, I was beginning to get a bit bored with that one, to tell you the truth, weren't you? It's time we had a few new records here at Shambles Radio, so if you've got any to spare that would be suitable, send them along, you all know the address. And maybe this is as good a time as any to drop a plug for our newest, hottest and most exciting project down here at Radio Shambles headquarters. Yes folks, I can let you into a secret here; we're about to open the fund for a home for fallen women, a haven for poor Protestant creatures that have forsaken the ways of biblical righteousness and dallied with the ways of Satan.' McGuffin felt himself coming in his trousers at the very thought of it. 'Remember what the Good Book says: If thou wilt be perfect, go and sell that thou hast, and give to the poor, and thou shalt have treasure in heaven. Pastor McCoy taught me that verse when I still walked in the ways of unright-eousness. So I'm going to dedicate the next record to him, to my buddy if he doesn't mind me calling him that, the best friend a man could have in the world, for he gave me a greater present than any other person could give me, he showed me the path to Jesus. So if you're listening out there, ol' buddy, this one's specially for you . . .'

Sadly, his ol' buddy was not listening. By now he was halfway across the Shambles, determined to kick seven shades of shite out of the renegade for fooling around with the equipment and making a reel out of him when he had only popped out for a moment. But all round the town they had been listening, and as they listened their glee at McCoy's discomfort was turned to wonder at the sound of the Fenian's voice. The Protestant heart is not easily melted, but Patrick Pearse had done the trick. He had done what McCoy could never do. They knew McCoy for what he was, a loud-mouthed ignoramus trying to bully pence out of them by shouting at them, but the Belfast man was a natural deejay. His voice, his timing, his presentation were perfect. As the music started up and he faded out, there was scarcely a dry eye round the Shambles. McCoy reached the studio a minute later, tore off his belt and was putting his intentions into practice when the first knock was heard on the outside door.

He stopped hitting McGuffin and went to answer it. A snotty-looking youngster was standing at the chapel door holding a grubby envelope. 'My mammy said to give you that,' he said, 'and she says to be sure you get the wee Fenian to read it out.' Inside was a scribbled note requesting the enclosed for the eldest in the family, gone but not forgotten, wishing him and his mates in the Kesh best wishes. The paper bag contained a well-scratched single record. It also contained (wonder of wonders!) a pound note. The record was a sentimental ballad, popular on both sides that season in the bulging prison camps of the province. He who pays the piper calls the tune, thought McCoy. If it had been the Pope himself singing he would have considered giving him air-time for a pound. He passed the record uncensored to the turn-table and handed Patrick Pearse the request to read. He blew his nose and interrupted the Shankill Warriors. They played it twice; then they played it a third time at the correct speed. Patrick Pearse talked them through the technical teething problems, his mixture of banter and Bible wisdom smoothing over the gaps in trans-mission.

After that he was never off the air.

Could the wee taig read out a request for my mammy, my daddy, my brother, my auntie? Birthday requests, anniversary requests, engagement requests, coming out of jail requests, going into jail requests. Some didn't want music, but asked instead to hear him read a passage from the good book. Sometimes they would have a favourite passage, or sometimes they would leave the choice up to the convert himself. McCoy would fling open the book on the floor, in the time-honoured way, and let the Lord guide his hand towards a particular text. Patrick Pearse would whisper it into the microphone while his old buddy coached him in the more difficult names. The listeners were capti-vated. A small contribution would gain you a mention on the air. Ten shillings would guarantee you a good three minutes, more after midnight if he could keep the Fenian awake. But a pound would get you a full request, with plenty of time to include all your extended family and the household pets by name, as well as your sacred musical choice in full.

Whole families clubbed their pennies together, vying with the

Though categorically proscribed, under pain of ferocious flogging, a radio had been smuggled into the dormitory. The daydogs had managed to slip the spare parts past Security and a couple of the boarders, with commendable ingenuity, had soldered them together into a makeshift receiver. They had rigged up an aerial across the dormitory, disguising it as a washing line festooned with grey Y-fronts and malodorous socks. When the lights were out and the footsteps of their guardians had died away in the cloisters below, they huddled round and tried to tune it to Luxembourg. The set howled like an animal in pain, threatening to bring the wrath of the priests down round their ears at any minute. But they persisted, fiddling and futtering, adjusting valves and aligning diodes. And just when they were on the point of giving up, the dormitory was suddenly filled with the high nasal voice of an American rock and roll star singing the blues. The number died, but with persistence they retrieved the signal and were rewarded with the epitome of erotica, a female vocalist pleading for love.

Frank, aloof from this behaviour, considered summoning the Dean. What was happening was nothing less than a scandal. Foreign filth was flooding in everywhere, threatening all that was true in Irish culture. To make matters worse they had forgotten already that it was coming up to Saint Patrick's Day, a day when all that was true and traditional in our culture should be upheld. He would go personally to Father Doherty in the morning and have the accursed contraption ripped out once and for all. He pulled his pillow over his head and feigned sleep.

But later that night, in the small hours while the others finally slept, a strange madness seized him for the first time. What uncontrollable compulsion was this, drawing him towards the radio to toy with the dial? It wasn't the dance-hall rhythms of Luxembourg that were calling him. He wanted news from the world outside, from the land he had crisscrossed with his father and from which he was now so effectively isolated. *Óm Sceol ar ardmhagh Fáil ní chodlaim oíche*; they had taught him the ancient poetry and it had struck a chord. He knew that nothing had changed. At the news from the high lands of Ireland I cannot sleep at night.

He reached out and plugged the set in. Slowly the valves began

101

to glow. Cautiously he adjusted the tuning wheel, hearing the static rise and fall as it slipped from station to station. Hilversum, Petrograd, Lyon. He could find nothing he could understand. He tried again and again, tuning meticulously, desperate for a voice that would speak to him from the great world outside. He had almost given up when he was rewarded. Through the wails of static he heard a voice, far away and very garbled, interrupted constantly by a cacophony of foreign tongues. The short hairs on the back of Frank's neck stood erect. He had heard that voice once before, in the public house in Pettigo, the night he and his father had first set out for the Yellow Meal Road. It was a voice he would never forget, the voice of the man with nine lives, Patrick Pearse McGuffin.

❖

One of the Patriot's few pleasures in life was to tune in to Athlone of an evening and listen to An Nuacht. It was a ritual well established in the bar; the drinkers who patronized the establishment knew to call for hush when the first peals of the Angelus reverberated from the old set placed high up among the whiskey bottles. The reception from Radio Éireann was often garbled, the voice of the newsreader competing with howls and wails from the ether. But none of this interfered with the Patriot's pleasure. He lumbered on to a chair and stood with his ear to the set, his face furrowed with concentration as word came through of battles in the Middle East and political skulduggery at home. He understood little of what was said. But sometimes a word or a phrase would fall into place and his face would open into an expression of pure pleasure at the recognition; in the silent bar there would be smiles all around and conspiratorial winks at the prospect of extended credit and generous measures for the rest of the night.

At the precise moment that McCoy was blowing into the mike across the square and calling the province to order, the Patriot was tuning in to Athlone in the firm expectation of hearing five minutes of the pure language of the Gael. He found instead his eardrums assailed by vulgar *Béarla*, the English of the Planter,

102

demanding that he repent his ways forthwith and ordering him to send his donation off immediately after these messages. He tried to change channels, hoping to find the Angelus elsewhere. But the set was old and stiff, unused to anything but soft Irish spoken civilly, and his fingers were uncouth. Everywhere he tried he found McCoy.

'The Lord giveth and the Lord taketh away; Blessed be the name of the Lord!' There was the skirl of an Orange Pipe Band and then the bellowing of the bigot once more, warning them that he that maketh haste to be rich shall not be innocent, and he that giveth unto the poor shall not lack. The Patriot let Eugene fiddle with the knobs in the hope that it was all a bad dream. But for all his efforts, he got the same result, McGuffin announcing the temperature in the downtown area (a breezy three degrees above freezing) followed by the big man himself trailing his upcoming sermon on the secrets of the Vatican, and biblical prophesy fulfilled.

The Patriot lifted the set and threw it across the bar. It landed in the sawdust and the outer case splintered into a thousand bakelite fragments. But its innards were made of sterner stuff. For a moment the valves flickered, then they righted themselves and the voice of McCoy once more filled the saloon. The Patriot left it where it lay. Without a word Eugene cleared the bar and bolted the door. No one loitered to remonstrate about their unfinished pints. The bar remained closed as all night long the voice of the tormentor boomed up at them from the shattered wireless, demanding money with menaces.

The vegetable man collared Eugene the next morning when he was dumping the empties in the yard. 'Did you ever meet the beat of that bastard across the way? It's a mystery how something hasn't been done to quit his warbling. I don't think one of us got a wink of sleep last night what with one thing and another!'

'You're not the only one discommoded,' Eugene told him.

'And did you hear that racket from your attic? Something was thumping away up there last night, rats or that. You'd need to put something down before we're all plagued.'

'I'll mention it to himself,' Eugene said, closing the conversation.

❖

Though he wasn't normally a great one for the radio, even Schnozzle above in Ara Coeli couldn't escape the consequences of what was going on in the Shambles. For one thing he could hardly ignore the swaying Eiffel Tower of scrap metal rearing up in the square, threatening to dwarf the spires of Saint Patrick's itself. Nor could he ignore Immaculata McGillicuddy, whose demands for direct action were becoming more strident by the day.

'Do we neutralize them? Yes or no? Just give us the word!' she insisted.

Schnozzle waved her question aside, and turned to the window. Below lay the Shambles. He could trace English Street and Scotch Street winding through the town. Irish Street too, where his people lived. There was a time when they would have paid with their lives for moving outside their designated areas. Such times weren't so long ago either, nor so strange to the people who guarded the honour of their territories. It wasn't as easy as Immaculata made it out to be. He was a Shambles man himself, born and bred in the timeless slums below. He knew all too well the uneasy truce that existed in the area, a truce that could be broken by precipitous action of any kind. Furthermore, McCoy's Tower of Babel would be well protected. He had seen from the window of the limo, as it sped through the area, the thuggish outlines of Magee and the Portadown bandsmen. He wasn't personally acquainted with these gentlemen, but he knew they wouldn't let Immaculata spoil their little earner without a struggle. He smiled to himself. It would make an interesting contest. The Protestant boys were strong and well armed, and no doubt the butcher had money invested in the radio. But Immaculata, on the other hand, had all the fanaticism of her order behind her, an unshakeable faith in the correctness of all her actions that he could only envy. Schnozzle wasn't a betting man but . . .

Then there was the question of Patrick Pearse McGuffin. Since

104

he ran away from the ghetto and threw in his lot with McCoy, Schnozzle had followed his progress with interest. It didn't take him long to conclude that Patrick Pearse McGuffin, in his incongruous new life as disc jockey and aspiring pimp, posed little threat to the foundations of the one true church. Immaculata was immune to the irony of the situation. Make a public spectacle of the turncoat, that was her solution. Schnozzle knew that the ways of God are infinitely more complex than our human brains can ever fathom. He sensed the divine hand at work and knew that all, in time, would be revealed. Already the germ of an idea was growing in his head. He would fight fire with fire. Tomorrow, if God spared him, he would take a run north and check his protégé. It was time Master Frank Feely got started at Maynooth. A boy like that would be qualified in no time at all. Schnozzle had plans aplenty for him then.

It's as well that His Eminence couldn't see the prodigy at that moment. Frank was lying under the blankets, the receiver pressed to his ear, listening to McGuffin pleading for donations. He was sharing his dream of the Rest Home with his listeners. And as he did so a strange new sensation began to creep down Frank's body. An image flickered into his mind, legions of unattainable Protestant women abandoning themselves to the lusts of the flesh. He thought of saying an Act of Contrition, but the lewd thought persisted. McGuffin's voice faded. He shook the set and the renegade was back once more whispering in his ear.

Small wonder then that in all the confusion he almost overlooked the arrival of his first real hard-on.

Five

Saint Patrick's Day. *La Fhéile Pádraig*. A festival older by a millennium than the patron saint whose name it bears. The turning of the stone. Winter gives way to spring; the boy gives way to the man. It is the most unsettling day of the year, a day for retrospection and a day for new beginnings. The rooks are rebuilding the rookeries and the hares are rutting in the woods. A day for killing the winter-fed boar and a day to start sowing the spring crop. A day for carnality and drunkenness.

A day when all men look to the past and all women look to the future.

Dean Doherty knew the problems that Saint Patrick's Day could bring. The lads might be quiet all winter, but the seventeenth of March would see a change in them, a restlessness that no number of retreats or floggings could totally control.

The nuns of Ireland had reason to dread the saint's day too. Even the isolated holy nuns of Caherciveen, the Little Friends of Mary. Though the girls in their charge might be special (and who could be more special than Noreen Moran who had been vouchsafed a vision of the Holy Mother herself?), yet the day would not pass without a ripple of restlessness running through the convent.

The bishops knew it, and the priests knew it, and went in trepidation of it, for if there were a secret in a man's life, though he could live with it for twenty years, it was round Saint Patrick's Day that it would come out.

And better than anyone else, Schnozzle knew it. As he rose to greet the dawn, he knew that the time had come for him to reclaim his blue-eyed boy.

❖

106

Four thousand miles to the west, on the bleak and beautiful Keeweenaw peninsula, it would be dark for several hours yet. But in the Roadkill Café, on the edge of the Reservation, Chastity McCoy was already at work brewing the first coffee of the morning. A dozen pitchers of beer, dyed green with a gallon of concentrated spinach juice in deference to the day, stood in readiness on the counter and Chastity, by order of the tribal elders, wore a green plastic shamrock on her apron and a leprechaun badge saying, *Kiss Me I'm Irish*.

Through the small kitchen window she could see the icicles hanging in grotesque formations from the gaunt trees. The woods were silent at this time of the year, but she could hear the groaning of the pack ice on the great lake beyond the bayou. Even with the stove lit it was bitterly cold. Saint Patrick's Day, the Indians had assured her, was by tradition the beginning of the thaw, marking the end of the long days of winter. The tribe would celebrate the saint's day with dogged sullen drinking. But Chastity could feel that the long-awaited spring was many weeks away. The overnight temperature had fallen to twenty below and there was a storm brewing somewhere over the bleak vastness of Lake Superior.

The Roadkill opened at six. There would be the usual trickle of early morning regulars, hung over from the night before. Business might pick up by mid-morning when the truck drivers stopped off. She would be on her feet till dusk. As she went about the familiar duties of the place, Chastity tried to shake from her mind the still vivid memory of her dream. She fried donuts and pared potatoes, saying to herself her morning prayers. But the after images lingered and couldn't be so easily dispelled. Just as Saint Patrick had heard the voice of the Irish people, their cries like the wind in the rushes, calling him back to them, she too had dreamed of her own father, calling her back to Armagh. She had seen his face again, gaunt with grief and bewilderment at her betrayal and had woken to the sound of his sobbing.

Why, she asked herself, as she did every morning, why had things turned out the way they had? How had she ever got mixed up in all this? Why had she let Alphonsus talk her into coming to this place? Would it not have been easier in the end to stay with her father, sleeping in the ice-cream van in the summer and in the chapel in the winter? Surely she could have put up with Magee and his advances for a year or two more till she was old enough to leave them for ever.

It had been exciting for a while, that first year in California, after Alphonsus had declared he was never going back. He had been a different man then, a man chasing a dream, sampling the hundred and one cults that the West Coast had to offer like a kid in a candy store. But Chastity knew it could never last. They were living on borrowed time. Nowhere was safe. They were a pair on the run. On the run from those they had outraged back home, on the run from the authorities here, uneasy and unclear of their legal status in an uncaring land. She had grown weary of the deceit and the paranoia, and the way they were forced to move from state to state, living in motels doing part-time jobs, passing herself off as older than her age, another piece of the restless tide of American jetsam.

So when they had come to the Upper Peninsula and he had told her that these were her people and that they would settle among them she had welcomed the decision with relief.

The Keeweenaw was the furthest they could go, a thin finger of land, surrounded by the endless grandeur of the lakes. A peninsula on a peninsula, set in the middle of an inland sea, guarded to the west by the Iron Mountains and to the south by the treacherous Seney swamp. In this remote spot Alphonsus began to feel safe at last. There had been white men here once, a century before when there was copper and hardwood to export, but they had rapidly plundered its natural riches and left it despoiled. The Indians had quietly returned. It was Chippewa land again, part of the reservation that straddled across to Canada over the rapids at Sault Saint Marie. The Chippewa accepted Alphonsus in their fashion. They needed a priest among them who respected their ways. They asked few questions, made few demands.

Sometimes when he had smoked strong marijuana in the woods Alphonsus imagined himself following in the footsteps of the earlier missionaries; Marquette and his band of Jesuits who had opened up this wild territory to the Europeans, travelling with the Ottawa to their summer hunting grounds and tracing with them the portages that lead to the headwaters of the Mississippi. He was happier, for a little while, than he had ever been before.

Except at night when he closed his eyes and saw again the mean streets of his childhood and the parish he had abandoned, and heard the desperate cries of his countrymen.

Though she had grown to resemble the Indians, with a broad face and black eyes, Chastity was weary of the reservation and the few pleasures it had to show. A run-down casino offered bingo and craps. A sawmill whined intermittently in the short summer months. There were shibeens aplenty. And for dining out there was the Roadkill up on the highway, touting for custom from the passing trucks. After a year she knew she would never be at home here. She had nothing to say to Wayne, slouched over the counter till noon every day; or Gary, swerving past in his pickup; or the women with their sanguine view of life, speaking Ojibwa, a language she would never understand. She found her thoughts wandering back to the ice-cream van on the Shambles and the days of her childhood. As a girl she had only ever thought of escape, from the tyranny of her father and the lecherous hands of Magee, from the stifling narrowness of the place, the incipient violence and sordidness of it all. She knew it was still the same, that it would always be the same. No power would ever assuage the hatred and bigotry of her birthplace. Why then could she never put the Shambles out of her mind entirely?

They were safe here, Alphonsus insisted, when she tried to broach the subject of her homesickness. Safe from the vengeance squads who might pursue her elsewhere; safe from the authorities looking for green cards. But she understood what he was really saying. She knew that he had brought her here to escape from his own troubled conscience. He was the one who would be running for ever. For the legacy of the Falls Road is not so easily discarded. Alphonsus knew, in his heart of hearts, that one day it would stretch out to reclaim him no matter what.

❖

Frank woke next morning aware of a strange stirring in his loins and the bed beneath him wet and sticky. The other postulants had long since reconciled themselves to the endless round of masturbation and absolution and paid him little heed. Outside the window a sad bird was singing; he listened to it instead of leaping out of bed as he usually did to be first at Mass. He heard the dim, distant sounds of the city awakening. The clip-clop of horses, and motor traffic rumbling over the bridge. The voices of women barging and children crying. Until now it had never intrigued him, this city of rubble beyond the grey walls, for he remembered only too clearly the images of dereliction he had first witnessed the day the Sisters had driven him here. He'd had no truck with the dayboys either. They were a scrofulous lot, albeit the hand-picked flower of Derry youth, well cowed by the casual brutality of their teachers, smelling of dirty feet and stale urine. He ignored them as they shuffled to the back of the class, their speech coarse and incomprehensible, their bodies stunted, their humour rough and vulgar.

But as he lay in bed, listening to the bells pealing above the chapel and the answering chimes from Saint Eugene's across the city, he began to wonder about them. What was life like beyond the walls? The thought excited him strangely. Before the day was out he would have to find out what lay outside the seminary. His hand reached down under his pyjamas and felt the brittle pubic hair that had sprouted overnight, and the stiff insistence of his organ for relief.

The cubicle door was flung open and the Dean of Studies stood above him. 'Why are those hands not above the blanket, boy?' he shouted, 'and what are you doing still in bed?' But his voice was restrained, nor did he lift his fist as he would normally have done, or the toe of his boot, to hoist the laggard from his warm bed on to the lino. This boy was his great hope, and he didn't want to spoil anything at this stage.

Frank mumbled an excuse. He had a temperature and a sore throat. The lie came naturally to him now, leaving, he noticed, no residual remorse. Maybe he would try and suffer for his sins, he added to the Dean, making a show of rising from the bed. Maybe catch pneumonia and be laid up for weeks, said the Dean

110

kindly. He put a friendly hand on his shoulder and pressed him back into the bed.

'Lie on until you feel a bit better,' he said, 'I'll have one of the other boys bring you up a cup of tea after Mass. We can't have you coming down sick on us, can we?' At the door he paused. 'And if there's anything . . . anything in particular troubling you, anything you'd like to discuss . . . well, you know where to find me.'

'Thank you, Father,' said Frank. 'I'll be as right as rain in a wee while.' Even as he spoke he felt his penis straining against his fist and the sperm welling inexorably up through its shaft.

'We can always sort these things out, you know. Man to man. With the help of Our Blessed Lady we can put the temptations of the flesh behind us . . .'

Dean Doherty closed the door and cursed quietly to himself. What a time for this to happen! What if the whole business unsettled the boy, just as he was about to go to Maynooth? Caused him to start having doubts? He'd seen sensitive boys like Frank before, getting themselves into a terrible state with scruples and worries, and no one able to help them. Why in God's Holy Name couldn't Schnozzle's blue-eyed boy have been more like the rest of them? They'd give you your fill of trouble all right, but at least you knew they'd turn out okay in the end; doubts would be the least of their worries. A regime of cold showers and early morning runs, a few rigorous sessions in the confession box and the problem would be as good as solved. But this lad was different. He couldn't start ordering the cold bath treatment for Master Frank. Whatever else happened, he mustn't do anything to upset the boy or cause him to do anything rash. Cardinal Schnozzle had his heart set on ordaining the lad himself.

Frank lay in bed analysing his feelings and examining his conscience according to the formula he had been taught. The act he had just performed had been pleasurable. But was it sinful? He could quote the opinions of some very learned and some very obscure men to say that it was so. The guilt that even now should

111

have been welling up in his breast failed to arrive. And he found that he didn't really care. He even thought about doing it again, and as he thought about it, his cock began to struggle back to life, trying to stand up, like a drunk man who has just been hit but who knows his drink is not yet finished. He had been taught often enough the routine for when temptation struck, how to say an act of contrition, examine his conscience and pray to the Blessed Virgin till the torment passed. But now that the time had come to put the emergency drill into practice, he found himself putting it off. What was wrong with him? Had he lost his faith as well as his vocation? Why was he not panicking, beating his head on the wall in anguish and despair at the utter emptiness of life, instead of lying there in bed trying to conjure up images of Dymph the Nymph? At the very notion of this houri his prick ached, bulging upwards purple and bold, demanding attention.

Afterwards he lay back and contemplated his life. He examined the problem from all angles, slightly taken aback by the cool, dispassionate way he was able to evaluate the situation. But perhaps that was the way it should be. For the first time he understood what Saint Paul meant. When I was a child I spake as a child, I understood as a child, I thought as a child; but when I became a man I put away childish things. The time had come to make some real decisions. Did what was happening to him mean he was not cut out for the priesthood? What would he do if he left now? Where could he go? Back to South Armagh, where they'd eat him alive! Disappear into the city below and live like an animal, not knowing where the next meal was coming from? He examined his conscience further. Why should he not become a priest? It was the only thing he knew, the only training he had. It would be a shame to waste all the book-learning he'd had to date. Besides how could he break the news to the Dean? Or Schnozzle? Could he really picture the Dean showing him to the door with a smile and maybe a few pounds in his pocket for the journey? Was Schnozzle Durante the sort of party who would let his investment slip through his fingers without lifting a hand?

Was he already damned, he wondered? One of those lost souls condemned from the beginning of eternity to act as a warning to others? Was it possible that he had no real feelings, no real conscience, and that his piety and spirituality over the years were nothing but a sham? What had happened to him overnight, turning him from the model postulant, humble, hardworking, deferential – the makings of a perfect priest – into the lecherous, cynical monster he felt he had become, wallowing in his own filth, the fate of his immortal soul hanging carelessly in the balance?

He listened again to the noises of the town. Why had he ignored them all these years? Those secular sounds now seemed to him the most magical, the most enticing, the most alluring in the world. Out there was real life, lived by real people, his people. The sort of people his father and mother, God rest them, had been; the sort of people his ancestors had been from time immemorial. Ordinary folk, rough and ready, but with hearts of gold. What was he playing at, living this artificial life among these artificial people, wasting his days and nights on dead languages and disputes in Canon Law? His mind was made up!

Before the morning was out he would have a word with Bosco Doherty.

Bosco was one of the louts who lounged in the back seats during history class, loud-mouthed and boastful, a part-time pimp, contemptuous of the authority of the fathers and openly sceptical of their sanctity when they weren't watching him. Frank had always treated Bosco with open contempt. Now he needed his services. He forced himself out of the bed eventually. Tonight he would put Bosco's braggadocio to the test.

Downstairs the Dean was deep in thought. He had been long enough in the job to know the confusion of emotions that must be running through the lad's head. He knelt before the statue of Saint Malachy and prayed for guidance in handling the situation. He'd had boys like Master Frank once or twice before, sensitive souls who were either all one thing or all the other. No give and take; always worrying, always trying to get to the root of things. You'd think they were exactly what the doctor ordered till something like this came along, and the next thing you heard they were for jacking the lot in and running away. Normally a good kick up the ass, or a few rounds in the ring with the gloves on and they would start to get things in perspective. But he knew

113

that wouldn't work with Frank. There was only one thing for it, he'd have to let him get it out of his system. It was a risky thing to contemplate, but he couldn't afford to lose this one, not if he was ever going to get the ruby ring and crozier. He looked at the statue for reassurance. Malachy was a man of the world, a practical man of his time. Dean Doherty decided he would do nothing hasty, for a day or two at least.

No doubt the lad would try to escape into the town one of these nights. That's the way they always behaved when the change came on them suddenly. The last one had killed himself falling off the chapel roof on the way back in. He'd sneaked out with the dayboys before they had tightened up security, and tried to climb back in at midnight in a state of mortal sin, only to impale himself on the railings below the dormitory. A terrible business! He couldn't risk any accidents with Frank. He'd issue instructions to the caretaker to leave some of the windows unlocked tonight, and maybe a ladder accidentally lying against the outer wall. He'd intimate to the other clergy to pass no remarks if they heard noises on the roof. But he knew the risk he was running. What if the other boys took advantage of the open window and he had a mass breakout to explain? And if the lad never came back, or came back maimed, or (God preserve us) got himself killed and the smell of sin on him, how could he ever explain that to Schnozzle? Might this be the very night His Eminence would call unannounced? Lately he seemed to do nothing but run the roads. If he wasn't in Belfast he was in Dublin; if he wasn't in Dublin he was in Cork. Nowhere seemed safe from his sudden visitation. The whole country was on its toes, for you never knew when your man would drop in without so much as by your leave, demanding to see the books and not showing any signs of moving till he was satisfied everything was in order.

Dean Doherty looked once more at the businesslike face of the medieval saint and thought he detected there a look of encouragement. He'd make a special offering to him if it turned out okay, a half-holiday and a Missa Cantata. In the meantime he'd put his trust in God that no lasting harm would come to the boy. And he'd send for one of the Redemptorists from over the border and have him on permanent standby till the crisis was over, ready to hear confession day or night. Chances were the boy would be less embarrassed by the outsider when the time came.

❖

'O my God I am heartily sorry for having offended thee . . .' Though it was Saint Patrick's Day, Sister Imelda had gathered her special flock around her for an English Literature tutorial. Some of the girls, whose fathers were paying good money, had examinations coming up, and besides what better way to spend the day, when High Mass was over, than in a study of poetry. Like Dean Doherty, Sister Imelda knew that the Ides of March could be an unsettling time for her charges. And as they recited the reassuring words of the Act of Contrition, her eye landed on Noreen Moran in the front row and she felt herself blushing modestly.

It was seven years since Noreen had come here from her far-off home in Donegal, escaping the aftermath of McCoy's raid on the Dancing Madonna. She stood now on the threshold of maturity. Even in the convent, where such things should matter least, everyone knew she was beautiful. 'Too beautiful,' the Reverend Mother whispered. 'Too beautiful for the outside world, where they will corrupt her and seduce her. A creature of such spiritual beauty belongs in the convent, safe behind its walls.'

Reverend Mother's word was law. From that day forth it was taken for granted that when she turned eighteen, Noreen would take the veil.

Sister Imelda led them through the Act of Contrition a second time to be on the safe side. Experience had taught her that girls of this age were ripe for the temptations of the flesh. Even girls as special as these, isolated in the Kerry mountains with not a man in sight and only exposed to literature of the most uplifting nature; even into this Eden of purity, reserved for those favoured by the BVM herself, even here, the serpent could raise its hooded head.

Noreen closed her eyes, forcing out all distractions, trying to concentrate on the words alone. A turmoil was raging in her soul, a turmoil that Sister Imelda, even in her wildest dreams, could

115

not have guessed at. The dream that had come to her in the night would give her no peace. She had always feared sleep, for she had been troubled by dreams night after night since she had been forced to abandon her father and Canon Tom and flee the wrath of the Sisters of the Faith. Night after night she heard in her dreams the Dancing Madonna calling out to her for help. But last night's dream was different and more troubling. In the hour before awakening, when the first soft bells of the chapel had pealed out their greeting to Saint Patrick's Day, she had dreamed suddenly of Frank, the strange silent boy who had come mute to her house in search of the miracle that would unlock his tongue. And dreamed too of Chastity and the night the Madonna had danced for the pair of them.

The débâcle that had ended her childhood still had this power to haunt her, the memory of that Christmas Eve with Frank and his father, snug and safe till McCoy had come among them. But what sort of a childhood had it been anyway, the nuns implied when she tried, once, to speak of her fears, with her father a spoiled priest forced to hide in ignominy in the wilds of Donegal and her mother dying of guilt before she ever got to know her? Noreen had never spoken to them about it again.

She finished the Act of Contrition and offered a prayer to Saint Patrick. It was foolishness, she told herself. What was Chastity McCoy but a wee bigot who had come briefly into her life only to betray her trust? And where was Frank? Killed long ago, if what the nuns said about the North was anything to go by. But there had been a second dream last night, one that she hardly dared recall. For when she fell asleep finally she saw Frank once more, a tall lad now, no longer solemn but laughing; she was laughing with him, running round her father's house where the heather grew between the rocks above the incessant sound of the sea. And she had wakened with the touch of his lips on hers.

'There is no such thing as a lapsed Catholic!' Sister Imelda confided when they were all settled. 'They all come back in the end, every man jack of them, screaming for the priest. Even James Joyce! Died begging for the last rites. Do you know what I'm about to tell you?' (They did, they had heard it often before, but they wanted to hear it again.) 'On his deathbed his last words were to burn everything he'd ever written before it destroys the country.' She had this on the authority of an old nun who knew a priest who heard it from the lips of the man who had brought the sacred viaticum to the old scribbler before he faced his final journey. 'Of course,' she added, sitting up businesslike and smoothing down her wimple, 'of course you'll hear precious little about that in the books they're pouring out about him nowadays. It's all an industry, you see, millions to be made out of filth, books like that sold openly in O'Connell Street and nothing the priests can do about it!' To Joyce she added a list of other infamous Irishmen who had likewise died screaming for the sacrament. One or two had been lucky, others decidedly less so. As a literary woman herself she felt reasonably sure she could name those now suffering the torments of hell. Throughout their lives these were men who had consistently tried to corrupt the morals of the race and lead it from the Church. Their deathbed agonies invariably culminated in a recantation of all their books, seeing in their last few moments the folly of their life's work.

The girls knelt and said a prayer for the repose of the soul of the late James Joyce, in the faint hope that he had made it to the Mercy Throne, followed by an Our Father and three Hail Marys for the repose of the souls of all Ireland's writers, past and present, said with a sigh of such complete anomie that no one doubted it was a bit of a lost cause. And then to cheer themselves up they said an Our Father and three Hail Marys for a happy death for the present company.

Sister Imelda settled herself once more and, in a stream of consciousness that Joyce himself might have envied, began to share with them her secrets on preparing for a happy death. She was a Mayo woman, and on a good day she could rival Chaucer or Boccaccio when it came to storytelling. Down the years she had amassed a stockpile of anecdotes and these she would plunder to illustrate both the infinite mercy of God and the concomitant danger of presumption. Start her off and she could go on for hours. There were stories with happy endings, involving exotic locations, slant-eyed pagans and Irishmen making it into heaven by the skin of their teeth and the fortuitous arrival of a priest, invariably Irish too, at their deathbed. There were stories of suspense to keep you on the edge of your seat, stories of poor exiles fallen from the faith, trying to reconcile themselves with God at the last minute through an Act of Contrition, when the flames were already leaping round the pot they were stewing in, or before they expired on the barroom floor in some sleazy city in the Far East, or as the ship went down with all hands in a distant, shark-infested ocean. And there were stories of such terror that they would haunt you for the rest of the day. Stories of young girls fallen from grace, maybe even girls who had once sat on those very benches they were sitting on now, who thought that an Act of Contrition was enough in itself to make things right again with God. Lulled into a state of deceptive euphoria, filled by the Devil with false presumption, they felt they could put off confession for a day or two, felt they could walk out and face the world without a worry.

Walk out and fall under the wheels of a CIE bus more than likely! It was then that your troubles really started!

She invited her wide-eyed charges to contemplate the horrors of hell. They sat in silence for a minute listening to the ticking of the schoolroom clock and the rustle of the mice under the milk crate. They listened, too, to the racing of their hearts. 'Now imagine an hour,' she said. 'A day. A year.' Her voice became slower. 'Ten years. A hundred years.' She paused. The clock was now ticking deafeningly. 'Now a thousand years. A hundred thousand times that and you have a million.' (She was no mathematician; Eng Lit was her subject.) 'The world we know no longer exists. God has destroyed the universe. The sun has been quenched, the stars obliterated. The human race, with all its pride and its sinfulness is no more. All material things have ceased to exist. Another million years passes slowly.' They listened to the clock. 'But your sin has not been forgotten; it has not been forgiven. That sin you committed on earth and never repented, because you were too proud; that insult that you threw in God's face, has not been forgotten and will never be forgiven. You cry out, but you can never be heard. You had your chance and you turned your back on God. You regret it now! How you regret it now, with every second that passes! The pain of the fire increases with every minute. It is in your eyes and burning your throat and

118

scaring your brain. You want to die, but you are already dead; you want it to stop but it will never stop! It will go on getting worse every minute of every day for the rest of time. You think you will never be able to stand it. But you've got no choice. Your cries fill Hell. The Devil's curses are the only answer you get. God cannot hear you!' She paused. 'But eternity is only beginning. Another million years tick slowly by . . .'

Noreen grew pallid and gripped the lid of her desk. The blood drained from her face and the pins and needles shot up her arms. Before they could reach her she had fainted on to the floor. Sister Imelda kept a little bottle of something strong-smelling in the wooden cupboard and the girls waved it under her nose as eternity receded and the colour returned to her cheeks. God knows, the girl would make a fine nun, Sister Imelda thought with satisfaction. Even, with the help of God to Whom all things are possible, a great nun, one who would be worthy of leading the Order, maybe even, dare she say it? a saint. 'We'll just say a special prayer to the Sacred Heart for a special wee intention,' she said, and there were tears of hope in her eyes.

Bosco Doherty had the same stunted body, the same bright shifty eyes, the same cowed look of all the Bog Doherty clan. But where the others were bowed in submission, creeping from classroom to chapel in terror of the priests, Bosco managed to bring into the seminary something of the insouciance of the streets. Each morning he lined up at the picket gate with the other daydogs, not permitted entrance till he had been searched, scrutinized and authorized by the doorman. But Bosco carried something more subversive than contraband tobacco or illicit secular literature. He carried in his head the folklore of his people, a pot-pourri of jokes and songs, sayings, stories and garbled local history. He knew everyone in the Bogside and everyone, if he could be believed, knew him. He claimed kinship with most of the families and with half the Waterside as well. He spoke knowingly of wild nights fighting, of guns and robberies, touts and grasses, kneecappings and funerals.

But most of all he talked about the women of Derry.

Every morning as they rose to greet the day with three Hail Marys, Bosco leaned forward and, risking the wrath of the Dean, demanded through clenched teeth to know who got their hole last night? Some of the coarser novices would stifle guffaws; Frank would blush and try to concentrate on the prayer. 'Me and Wanker got ours,' Bosco would persist through the Glory Be. 'I'll tell you the full bars during Church History.'

It was useless for Frank to remonstrate that he didn't want his ears polluted with this filth; useless also to point out that it was nothing but scatological fantasies produced by an over-fertile imagination. In spite of his better judgement he had found himself listening to these bulletins of alcoholic excess and sexual orgy. On the railway lines, behind the gasometers, in the backs of disused cars, in his own house once, when his mother had gone to confession. Bosco mentioned the names of girls casually and disparagingly; Catriona, Sabrina, Molly and Millie; what he had done to them and what they had done to him, and how often they had done it. Sometimes the stories would be serious, but more often they would be wry and funny, for Bosco as a storyteller was, in his own way, a match for Sister Imelda any day, able to spin a tale with delicacy and virtuosity. In an environment devoid of any other entertainment his talents were eagerly anticipated.

Of all the characters who featured in these adventures, none did so more regularly nor more heroically than Wanker McCann and Dymph the Nymph.

Wanker could, and regularly did, satisfy half a dozen women in the one night, 'and so far he hasn't had any complaints, if you know what I mean,' Bosco added. The spotty postulants, who would never have such demands put on them, nodded sagely like true men of the world. There was no woman, no matter how snobbish, that Wanker couldn't pull with his charm. There was no snooker, however devious, he couldn't extricate himself from. There was no man in Derry he couldn't outdrink. Wanker was King of the Bog. Against invaders he had proved himself with the petrol bomb. Nor (it was implied) had his contribution to the national cause stopped there. As often as not, said Bosco, if you ran into Wanker on the street he'd be carrying, and if you

120

should accidentally notice the bulge in his pocket you'd be well advised to keep it to yourself.

Frank had known this paragon by proxy all his growing years; tonight, by arrangement, he intended to meet him in the flesh.

He spent the hours between Masses and devotions making a recce of the building and trying to plot his escape route. He discovered the window in the attic where the broken bars had never been replaced, and after lights out he climbed nervously out on to the chapel roof. In his study below the Dean heard the creak of the slates, crossed himself and prayed anxiously that everything would turn out for the best. Frank inched his way to the edge of the roof and looked down.

The city lay spread before him. It was as magical now as it had seemed that first time he had set eyes on it from the far bank of the Foyle. Even in the darkness he could make out the spires of the Long Tower church rising above him against the purple sky. As his eyes adjusted to the gloom he could trace the pattern of narrow streets fanning out from the cathedral, could see below him the concentric layout of the old town, could make out the thick stone walls with the four gates facing the four points of the compass and the defiant outline of the Protestant cathedral sheltering at its heart. Directly below him, running down the hill into the hollow called the Bog were the houses where the dayboys lived. The street was dark, except for the pale lamps glowing above the public houses. But there was movement and laughter, footsteps on the cobbles and the sound of women's voices. Frank's heart quickened.

He edged cautiously towards the parapet at the back of the building and peered down. He could make out a dark, narrow alleyway running along the side of the chapel. And, as if in answer to his prayers, there was a ladder propped up against the gutter! It stretched across to the roof of the shed opposite, and if it were strong enough it would be no great problem getting across there, and then only a matter of jumping down into the lane. He lowered himself carefully over the ridge and groped with his feet for the head of the ladder. He couldn't feel it! He lowered himself further, and felt himself slipping. Holy Mary, Mother of God, he prayed

121

aloud, dangling seventy feet above the alley. But just as he knew he could hold on no longer his boots touched the top rung. The ladder slithered down the wall, steadied itself, began to list over. He clambered down it before it toppled, and landed on the roof with a jolt. He was further above the street than he had reckoned, and in the darkness it was hard to guess how far he would have to jump. This was no time for his nerve to fail him! He lay flat on his stomach and eased his legs over the side. Then with a whispered prayer to the Holy Ghost he took a chance, wriggled his body over the edge till he was holding on by his fingers, and let himself drop down into the back lane.

There was the sound of a footfall in the alley, and a figure emerged from the shadows and beckoned to him to get up and follow. Bosco Doherty, as good as his word! Frank struggled to his feet, wincing at the sharp stab of pain from his ankle, and limped after the retreating figure of the dayboy.

They kept to the malodorous back lanes till they were out of sight of the seminary. And though Frank's ankle ached, Bosco refused to slacken his pace but dodged ahead from doorway to doorway, ordering him impatiently to keep up. They skirted round the town under the shadow of the walls until they stood overlooking the Bog. The houses clung to the contours of the hill, row backing against row, redolent of soot and babies and cabbage water. Women crowded every doorstep, young and old, arms folded defiantly across their chests, listening to the bars, the news. They greeted the boys as they slipped among them with cackling badinage.

'Who's your wee friend?' screeched an aged hag, staring shamelessly at the blushing Frank. 'Are you going to make a man of him tonight?'

He kept his head down, concentrating on his feet in the gutter, but the women were alert to his embarrassment and glad of the diversion. Their derisive laughter followed him down the steep street.

'Has the cat got your tongue, Bosco Doherty? What the frig's wrong with him?'

Bosco gave them two fingers cheerfully, and some of them hobbled over from their steps to cuff him playfully round the ears. He lit a Woodbine which he cadged at one of the doorways, cupping his hands round the match to shield it from the wind off the river below. The nicotine gave him a renewed burst of energy; he skipped off down the rest of the brae, dodging the potholes and puddles and piles of brock, shouting over his shoulder to Frank to quit hobbling and get a fucking move on.

At the foot of the street the women were bolder, and Frank shied from their voices and their touch. They stood in the middle of the street, blocking him, their hands rough on his face and arms as they reached out to him. Bosco, elbowing his way through, laughed at his timidity. Freed from the seminary, where the authorities had attempted to enforce on him some conformity of demeanour, he had reverted to the brisk side-stepping trot favoured by the locals. He was at home among these people. He smoked his cigarette with an ostentatious air, and taking Frank by the shoulder, pushed him through the women, giving as good as he got.

'Hi Bosco!' one crone shouted from an upstairs window, 'I seen Dymphna just after going into your house, so I did. Don't tell me you're taking the wee lad down to meet her?'

The mention of Dymphna occasioned general laughter the length of the brae. Some of the younger women encouraged them with cries and gestures that only Bosco understood.

'Tell her I said she'll be done by the polis for cradle snatching so she will!' they cackled.

'Sweet Jesus, Mary and Holy Joseph, would you listen to the tongue on that one! Go in and wash your mouth out this minute you!'

'Mind you, I don't see you kicking him out of bed!'

'God forgive you! Did you hear what that one is after saying?'

'Pass the wee lad on till us when she's finished with him, Bosco!'

'If there's anything left of him after that one!'

In the ensuing outburst of merriment, Bosco and his charge made good their escape.

✢

'YOU ARE NOW ENTERING FREE DERRY' warned the gable hoarding. Bosco stopped and invited Frank to admire it. 'Free Derry,' said Bosco. 'Stay close to me and you'll be okay.' Across the open ground, strewn with the rubble of occasional riots, stood the Lone Moor public house. No sign distinguished it from the rest of the houses round it, but a small crowd of boys, collars pulled up against the wind, huddled against the leeward gable, sharing a cigarette with two older men and watching the progress of Bosco and Frank down the lane. Where the women were loquacious, the men were dour. Bosco approached carefully across the waste ground, sidling up to them with Frank in his wake. For a while no one spoke. Bosco cleared his throat and spat on the ground. One of the older men then greeted him with an imperceptive nod. 'Yes, Wanker!' said Bosco with a curt shake of the head, and allowed the great man to relapse into his surveillance of the corner.

The minutes passed. One of the younger lads, suddenly overcome by boredom, aimed a kick at Bosco's privates. Bosco was on him like a terrier. He grabbed him round the neck in an armlock and twisted him till he could kick his backside. The youth finally told him to lay off for fuck's sake, and with a parting clip round the ear, Bosco dropped him on the ground. Wanker's sidekick, who had been watching the tussle with interest, moved over and landed a few kicks on the recumbent boy, who scrambled to his feet and got out of range as fast as he could, apparently none the worse for wear. 'Yes, Dog!' nodded Bosco, revealing him as another of the characters Frank had come to know vicariously. Stories had circulated for years about Dog Doherty. He featured in many of the fables about Wanker, often cast in the role of recipient of the greater man's wisdom, the straight foil to his wit and repartee. But the Dog also featured in his own right, in stories of sudden viciousness and unexplained savagery. 'A bit of a psycho!' the other dayboys called him, and Frank noticed that Bosco treated him with deference bred of fear.

'Are you buying?' demanded Dog. He spoke to Bosco but he was watching the stranger. Some of the others pulled away from the wall and began to shuffle nearer, surrounding Frank menacingly. Bosco said something he couldn't catch. The native speech was fast and clipped, delivered from the side of the mouth like a trainee ventriloquist, and he found it hard to follow their negotiations. Halfway through each utterance, the speaker would turn away and stare into the distance, as if disowning his words. But he knew that the topic under discussion was whether the newcomer had entered their company with the price of a drink on him.

Frank had indeed a little money saved. It wasn't much, but it was all that stood between him and the total penury that his vow of poverty demanded. It was against the rules of the seminary; what would a boy want with money, the Dean often declared, but to satisfy his baser carnal desires? These desires of the flesh took the shape of Mars bars mainly, smuggled into the austere world of the novitiate by dayboys at greatly inflated prices. Frank knew it was wrong for him to horde his pennies after devoting his life to God, but there was enough of County Armagh in him yet, despite the civilizing influences of the Fathers, for him to keep the matter to himself. Many of his classmates came from the farms and licensed premises of the archdiocese. They were the firstborn of their families; they would never lack for anything in life. He knew he had no such back-up to rely on. He was a penniless orphan who had only his wits to fall back on.

During his years in the college he had converted his mental agility into cash, payment for a composition or a Latin translation here and there. Bosco Doherty had demanded more than half of it to act as his guide. Frank had the rest of his life savings down one of his socks, enough, if the worst came to the worst, to get him to the ferry boats and a new life in England. Bosco's percentage had been an all-in fee, that much had been clearly negotiated; there would be no more to pay, for Bosco would see him right and handle all expenses and incidental extras. But standing in the pale sodium light on Free Derry corner, Frank knew the arrangement had broken down.

He thought about remonstrating, but caught the manic eye of Dog Doherty and remained quiet. This was no place to try asserting himself, no place either to renege on the deal with Bosco and demand his deposit back. Wanker and the Dog were now deep in conversation, their shoulders twitching, heads jerking, mouths contorted. Next minute Dog was beside him. He clicked his fingers peremptorily and held out his hand. Frank hesitated. He could feel the crush of the corner boys at his back; he could see into the eyes of the psychopath in front of him. Inwardly he cursed all Derrymen with a venom and a vocabulary he hardly knew he had. But he reached into his sock and fished out all his worldly goods, dropping them one by one into Dog's outstretched palm. Dog dropped on to one knee and felt his leg, locating the last florin under his instep. 'You're buying, fella,' he said, 'so why the fuck are we standin' out here?' Wanker threw open the door of the Lone Moor and signalled for the others to follow. Bosco winked across at Frank and beckoned him in. The younger lads pushed inside behind them, but Dog began to use his boot. They were apprentice Derrymen, not to be included in the company till they had served their time on the cold street corners. Their sporadic kicking on the door was to punctuate the rest of the proceedings.

The decor inside the Lone Moor was as uninspiring as the outside. Four tall stools stood against a high narrow bar, and a pair of hard wooden chairs flanked the only table. The rest of the floor was empty. Behind the bar were piled crates and boxes of empty bottles, and above it on a shelf stood a line of glasses. The floor was covered with the remnants of a faded oilcloth. The only hint that this was a place of recreation and entertainment was the television set, incongruously large, perched on a ledge above the barman's head, showing only a distorted test transmission. The sombre surroundings temporarily dampened conversation. Wanker ordered bottles of stout monosyllabically, and the barman, similarly tight-lipped, set them on the counter when he had checked the money. Dog, without opening his mouth, was demanding information about the greyhound racing from Celtic Park, nodding his head in the direction of the television set till the barman caught his drift and answered with a grunt and an expletive. Apparently satisfied, Dog let the matter drop.

Bosco handed Frank a bottle and a glass without comment, and sat watching him as he poured it. Frank knew it was an initiation. It had been many years since he'd watched his father pouring stout, but it's a trick once learned never forgotten. The head foamed yellow scum, some of it erupting over the side of the glass, and though Bosco laughed and tried to involve the others, they took no interest. His first hurdle over, Frank lifted the glass to his lips and took a swig. Old memories flooded suddenly back; his father in damp public houses, holding forth to all and sundry as the rain lashed against the window, ordering bottles by the neck. He had tasted enough of the dregs of those bottles to remember the taste for ever. He took another swallow and knew he would never finish it. Bosco kept his eye on him but said nothing. He lit a cigarette and passed it over to him. They all looked on as he took a draw on it. He felt the tears spring to his left eye as the acrid smoke stung. Wanker downed his glass in two gulps and motioned to the barman for the same again. The others emptied their glasses and turned towards Frank. He tried another mouthful; he felt himself gagging. He reached for the bar, his glass only half empty, but the Dog was at his elbow. The porter had loosened his tongue.

'Drink!' he said. It was an order not an invitation.

'I'm all right for the minute,' Frank told him.

'For fuck's sake!' said Wanker.

'. . . fuck's sake,' echoed Dog.

'Get it . . .'

'. . . fucking down you!'

'For the love of fuck!'

Frank took another mouthful, forcing the porter down. He wiped his mouth, and tried to catch Bosco's eye, pleading for release.

'You in a hurry, fella?' asked Wanker.

'. . . in a fucking hurry?' the Dog said.

'You too, Bosco?' Wanker suddenly turned on him.

'The sister's at home,' said Bosco by way of explanation.

'His fucking sister!' Dog said.

Wanker leered; he pressed his contorted face close to Frank's, revealing deformed gums and decayed teeth. He went to say something, then instead twisted his face into a grimacing gargoyle of a wink that apparently spoke more eloquently than any words.

'Dymphna!' shouted the Dog.

'Dymph the nymph.'

127

'. . . fucking Dymphna.'

'. . . fucking right!'

Bosco tried to laugh. He offered cigarettes and attempted to change the conversation. But they were not to be so easily waylaid.

'For fuck's sake, Bosco!' said Wanker.

'Fuck off,' said Bosco defensively.

'Have you no sense?'

'Fuck off!' Bosco repeated. He tried to order another four bottles, but the barman, who was slouched across the counter taking a desultory interest in the conversation, ignored him.

'She'll suck him in . . .'

'. . . and blow him out as bubbles,' said the Dog. They laughed bitterly.

'Fuck off,' said Bosco, joining respectfully in their laughter.

But the conversation that had started so promisingly began to falter. The Dog scratched his head and laughed after the others had stopped, but Wanker had grown weary of the topic. The barman recognized that the crack was over and moodily turned his attention once more to the blank television screen. They went back to drinking their porter in silence, and though the Dog muttered 'fuck' a few times in an effort to get the ball rolling, no one took him on. Another four bottles appeared and then another four. Frank worked his way through them, praying that each one might be his last, but they kept coming faster than he could sip them, piling up in front of him accusingly.

'Your man,' Wanker said, indicating Frank, 'your man's a very quiet cunt.'

Bosco shrugged.

'The quiet man,' said the Dog.

'Going on for to be a priest?' Wanker addressed him for the first time. Frank opened his mouth to deny it. Wasn't this his first day of freedom, his first day as a layman, free to go and do as he pleased? He felt the acid rising in his throat, making any effort at speech impossible. He nodded.

'You're not a fruit?' demanded the Dog after a pause. 'Hi, Bosco, your wee pal isn't a fruit is he?'

'Fuck off,' Bosco said.

128

The Dog grabbed Frank suddenly, clutching his balls playfully but firmly. He pulled him off the stool and pretended to bugger him, pushing his bony pelvis roughly against the boy's back. 'Is it a good ride you're after?' he laughed, twisting Frank's balls in his fist. Bosco laughed, but Wanker turned away without interest. 'Leave him alone, can't you, for the love of fuck,' he growled.

'He's only got Dymphna to handle later on,' added the barman, hoping to get the conversation back on to that particular track.

The Dog released his grip. Frank vomited, suddenly and copiously, over the Dog's shoes, over the floor, over the stools. The dark liquid shot out of his mouth in an uncontrolled, foaming torrent.

'You've just boked all over me!' yelled the Dog. 'For fuck's sake, Wanker, he's just boked all over me!'

Wanker grinned at his companion's adversity. 'For fuck's sake!' he laughed.

'For fuck's sake, fellas,' pleaded the barman. He vaulted over the bar and advanced with a bucket of sawdust. Frank caught his eye and tried to apologize, but he felt the vomit rising again in his throat. Bosco led him outside. The corner boys gathered round them, demanding money, but he scattered them with a few well-aimed kicks. He propped Frank up against the wall, under the great black letters proclaiming the freedom of the city and let him take a few lungfuls of cold air.

'Didn't I guarantee,' he said proudly, 'that you'd have the time of your life?'

❖

It wasn't over yet. The next few hours were a slow journey through purgatory, a long descent into hell. Uncontrolled, his faculties no longer his own, he followed his mentors through the dark recesses of the populous city. Later, when sobriety returned, he would struggle to recollect the nightmare, to piece together painfully the catalogue of terrors and horrors of that night. He would try to recollect what sins, venial and mortal, he had committed. But he would find most of it blanked for all time from his memory.

Had he killed anyone? He didn't know. He knew now how easy murder might be, to kill and maim under the influence and have no recollection of it on awakening. He remembered wanting to kill, was it Bosco or the Dog? Or even (foolish thought!) Wanker himself? He remembered Wanker showing him his piece, removing it suddenly and dramatically in some stinking jakes and pointing it towards him, but whether in a spirit of anger or sudden camaraderie he could no longer tell. He remembered some argument about his behaviour with the billiard cue, and the way the others had seen something in his countryboy's eyes that had impressed them. He had been sick, and sick again. On a carpet, when there was shouting above him, and on a street under a pale flickering light. But he had got his second wind; cleared his stomach and declared himself fit to graduate to the whiskey. He had been sick again, but it was a different sensation. The universe had started to spin and not even God could steady it. Afterwards there had been laughter, violence, backslapping. They had crossed the wide river, its dark waters lapping the bridge. There was shooting in the distance. More steep streets, more mean public houses. He remembered singing and shouting, a fight that had been none of his doing, and another fight that he might have provoked, and that the Dog had finished for him.

Then there was Dymphna. It would be necessary for him, in the long aftermath, to recollect what he could of her. Penitence demanded a full examination of conscience, but how could he examine his conscience if he couldn't recall what she had looked like nor what had happened between them? He had few details on which to build his repentance, for some part of his addled memory insisted on drawing a veil of discretion over what had gone on in the dark little bedroom to which Bosco had eventually led him, at the top of the creaking stairs that swayed and cart-wheeled as he crawled up them on all fours. He could remember the stale smells of poverty. He could remember the bed with its warm rough blankets, smelling of old urine. He thought he could remember soft, pneumatic thighs arching over him in the dark. But her face? Her body? He couldn't recollect! Had he, in the fetid darkness, entered her hot, wet body, squirting his load into her almost as soon as he had mounted her? He couldn't remember. Or had she straddled him, taking her pleasure slowly above him as he fought to keep his erection? Did he recall thick mottled buttocks and coarse pubic hair, a fat girl cursing his clumsiness? Or was hers an emaciated body, ribs protruding under scraggy breasts, teeth long and bucked, with bad breath, clutching him with her nails while he arched into her unseen body in an ejaculation of hot pain?

These and a thousand other cameos flitted through his brain next morning, each one more terrifying than the last. None could be pinned down, for they danced before him daring him to contradict them. He lay where he was (where was he?) afraid to open his eyes or move lest new horrors awaited him. Would he ever truly know what had happened? Had he really sinned grossly against holy purity; had he submitted his body to the indignities he now imagined? A bell tolled close at hand. Slowly he focused on the familiar sounds of the seminary. He could not remember getting back in last night. It seemed unlikely that he had climbed the shaky ladder, risking life and limb over the chapel roof. Had he been smuggled in with the daydogs, somehow foiling the security check at the gate? He remembered now that it was the Saint Patrick's Day weekend. The dayboys would be at home, apart from the few who were drafted in to swell the choir. He could hear them singing below him in the chapel now. Gingerly he opened his eyes, wincing at the dull light from the window.

He was back in his own narrow bed, right enough. He slowly ran his hands over his face. There was a bruise under one eye that throbbed when he prodded it. The result of a fight or a fall? He forced himself to sit up. The painful unfinished business of his conscience would have to wait till he got to confession. It was time to examine his body.

He was still fully dressed. He felt in his sock, then in his pocket. Not a penny. He was as helpless as the day Schnozzle had found him. Carefully he lowered his trousers. His penis tried to rise, but sank back at once, as if fearful of the cold light of day. He examined it. Were there any swellings, any signs of lesions? It lay in his palm, flaccid and raw. How could he tell where it had been the night before? Was it possible it had been inside the thrusting

131

belly of a Derry woman? It stirred in his hand as yet another of the possibilities of the evening swam before him. He saw himself masterful and virile, astride the willing Dymphna, her long hair etched against the clean white pillowcase, her eyes closed in ecstasy, her small mouth open in a groan of pre-orgasmic pleasure. Had it been like that? Could it ever be like that? The image faded and he felt his erection die as a wave of nausea swelled up from his gut and rose inexorably up through his whole body.

He felt a little better when he had finished vomiting bile. He lay face down on the bed, struggling with body and soul. Never again! Never again, he groaned. He would start a novena; perhaps to Our Lady of Ballychondom, the Silent Madonna, wherever she might be in hiding, praying that he hadn't got the clap. He would renew his devotion to his Guardian Angel. He had been neglecting her recently, but perhaps she had protected him more than he knew last night. Kept him pure for the day when he would prostrate himself before the altar as a postulant, and rise as an ordained priest of the Church? The turmoil in his stomach eased slightly, though he knew it would be back to torment him for the rest of the day. Never again! He vowed he would renew his Pledge that very day. He would sport his Pioneer Pin with pride. And when the time came for him to take a drink, he would do it like a real priest. What call had he to be drinking cheap porter with corner boys? As a priest he would touch nothing but twelve year malt. Where was the attraction of the fleshpots and the stews of the restless slums? He could live happily without the likes of Wanker and his cronies, without the dubious charms of the elusive Dymphna. Never, ever again would he subject himself to the indignities of the great unwashed; never again would he lower himself to their level, acting like a farm animal, swilling stout in a public house to please and impress a scuffle of louts. From this day forth he'd see to it that that class of lig treated him with the respect he was owed as one of God's anointed. He felt the nausea return, an acrid taste of stale stout and cheap tobacco. Never again! The only cigarettes he'd smoke from this day out would be long and smooth and cork-tipped. He made himself another promise as the waves of sickness ebbed and receded through his body. He vowed never again to set foot on the streets of the Maiden City.

He vomited once more in the latrines and washed his bruised face in cold water. Should he face the Dean? He decided not. If the Dean wanted to see him he knew where to find him. Timidly he made for the staircase and God knows what reception that awaited him below. By rights he should be at Mass; he could hear them chanting the Credo in the chapel. But Mass would be an empty ritual to him in his present state. How could he approach the altar rails in this physical and moral condition? He needed time to think. He needed someone with whom he could talk over his predicament, someone who would help him examine the conflicts in his soul, examine them rigorously. He needed absolution for the sins he had committed and the sins he had contemplated. Nervously he opened the refectory door and peered inside.

The Redemptorist was sitting at the table, alone, picking his teeth with a match. He looked up as Frank peeped round the door and smiled when he saw the haunted, disfigured features of the novice. He reached under his plate and felt for the fee (sale or return) that the Dean had discreetly left for him and pocketed it quietly among the folds of his habit. From another pocket he pulled out his travelling stole and casually laid it round his neck like a cravat. Frank hesitated at the door. The Redemptorist reached across for the teapot and held it up to show Frank that there was a drop still in it. He came into the room nervously, shutting the door behind him. 'The very man,' said the monk, speaking at last. 'I thought you weren't going to show at all; I'd nearly given up on you.'

'Bless me Father for I have sinned,' Frank croaked.

The confessor brushed aside the formalities with his hand. 'I can see that by the state of you. So why don't you sit yourself down here and tell me all about it, blow by blow, in your own good time,' he said, pouring them both a cup of strong tea.

The Dean had reason to congratulate himself on his foresight in hiring the mendicant confessor, for no sooner had he shown him out the back door than there was a flurry of horns in the street outside and the gates were opened to His Eminence and his entourage. The Dean crossed himself angrily. Today of all days! It was as if the bastard had the gift of second sight. The boy was hardly presentable, but at least he was shriven and washed, and had at last stopped throwing up every five minutes. Thank God he hadn't arrived twelve hours earlier. He'd have found the bird well and truly flown, and no amount of special pleading would have saved his bacon. He watched the cars draw up in the cloistered yard below and one of the Sisters jump out and hold the door open. If he could keep the boy offside for an hour of two it would give his face a chance to get back to normal. There might be a bit of cold beefsteak in the kitchen. He could pretend he got it on the hurley field, and put his general malaise down to a touch of the 'flu. But Schnozzle was the suspicious type. Cursing his luck, the Dean hurried down to greet his guest with a firm handshake, tracing the sign of the cross in the air and assuring him that his door was always open.

For once Schnozzle seemed impatient to be gone.

'I'll not take up any more of your valuable time than is strictly necessary. Yours *or* mine,' he announced.

The Dean tried to look crestfallen, as at a pleasure suddenly granted and as suddenly withdrawn.

Schnozzle cut short his fawning. 'I've come for the boy. It's time he was out of here; you've taught him all you can. Fetch him down here. We've a long journey ahead of us.'

'Your Eminence is never returning to Armagh tonight?'

'The lad is going to Maynooth. It's time for them to make a man of him. He's wasting his time here. You agree with me?'

'Well of course we've done all we can for him. A most promising pupil, the makings of a grand wee priest. I think we can agree he's a credit to us all, Your Eminence.'

Schnozzle grunted dismissively. He grunted again, but this time there was a note of interrogation in his tone, for he had just seen his protégé approaching through the cloisters. Behind him marched Sister Immaculata, carrying Frank's few belongings in a canvas holdall. The boy's face was puffed and purple and his eyes were bloodshot. He walked with a limp, as if he'd taken a heavy fall. The Cardinal looked quickly across at the Dean.

'Do you think the poor lad's fit to travel at all?' blustered the Dean. 'Sure he's been in the sick bay all week. I think it must be a virus. I was on the point of having the doctor in to have a look at him.'

Schnozzle said nothing. He ordered Frank into the car with a curt nod of the head. The Dean, sensing the unspoken accusation in his movements, was trying to explain about the accident on the football field, assuring him that he'd be as right as rain in a day or two. The Cardinal ignored him, turning instead to look disdainfully at the shabby buildings around him, mentally finding fault with every aspect of the seminary.

'He's been wonderfully well treated, haven't you now?' pleaded the Dean through the half-open car window. 'Sure he's a great credit to us and no mistake. He'll not forget us I'm sure when they make a grand priest out of him up in Maynooth.'

At a signal from Schnozzle, Immaculata closed the window and started the engine.

'You'll remember us in your prayers, won't you now?' begged the Dean after the retreating limousine.

From the snug interior Frank looked a last time on the buildings where his innocence lay immured. From which he had so recently and so disastrously escaped. There would be no more of that, he thought, allowing himself to appreciate the heavy plush of the interior, the silent engine, the reassuring presence of the bulky bodyguard in the front. There was not another car like this in Ireland. Derry, in all its daytime drabness, slipped past the darkened windows.

He settled back into the seat and closed his eyes. 'That's right,' said Schnozzle soothingly, 'you look as if you need a rest. What have they been doing to you in there?' Frank didn't answer. 'Things will be different in Maynooth,' he assured him. He patted the boy's knee, letting his long hand linger for a moment there. 'Very different. What you need now is a bit of fattening up.' He squeezed Frank's thigh gently before removing his hand. Inside the car it was warm and comfortable, with a lingering hint of incense. The sullen Tyrone countryside slipped past unnoticed.

135

They said five decades before they reached Aughnacloy and the old border posts. Schnozzle paused for a rest, proffering long, white cork-tipped cigarettes from a silver case. 'We'll be in County Kildare in no time at all,' he said. 'A few years in Maynooth and we'll not recognize you.' Frank nodded deferentially. It was clear that his future had been mapped out for him. 'And then,' the Cardinal said, 'with God's help we'll be seeing plenty of you.'

'In what way, Your Eminence?'

By way of answer Schnozzle bent over and switched on the radio. A blast of the Reverend McCrea and his pack of cards filled the car. Schnozzle let it play till the song was over and McGuffin was back on, wearily begging money for his fallen women.

'But I know nothing about the radio,' Frank said.

'Radio! Would you listen to the boy!' Immaculata shouted.

'Radio is all right for the likes of a country ignoramus like McCoy,' the Cardinal explained. 'Down in Maynooth they have a new course starting up. Bringing the Church into the Irish home through the medium of television.'

'Television?'

'You're signed up!'

'. . . but . . .' Frank started to remonstrate.

'No buts. It's all arranged. There's two days a week training in the RTE studios where you'll pick up the tricks of the trade. The place is full of hot air merchants. If you're your father's son you'll not be long in learning the ropes.'

And with the matter of Frank's vocation taken care of, he produced the beads and began intoning the five joyful mysteries as the car sped silently towards the spires of Maynooth.

TWO

Six

Above in the belfries the bells of Maynooth pealed out their joyous message to the town. They had been ringing since dawn, for this was a great day in the college, the most important in the year. Ordination day! And though the ceremony was now over and the reception in full swing, still the carillon chimed above them.

The Bursar took Frank aside and filled his sherry glass. 'A word in your ear, Father, when you have a minute,' he said winking confidentially. A frisson of pleasure ran down Frank's spine when he heard the title used, not as a joke, but seriously at last. Father Frank! A priest at last, his own man.

'I'll join you in the library in a moment or two,' he told the Bursar. 'I've promised to dance with someone's mother and she'll never forgive me if I stand her up.'

The Bursar chuckled. 'You're a fierce man for the women altogether.' Frank watched him as he ambled through the crowd in the banqueting hall. He knew what the message meant; the suits must be ready.

Over the years of his novitiate Squeaky (the Bursar's castrato-like voice had occasioned the sobriquet) had lectured them weekly on Management and Administration in the Modern Irish Parish. As often as not his lectures had turned from the finer points of line management techniques to the pressing problem of clothes. Squeaky attached a lot of importance to appearance. 'Never let me catch a young priest in anything but the best of worsted,' he would warn them weekly. 'You'll get no respect from the ordinary people if you're running round like jack the lad in man-made fibre. Formal wear or casual, it's worth taking that extra bit of care. A few quid spent on a good tailor is an investment for life.'

139

The boys used to laugh at this sales pitch, for it was no secret that the Bursar's brother, whose vocation had floundered somewhere along the line, now ran a clerical outfitters in Grafton Street, and that Squeaky would arrange credit for you on the first couple of suits.

Frank, though he joined in the general laughter, had taken the old man's advice. Unlike the others he had nothing but his wits to get him started. He had accepted a card from the Bursar at the beginning of his last year in the college, and had made the trip to Dublin one Saturday afternoon to be measured in the back room. Credit, the tailor assured him, lingering over the inside leg, would be no problem for a young man with prospects like himself. A couple of suits would be made up in time for ordination day, and an overcoat while he was at it. A dozen dog collars were added free, and Frank signed for the lot.

He surveyed the scene before him, a fixed smile on his face. The room was full of noise and cigar smoke and the smell of ground coffee and fine sherry. Eager young postulants (he had been one once!), overawed by the splendour of the occasion, glided from group to group, pressing ornate hors d'oeuvres on blushing family groups. They were ravenous too, he noticed, for there was nothing like a two-hour concelebrated Mass with all the trimmings to work up an appetite. Was it only this morning, he asked himself again, that he had prostrated himself along with the others before the altar, and heard Schnozzle proclaim him a priest for ever according to the order of Melchisidech? The parents and relations, up from the country and dressed to the nines, had wept and smiled and wept again; they had been introduced to a hundred clerics and shaken a hundred priestly hands. There had been photographs by the score, the occasion recorded as scrupulously as any society wedding. They had stood on the chapel steps, in large groups and in small groups, the older men smiling indulgently on their sporadic horseplay. Then the reception; another hundred hands to shake, another hundred stories and jokes to rehearse. The tea was passed, and then the sherry. Soon the men would be asked if they wouldn't take a ball of malt, seeing the occasion that was in it, and they would make a show of declining, tapping the Pioneer pin on the lapel of the hired suit; and then they would make a show of accepting, lest a refusal might be construed as giving offence, and the decanter would pass among them. Nor would they be any strangers to the Jameson, the same boys. Weren't they publicans almost to a man, part-time Pioneers exempt on special occasions? And what occasion could be more special than the present one, witnessing one's own flesh and blood ordained as a priest of the Church? So special that they had closed the bar for the day, or left it in the charge of a local girl under strict instructions to watch the till. Even so the thought of it would never be far from their minds all day, like a stone in a shoe, nagging away.

Frank himself had only the one guest, Major-domo MacBride down from Armagh for the day. He knew where he'd find him if he needed to, in the kitchen tucking into the brandy and water, inspecting the facilities and swapping stories with the cooks. More at home there than out here hobnobbing with the clergy. He wondered how his own mother and father would have fitted in with this crowd. Would his father, so proud of his ability to pass himself off in any company, have carried it off, or would the fourth whiskey have loosened his tongue too much? And his poor mother; would she have been proud of him? Or would she have been suspicious of his success, on the lookout for the trick, the catch? He had found himself thinking about them over the last few months as the great day came closer, remembering things about them long suppressed. A chance remark by Squeaky one afternoon, nothing more than a throwaway jibe about Irish condom production which had duly got its guffaw, had set his mind back to a time he thought he had forgotten for ever, a submerged dreamtime when he had been briefly happy. Sitting in the stuffy classroom, joining in the raucous laughter of his fellows, he had smelt once more the peat smoke from the damp fire, and heard the sound of his father's voice, singing in the night. And though he had dismissed it from his mind, the memory refused to fade completely, but returned to trouble him in the days before his ordination.

He made his way through the throng, pausing with each group as they called out to him, pressing him with introductions and reintroductions to their families. The lads were running round like

141

bridegrooms now, blushing at compliments, feigning embarrassment at childhood reminiscences, kissing hatted aunts not seen for years, laughing at the Archbishop's jokes. There were more introductions. He accepted, yet again, their invitations to drop in on them any time, to take them as he found them. By tonight they'd be packed and gone, back to the towns and villages they had come from, to streets bedecked with bunting and the whole townland out to welcome them. They had earmarked jobs for themselves, and their placements had been duly ratified by the authorities. The list had been published the previous night, and they had gathered round the noticeboard to confirm their postings and to check on those of their friends. Frank had hardly given it a glance. There was no parish waiting for him. His future lay elsewhere. He thought again about the offer he had been made and a thrill of pride tinged with nervousness ran through him.

The Bursar appeared at his elbow and steered him into the library. 'The suits are upstairs, Father. I got one of the younger lads to pack them with the rest of your things. You'll not be disappointed, I can assure you of that.'

'And you can tell your brother that I'll get the first instalment to him . . .'

The Bursar held up a silencing hand. 'Would you listen to yourself, man! Since when did a tradesman go chasing after a man of the cloth for a few pounds? You'll see him right in your own good time.'

'It may take a wee while. The show doesn't start till the autumn. I was thinking of taking a while off to look up some old people I once knew, though that's between you and me.'

'Are you now? I couldn't but notice that you were all packed up and ready to leave us. What does our long-nosed friend think of that? Or maybe you haven't asked him?'

'It's only for a few days. He'll hardly know I'm gone.'

'Won't he now? I wouldn't bet on that one.' The Bursar lowered his voice. 'He's expecting great things from you from what I gather. I'll tell you what I heard, for what it's worth. It seems that the gentleman in question has been getting very hot under the collar of late about our public image. Especially on the TV. That business last year with the Little Sisters and the newsreader didn't look too good in hindsight, though mind you I won't hear a word against them myself.'

'But I haven't even signed a contract.'

'Contract! Since when did the clergy need to get bogged down in red tape to preach the word of God?'

'You've no idea how much I still have to learn.'

'A good-looking boy like yourself? What more do you need to know? The sooner, Father, you get this new chat show of yours on the air the better, before the country goes to the dogs altogether. I sometimes think that scut John Joe has done it deliberately, allowing a crowd of atheists to take over down at Montrose.'

'I suppose I should have a word with His Eminence,' said Frank dubiously. He looked across to where Schnozzle was deep in discussion with a coterie of senior clergy, while Immaculata and a handful of the more presentable Sisters slouched watchfully nearby.

'Take my advice and leave well enough alone. He's busy at the moment with one thing and another. He'll know where to find you when he needs you, never fear.'

'That's true enough,' Frank agreed.

'Anyhow,' said the Bursar, proffering Sweet Afton, 'where was it you said you were heading?'

Frank took a contemplative draw on his cigarette before answering the older man. He knew he could trust nobody; mention Ballychondom and Schnozzle would hear of it within the hour. 'Nowhere you'd have heard of. Just visiting a few old friends,' he said.

Was it madness on his part, this scheme to revisit Ballychondom, and maybe jeopardize his chances with Schnozzle? Would the old people be alive, Moran and the Canon? And what about Noreen? She'd be a grown woman by now, maybe married with a couple of kids. Was it their approval he wanted? What right had he to expect them to remember him? 'But I must be about my father's business,' he muttered, turning away from the ballroom without a backward glance.

Upstairs on the bed his case lay already packed. It contained all his worldly goods, all that he needed for his new life. His stole,

143

his letters of credit, his papers, his diploma in Advanced TV Techniques and the new rig-outs. He took one out and tried it on. Squeaky was right, it was worth every penny. He looked at himself in the mirror. A good-looking boy, he thought; they can't all be wrong. He flashed himself a quick smile as he ran a comb through his brilliantined hair, the only legacy he had brought from his days in Derry. From downstairs came the sounds of female laughter – a strange sound in this male bastion – and he heard the tinkle of the piano as Squeaky struck up the opening chords of 'Boolavogue'. One part of him wanted to join them, say his formal goodbyes, prolong even for a few moments his departure. But he paused with his hand on the doorknob. Let them get on with their lives, he decided. This is where we must part. There was no doubt he would miss their company and the warmth of the companionship, but those days had now come to an end. He didn't envy them their sinecures, cosy parishes in the midlands, growing portly and self-important, swilling tea with all and sundry. He knew he was cut out for better things.

Outside it was raining gently. He slipped unnoticed out of the college and down the driveway. He passed a bus stop and hesitated. Should he wait for the bus? A group of women, struggling under piles of paper bags, passed by, saluting him as they went. He grinned. Bus indeed! There was an undertakers on the corner, with a sign in the window promising car hire. He marched in and coughed for attention. The undertaker hurried from the back room to greet him. 'Sure what can we do for yourself, Father?' he asked solicitously. Frank told him. 'A car? I've got the very job for you, Father. I'll just get the boy to fill it up and bring it round to the front. You'll have no trouble with this one, Father, she's a real beauty.' Frank indicated his willingness to sign something, pay a deposit. 'Will you get away, Father, there'll be no need for anything like that.' He pressed the keys into the young priest's hand and opened the door for him. 'And a safe journey to you, Father,' he called.

Frank eased the limousine carefully through the crowded streets. On all sides the ragged people parted to let him through, saluting him as he went by. He sped out through the townships on the edge of town, on through the shanty town that straggled beyond it, and was suddenly in the country, heading west. The road was deserted, rutted and potholed, barely passable in places, with the burnt-out carcasses of old abandoned vehicles littering the verges for the first few miles. But the big car rode over the pitted surface effortlessly. The rain was heavy now and the wind was cold; but the interior was warm and snug. He pressed the radio and the car was filled with country and western music. He fished in his pocket for a packet of Sweet Afton and lit one at the glowing lighter that beckoned from the dashboard. Ahead lay the plains and then the hills of the borderlands. After that came the mountains.

But he was a priest now, and he had nothing to fear from this land or its people. He'd be in Ballychondom by nightfall.

❖

Noreen walked over to the window of her old bedroom for the tenth time and gazed out on to the road below. She sighed and returned to the bed. How strange and unsettling it felt to be home again. Ten years under the nuns had changed her into a woman, a woman that even Sharkey took a moment to recognize. But at least her father seemed pleased with the transformation. 'Would you look at herself!' he remarked to the Canon as she stepped out of Sharkey's pick-up. 'By God but the nuns must have fed you like a fighting cock for you're well filled out.'

The Canon concurred. 'It was money well spent, by the look of things. I can vouch for the good Sisters; they love the grub. And more power to them. I've never risen from the table after a feed anything less than full as a tick.'

'Who would begrudge it to them?' said Cornelius.

'Would you listen to the pair of you,' laughed Noreen, kissing her father lightly and shaking the Canon's outstretched hand. 'You'd make a body think it was the only reason I went to the convent.'

The Canon smiled. The nuns had done a good job. Noreen had acquired a light-hearted, flirtatious way of speaking that suited her; she managed to sound both respectful and familiar at the same time. And though the banter sounded natural on her

145

lips, he knew it was the result of hours of hard work under experienced hands. She'd been practising it on the young priests that you'd find hanging round the convent, finding out how far you could go and when to draw the line. Any young lady who had learned that art could go far.

'God but I'm starving,' she said as Cornelius opened the door and they caught the whiff of warm soda bread. 'Someone's been baking.'

'The native speakers knocked up a few wee things,' said Cornelius. 'Sit down there and I'll wet the tea.'

'Are you telling me that Páidi Mhici Óig is still alive? He must be a hundred if he's a day.'

'He's as good as the last of them,' her father said. 'The last of the Mohicans. We'll not see their like again when he goes.' As he spoke they heard, over the keening of the wind, the sound of a fiddle from the cabin in the glen. It was a tune both lively and poignant. 'He's wound up the gramophone in your honour.'

'The damn thing will be going all night, enough to drive you astray in the head!' the Canon complained, as they heard the needle jamming. 'The old blackguard's as deaf as a post!'

'Maybe I'll get a run up to see him later,' Noreen told him. 'Now sit down the pair of you. I haven't forgotten where everything is,' she declared, filling the kettle.

She looked at the once familiar room, its armchair and table, the bench and the day bed in the corner. 'God but the old place hasn't changed a bit. Have you done nothing since I left? I suppose the pair of you have been sitting in those chairs all the time jarring away, with never a thought of putting up a bit of wallpaper or changing those curtains.' She ran the material through her fingers and grimaced dramatically. 'I declare you've never even washed them in all that time. Men are a right caution, the nuns were right!' she laughed.

She looked at her father and the Canon. The Canon hadn't changed at all; still the same old sour puss on him, she thought, not that he wasn't a big softie when you got to know his little ways. But her father had aged. His hair, that he'd been so proud of, was now white and his movements were those of an old man. As a girl she had always thought of him as going on for ever, but she saw now what the years of banishment had done to him. It had shocked her when she first caught sight of him from the truck, and she hoped it hadn't shown in her face or that he hadn't detected it in her voice when she assured him that he didn't look a day older. She poured the tea; they all laughed as she tried to remember how they liked it – her father's two and a half teaspoons of sugar, the Canon's insistence that the milk be poured first. The light faded and they sat over the teacups, tentatively recalling old times before the trouble.

They spoke carefully of those days, anxious not to open old wounds or start old controversies. When Noreen suggested a decade of the rosary it came as a relief and they prayed briefly and silently for the poor desecrated Madonna, not daring to articulate aloud their fears for her ultimate fate. Her father grew tired but he wanted to talk; when he had first seen her face through Sharkey's windscreen he had seen again the face of her mother, and the image would not leave him. He was talking about her now and there were tears in his eyes. Noreen thought once more about the news she had for him. How was she going to break it to him? They had warned her that he might take it hard. There was a tremor in his voice now and she knew it would not be long before he lost control of himself.

'Have you both turned into Pioneers or what?' she joked, trying to break the mood.

'My God,' exclaimed her father, jumping up, 'but it's not like me to forget my manners. What was I thinking of?' On the sideboard he had a bottle of cream sherry. He uncorked it ceremonially and poured three glasses. He handed one to the Canon and another to his daughter.

'Don't go pouring one of those for me. Sure I never touch the stuff,' she protested, allowing herself a demure sip.

'Your very good health!' said Cornelius, his voice overcome with emotion, 'and welcome back to Ballychondom.' They raised their glasses. It was a solemn moment.

He pressed her for a refill. 'Just a wee drop,' she agreed. 'Jayney Mack, you've filled it up. One glass of this and I start to get tiddly.'

The men laughed. 'Well tell us all about the good nuns,' said

147

the Canon after a while, when the sherry had begun to work. 'How did they treat you at all?'

Though they had singled her out from the earliest days as someone special, Noreen soon realized that she could never be at home there either. There was an intensity about her, a loneliness that set her apart from the other girls. Her classmates had allowed the memory of their visitations to fade as the years went by. The nuns had learned to accept this, to understand it as part of the divine plan. By the time they left the convent they would recall little of the night the Virgin had appeared to them. They would settle into family life, making attractive wives for Fianna Fáil TDs or Fine Gael businessmen. But once in a while a special girl came along. One for whom the resonances of her vision still vibrated. Noreen was one of these. The memory of the Madonna dancing for her in the damp graveyard still stalked her secret thoughts. She saw Her every time she closed her eyes; an image of three children bound together for ever. The nuns earmarked her as one of their own; she ate with them and prayed with them, they took her into their confidence and whispered to her their most secret dreams and hopes. But despite their attention she had always kept a part of herself back from them, a part of her soul that was not for scrutiny. They sensed her resistance and redoubled their efforts. She pleaded with them to be allowed to visit her father for one last time, and they had let her go only on the promise that when she returned she would take the veil and live among them for ever.

But her doubts and fears were not something she could confide in her father. They had grown too far apart now for that ever to be possible again. Instead, forcing a note of gaiety into her voice, she assured him that she had been a great favourite of the Reverend Mother herself. 'By God but that's some honour, eh Father?' said Cornelius, winking across at the Canon.

'She was great gas,' said Noreen, 'not at all what you'd expect. We were as thick as thieves.'

'Sure you were having such a great time,' said the Canon, his tone suddenly tetchy at the image of the Kerry nuns living on the pig's back, 'I'm surprised you could spare the time to tear yourself away.' Noreen tried to laugh it off, but there was no denying the querulous edge to his voice. His bark is worse than his bite, she thought, but maybe it was as good a time as any to tell them the big news.

'As a matter of fact,' she said, lowering her eyes and her voice, 'I've been meaning to tell you since the minute I got home. I've got great news!'

'What would that be?' asked her father, half rising from his chair. Noreen hesitated. How could she tell him that she would soon have to leave him, that this would be the last time she would ever see him? 'I'm going to enter,' she said quickly. 'The nuns have been praying for a vocation and their prayers have been answered. Reverend Mother thinks I'll make a great nun.'

The room fell silent. Cornelius was the first to speak. 'Well that's great news altogether,' he said dubiously. 'Did you hear that, Canon? A nun in the family.' He was putting a brave face on it but she knew he was shattered. She could only guess at how long he had looked forward to this day. And here she was, no sooner back than announcing that she was leaving for ever. He slumped back into the chair, a confused and defeated look on his face. She knew how he must be feeling, wondering who would care for him now. She had been bracing herself for this moment since she left Caherciveen, but nothing could have prepared her for the look of despair she saw in her father's face.

'A little drink is called for here,' said the Canon uneasily, glad of an excuse to open the whiskey, for too much sherry had left a bad taste in his mouth. He too, she knew, was hiding his disappointment. 'You'll not regret it,' he tried to assure her, 'not for a minute. What higher calling is there for a young girl than to serve God Almighty through a religious order? And the Sisters of Caherciveen are a lovely order, a civilized order. You'll want for nothing. And don't spare a thought for the pair of us, here on our own. God knows we've managed this long, we'll manage again. Haven't we always Mister Sharkey to take care of us in our old age?'

'Someone's prayers have been answered at any rate,' Cornelius cut in, for he wanted no unseemly invective from the Canon at a moment like this. 'If your poor mother had lived to see this day, she'd have been a proud woman.'

'I'll be praying for you both, every minute of the day,' she assured them, the tears now streaming down her face.

'Sure you will,' said Canon Tom. 'It'll be a great comfort to your father and myself to know that.'

Alone again, she stared at the ceiling, tracing the familiar crack across to the window. She had looked forward to this day for so long. She had pictured to herself the little parlour and the once familiar stairs, and her father as she remembered him, upright and strong. And now she was home again, and her great news told, and the sense of sadness crept over her like a mist creeping over heather. Feelings of disappointment and anticlimax mingled with anger and regret. The house was a dump, she could see that now, after the marble halls and perfumed chapels of the convent. Her father was an old man and the Canon, God forgive her, an old grouch you couldn't please. The place was even smaller than she remembered it. One part of her ached to escape from it, to get away from it and them and their talk and memories, back to the convent and the quiet, cultured life that the nuns could offer her.

Silence had fallen over the house now as evening drew in. The Canon was probably asleep by the fire, and she could hear her father's slow footstep in the yard, getting in more turf. Somewhere outside she heard the voice of Paddy Mhici Óig, keening a snatch of one of the old, sad songs. She remembered her last night under this roof with Chastity McCoy. It made her blush to recall that evening. God, to think what they had said and what they had got up to. She'd never met anyone like her; the way she played with the doll, like it was a real baby, talking to it in her strange accent as she undressed it for bed. Chastity had crept out of the house under the very nose of her father and together they had run across to the chapel at midnight to hear Mass and to kneel before the silent Madonna in the churchyard. They had been close for a few hours, closer than she had ever been with anyone before or since. Mind you, she told herself, they were only a pair of children, and by next morning Chastity had gone and the Madonna with her. She thought of Frank, too, and how quiet he was, sticking close to his da. The room and the smell of turf and the noise of the Canon snoring below brought it all back to her more vividly than ever. She went to the window again. She imagined an ice-cream van coming slowly down the hill, its one headlamp picking out the snowflakes that swirled in front of it. And for a second her heart leapt.

She flung herself down on the bed and wept into the pillow. She was behaving like a spoiled child she told herself, allowing these old memories to disturb her. She blew her nose and dried her tears. She was merely feeling sorry for herself, giving in to self-indulgence and self-pity, which was a sinful pleasure. She knew what she must do; make herself busy, say a wee prayer and maybe read from an inspiring book. Ask Our Blessed Lady to fill her mind with serene thoughts.

She forced herself off the bed and wiped her face. At the top of her suitcase she found the prayer book she had been reading on the bus. She read a page aloud, but for the first time the words made no impression. It had been different in the convent; different, too, on the bus that brought her to Donegal, with the country women taking sly looks at her and nudging each other and smiling at her if she raised her eyes for a second, the way they would smile at a real nun. On the bus she had concentrated on the lovely words, letting the hills and the fields slip past unnoticed. The nuns had taught her how to behave in public, how to devote every moment of the day to prayer and meditation; how to exercise discipline of the eyes, to stop the outside world distracting you from your higher duties. But here in the quiet of her own bedroom, where she had expected to feel so secure and at home, she could no longer concentrate. She let the book slip to the floor, its pages scattering on the dusty linoleum. She ought to pick it up, she knew. But she lay on. She ought to get off the bed this very moment and say a prayer. Didn't she know a dozen saints to turn to when things went wrong, wonderful understanding saints who knew the meaning of hardship and disappointment? Weren't there a thousand special prayers she knew for dealing with doubt and temptation? She'd lie on for a moment more and then she'd say the rosary, all fifteen decades, and offer it up for the Canon's special intentions, to make up for having thought of him as an old grouse.

'Never give in to the sin of sloth!' The voice in her head was Sister Imelda's. 'The sin of sloth is the father and mother of all the rest. Feather beds and central heating will be the ruin of this nation! Never get into a habit of sloth, my dear children, for it can get a grip on you and open your soul to the devil. Up you get and say a prayer! Do something useful, that wee thing you've been meaning to do all day but keep putting off because you haven't the time. Sure there are only twenty-four hours in the day, and our time on this earth is limited, so we should be praising God and His Goodness every one of them.' Maybe she should say just one decade of the rosary while she was lying there. Unpack her things. Go down and make a start on the dishes.

She had never felt like this before. Never experienced this mixture of disturbing emotions, at once unsettling and unspeakably sad. Something was exciting her strangely. Her hand moved slowly down over her soft, plump belly. She pulled it back. Touching yourself like that, even with all your clothes on, was an occasion of sin. But her hand returned, and this time she didn't pull it back. One part of her watched in detached and terrified fascination as it searched out the moistness between her legs. There was an emergency prayer the nuns had taught her for such occasions. She started to say it aloud, her voice becoming faster and faster with each passing second. But she abandoned it before it was finished, and closing her eyes she gave herself over completely to the urgent demands of the flesh.

A car with a powerful engine drew up silently outside the house. A door slammed and another opened. There was the sound of surprised voices in the hall and laughter. But Noreen heard none of these. She heard only her own sobs of anguish. A mortal sin! She had committed her first mortal sin! She knew the gravity of what she had done even before she came to a panting halt. The bed which had minutes before shaken to her ecstasy now reverberated with the violence of her remorse.

From below there came the sound of muffled laughter, her father's voice loud and excited and the Canon's high with interrogation. Desperately she tried to say an act of perfect contrition. It was no good! She couldn't do it. The dreadful sin of despair had descended over her like a malevolent cloud. She knew she

152

must not give in to it; she must fight it, not allow herself to wallow in self-pity. She tried to think of God, His infinite goodness, His divine love, His abhorrence of sin. Each time she tried to concentrate the noise from the parlour broke into her thoughts. They must have company in, a rare treat round these parts she imagined, probably some distant neighbour imported just because she was home. How could she face anyone on a night like this? How could she sit and make small talk, drink tea and tell tales about her time away, when with every second that ticked away her immortal soul was sinking deeper and deeper into Satan's grasp?

Somehow she needed to clear her mind of all worldly things. But how could she when she could hear them at it downstairs? And worse still she could feel the dampness between her legs, and yes the first unmistakable twinges of returning desire. She got off her knees and went to the window. The stranger's car sat brooding in front of the house. It had stopped raining but there was the smell of a storm in the air. Round Errigal, the clouds were dark and menacing. What if the house were struck by lightning and burned to the ground before she had a chance to escape? What if she had a heart attack? At the very thought of it her heart missed a beat and she felt herself go weak. She clutched the window frame for support, knowing for certain that she was fated to die before morning.

Through her sobs she became aware of her father's voice, calling insistently. Then she heard his footstep on the wooden staircase. He mustn't find her like this! She ran to the bedroom door and tried to control her voice. 'Ah there you are at last,' he shouted, his hand resting halfway up the banisters. 'We were wondering what had happened to you. Tell me, did you sleep?' She stammered an answer, keeping the door half-closed. 'Anyhow, come on down into the parlour. I've got a great surprise for you. Wait till you see who's arrived. Just landed in on top of us out of the blue! I'll not spoil it for you. Get yourself decent and come down.'

She dabbed some water on her puffy eyes and blew her nose. Shakily she descended into the hall where her father was still talking excitedly. 'He's just this minute come up the whole way from Dublin, so he'll be needing a bit of a lie-down himself later

153

on. And wait till you see the motor he's driving! We've been having the great talk.' He flung open the door dramatically. 'Wait till you see the cut of him, you'll hardly recognize him as the same boy.' Noreen allowed her father to usher her into the room. There on the hearthrug, ball of malt in hand, warming his backside before the roaring fire, stood Father Frank.

❖

She never knew a man who could take so long to say goodnight, but her father went to bed eventually. He'd announced his intention of turning in a good hour earlier, after himself and Father Frank had got down from putting the Canon to bed. But though exhausted with the day's excitement, he had lingered with them, unwilling to give up the pleasure of the company. Laboriously he went through the ritual of locking up; God knows why, she thought impatiently, for there isn't a soul within miles except for the native speakers above in the bog. He opened the back door and for a moment they heard music coming from the cabin, the insistent beating of a bodhrán, the skirl of a fiddle and the odd 'yahoo' of encouragement. The last remnants of the Gaelic culture were making a night of it. She could hear him now in the outside lavatory, the pipes hissing and spluttering as he pulled the chain in deference to the guest under his roof. Then he was back again, creaking the bar on the back door into position, and popping his head round the door one last time to say goodnight again, and to remind them that if they sat up to make sure the fire was damped down before they hit the hay. His footsteps retreated up the stairs at last, and they heard him kneel heavily at the foot of the bed to say his prayers; then the creaking of the springs as he settled himself under the blankets.

'He'll be snoring in a minute,' said Noreen, breaking the silence between them.

She was aware that the priest was looking at her and she was trying not to catch his eye. He spoke at last. 'You're very quiet altogether, Noreen,' he said, 'don't tell me the good nuns down in Caherciveen made you take a vow of silence. I always heard they were great gasbags.' She smiled but made no reply. 'I suppose we've been boring you to death half the night?' he asked. She turned quickly to look at him and he noticed the tears on her cheeks.

'Father, I've got to speak to you.' There was no denying the urgency in her voice.

'What's all this "father" business? Call me Frank!'

'You don't understand,' she stammered. The tears were flowing freely now. 'Father, you've got to hear my confession.'

He paused, the cigarette halfway to his lips, and let the match burn slowly down. Then he rose and walked deliberately to the door. 'I'll tell you what,' he said. 'I'll put a few sods of turf on that old fire.'

'I mean it, Father!'

'Of course you do. I've a feeling we're going to be in for a long session, and we may as well be warm. Sure some of you girls are fearful sinners altogether,' he chuckled.

Noreen felt anger rising. 'I mean it! I wouldn't be asking if it wasn't an emergency.'

'An emergency? That sounds ominous.' Still his eyes were laughing. 'Well just hold on for a wee minute,' he said, filling the bucket from the creel in the kitchen. 'You'll hardly die on me in the next five minutes. There's nothing to beat a good sod of turf.' He lifted an armful of peat and expertly built up the dying fire, poking it gently to get it to flame. It was the way Noreen herself had shown him when he was a boy, unfamiliar with the ways of turf. 'Now why don't you slip those shoes off and make yourself comfortable, and I'll just slip off this old dog collar, for the Canon will hardly be dropping in again tonight . . .' she found herself laughing in spite of herself '. . . and make myself comfortable, and then we'll sit here for a bit and you can tell me all about it in your own good time.' She noticed that as he spoke he had taken from his pocket the folded purple stole and laid it casually round his neck like a cravat. Without that there could be no confession; but with it on he was open for business. She felt a flutter of hope in her heart. Perhaps it wouldn't be that hard after all.

And it wasn't that hard. Not hard at all to tell a young man like Frank what was burdening her soul. He knew how to make

155

it easy for her; when she faltered he made her laugh, with his comments about 'those old nuns and the stuff they fill your heads with'; when she blushed and tried to tell him it was a sin against holy purity that threatened her eternal rest, he didn't look shocked or anything, but just chuckled quietly and said 'aren't those nuns obsessed with sex, and half of them out of date and out of step with modern thinking! Isn't it the most natural thing in the world?' Then she was telling him what had happened, hardly faltering, and he was nodding and agreeing, and when she hesitated he prodded her on gently and she told him more; and he gently coaxed her for more details, where exactly? how exactly? was it over the clothes or under the clothes? how long did this go on for? is that a fact you're telling me? did you give yourself pleasure doing that? was it a sinful pleasure would you say now? And she was spilling the whole beans, leaving nothing out, finding words she didn't know she had in her; and the next minute he had his right hand in the air tracing the sign of the cross and she knew she was absolved. A great weight lifted from her shoulders and a great rush of love, for him and for the whole world, surged through her. She dried her eyes and blew her nose once more and started to laugh; she found she couldn't stop she was that happy and relieved.

They began to talk freely at last. He told her what he could of the fate of the Madonna, and how his father had gone searching for Her and had rescued Her from McCoy. He had returned with the precious statue to the Shambles but they had followed him and killed him, and the Madonna had never been seen again. Then he told her of his time working in the Palace and made her laugh with his stories of the major-domo. She quizzed him about Chastity and he told her what he knew. But a silence came over him when he tried to speak of the death of his mother and she understood better than to force him to remember it. Then he told her of his years in Derry, and his time in Maynooth. And as they talked their roles became reversed. She was listening to him now, and giving him her advice; listening to the little problems a man like himself had to face, with the Cardinal soon to be on his tail night, noon and morning. He had no choice but to go along with Schnozzle's plans for him; jobs were hard to get if

156

you didn't have an uncle in the clergy already, and she was able to sympathize with him on that score. Then he told her about the wee personal problems a man had, and how nobody else could understand the temptations of the flesh that confronted you daily, not that he'd have been much of a ladies' man anyway if he hadn't taken the cloth, sure what girl would give him a second glance? And she was saying nonsense, he was very attractive, sure all the young girls must be mad about him, and they laughed.

Then he was serious again; they talked about holy purity and how hard it was to live that way nowadays, wasn't Ireland out of step with everywhere else, the clergy an old-fashioned crowd of stick-in-the-muds. She was nodding and saying yes, and he confided in her how near he was to throwing it all up and going to England, if it weren't for John Augustus, alias Schnozzle Durante, who'd have him fetched back to face the music; he had his touts and informers everywhere; and she was pleading with him not to do that, you make a lovely priest, you're needed here. Then she was beside him, or he was beside her, and one thing was leading to another; and they both said this was silly and they should stop now and say goodnight and they could both laugh about it in the morning.

But they didn't stop. He took her in his arms and kissed her and she let his lips linger on hers and felt his heart pounding on her breast. Then she pushed him away, firmly but gently. 'If the Reverend Mother could see me now I swear she'd die on the spot!' she said.

'You're never going back to that convent!' he told her.

'I have to. I promised them.'

'Then break your promise. You'd be wasting your life in a place like that.'

'What else is there for me? If I don't go back what is to become of me?'

'Come to Dublin with me! We'll run away together, the pair of us!'

'Is it mad you are altogether, Frank Feely?' She was trying to make light of his proposal with a cod Kerry accent.

'Schnozzle Durante need never know a thing!' he protested. 'I have a contract with the TV station. I'll need researchers, scriptwriters, you name it! We could be together.' She shook her head sadly. She had seen what had happened to her father when he had tried to outwit them, the wasted, lonely life that had been forced on him.

'That's only a dream, Frank,' she said. 'They'd never stand for it.'

'We'll make them!' he declared.

'They'll beat you in the end.'

'But there's something you don't understand,' he stammered. She was silent for a moment before she dared speak.

'What do I not understand, Frank?' she whispered.

'That I love you,' he said, suddenly.

Noreen looked at him. When she spoke at last her voice was so soft he had to strain above the hissing of the damp turf to hear her words. 'If they heard you say that they would only turn it into something sordid, a nine days' wonder for the gutter press. Never say it again! Please, Frank.'

'But it's true, I know it. We were meant to be together.'

'We can never be together. We can never meet again. You have your life to lead, and a great life it will be with God's help. I have the convent to go back to.'

'We'll defy them.'

'No one defies them. Look around you. There's plenty of talk but talk is cheap.'

She kissed him quickly on the lips, pulling away from him before he could encircle her in his arms. She fled up the stairs ignoring his entreaties, and threw herself on the bed, weeping uncontrollably. In one night her world had changed utterly. She knew that she could never return to Caherciveen.

The plaster statue on the bedside table, a souvenir brought back by Sharkey from Lourdes, began to weep silently. Slow tears, salt tears, tears that even the most intransigent Trinity professor could not have gainsaid, etched funnels down her chalky cheeks. And on the facing tallboy the Little Child of Prague, normally the most undemonstrative of icons, began, despite its cumbersome raiment, to semaphore a warning with its orb and mace.

THREE

Seven

The house lights dimmed and the group on stage, after a momentary hesitation, burst lustily into song. From the darkness behind the cameras Father Frank surveyed the sea of blue hats in the auditorium, checking for familiar faces. He spotted one or two and noted where they were sitting. People always liked to be remembered. Most of them, he knew for a fact, were complete head-the-balls, but what harm was there in a quick mention? It was these little touches that made the show so popular. At this moment every home in the country would be tuned in to the opening credits. In the saloon bars they would be calling for hush till they saw who was on the bill with him. In the convents they would have finished eating early and settled down to watch the only TV permitted all week. The show had long ago grown away from its humble beginnings; though he stuck with the original title, 'Father Frank's Half Hour', it now dominated the nation's screens for the better part of Sunday night, three hours or more. During the entire evening he would be in command.

Frank could be the most relaxed of chat-show hosts even when things weren't going smoothly. Tonight, he could see from the running order, should present no problems. There were no big stars, but the audience liked that from time to time, for it gave them a chance to air their views in public for the edification of the nation as a whole. The juggling nun from Athlone had made it to the studio okay and was having something backstage to steady her nerves. The guest star, an American comic with an uncle a priest, was keeping her company. His regular panel of celebrities had assembled and were looking after themselves in time-honoured tradition. The Grand Old Man of Irish Letters had been delivered by the boys in the white coats. Whingeing

Maire, the romantic lady novelist with a 'past' was there too, looking like the dog's dinner in chiffon and lace, the way they liked her. The Easter Week Boy Scout was hitting the sauce in the wings and would be wanting to hog the second part with hazy reminiscences of the Rising.

And of course the Sisters were there. He had learned to live with their ubiquitous presence over the years. A pair had taken over the hospitality suite and were getting stuck into the Jameson. Others hung around the set, getting in the way of the camera crew. Quite a few had tried to mingle with the audience, he could see from the monitors. They would sit stony-faced and sullen through his opening monologue. He shuffled his notes once more, scanning for anything that he had overlooked.

The singing family from Rathmines, despite a lack of consensus on key or tempo, brought 'The Old Bog Road' to a successful coda, and Father Frank bounded on to the stage leading the applause. They clapped and whistled when they saw him, and he encouraged them by pretending to be embarrassed. Then he made a show of pleading with them to stop, and they renewed their efforts. He turned his back on them and made out he was leaving, having nothing more to do with them, and they all laughed and clapped the louder when he came bounding back again, with that boyish grin on his face that assured them he had only been codding.

'*Go raibh maith agaibh*, thank you very much, Reverend Fathers, Sisters, ladies and gentlemen. And anyone else I might have left out! The Singing Sullivan Family from Rathmines, give them a big hand' – he paused for the renewed applause – 'proving to us all once more that if it's talent you're after you don't have to go to Nashville, it's to be found right here on your doorstep, so to speak.' Some of the audience, sensing that he might be less than serious, started laughing, and Father Frank stared straight into the camera with a cheeky grin, giving nothing away. 'We'll be hearing from them later on in the show. And what a show we have for you tonight, ladies and gentlemen! Some familiar faces, some new faces whom I know you'll welcome in your own way. Mother Immaculata is here as usual, of course, and will be giving us the benefit of her sagacity . . .' orchestrated oohs greeted this pomposity as he knew they must '. . . her sagacity later on in the show. And of course we have our usual panel with us tonight. Our very own Maire, that doyenne of belles lettres. And The Greatest Living Irishman, *tá sé anseo fosta agus beidh sé linn roimh i bhfad*. A certain party who was a chissler of a boy scout in Easter Week is here too, in great fettle as usual and needing no introduction from me . . . and who else? . . . oh yes we have a very funny gentleman come all the way from the States, it's his first time in Ireland so I'm sure you'll give him a warm welcome . . . and we have the McAntaggart School of Dancing later on in the programme showing us their terpsichorean skills. They're practising backstage.'

While they were laughing he turned dramatically in the direction of the wings and shouted, 'Go easy there girls, the building's not insured!' They all laughed again. The McAntaggart School, big girls all God bless them, were regular guests.

'But enough about us up here,' he said, jumping from the stage and picking up the hand-held microphone. 'Let's have a look at who's in the audience tonight. Is there anyone here from Cork?' A phalanx of hands shot up to simulated jeering and cheering. Frank cracked a couple of one-liners about Cork people, and then a couple about Dublin people to show he was neutral. Then he made a few remarks about Kerry that went down well as they always did, and threw in a reference to Mullingar because it always got a laugh. He walked up and down the makeshift aisles, thrusting the mike at various groups and asking them where they were from and what they were called and who they were with and if they were courting, while the cameraman scampered after him getting them in close-up.

'He's a right gasbag,' grumbled the Tyrone man, who was watching the show in the Patriot's snug.

'You're only interested in the dancing girls,' Peadar said. 'Why can't you shut up and listen to the man?'

'A fiver says he won't risk the juggling nun,' the Tyrone man said.

'You're on, you bastard!' Peadar told him.

'Any more of your talk and the pair of youse are banned,'

Eugene told them. Out of the corner of his eye he had seen Snotters MacBride hurrying across the Shambles towards the bar to watch the show.

Not that there would be much to see tonight. The picture was a snowstorm of dancing dots that made your head reel the more you concentrated on them. Through the murk they could dimly discern Father Frank and his studio guests. The Patriot had spent the best part of the afternoon in the attic fiddling with the aerial, with Eugene shouting up to him when the test card looked better. But McCoy had remembered that it was Sunday night and had ordered Magee to turn up the voltage on the transmitter and jam all incoming infamy. Jagged arcs of blue lightning crackled round the top of the scaffolding. 'Father Frank's Half Hour' was fighting back, for there wasn't enough electricity on the Shambles to keep him out completely. All evening it would be a battle between them, Father Frank's suave professionalism periodically skewing off into painful distortions of white noise through which the voice of McGuffin could be heard, screaming like a lost aviator in distress, demanding their money and their repentance.

'Right then, *a chairde*,' Father Frank said, bounding back on to the stage, 'I can see we have a great audience in tonight, and we'll be giving you all a chance to air your views, perchance display your collective erudition . . .' they oohed again on cue '. . . but before we do so I want you all to meet a very special lady who's come all the way from Athlone to entertain us. Now I know she's a bit nervous, and you'd be nervous if you knew what it is she's going to do, so I want you to give a special warm welcome . . .' Frantic hand signals from the floor manager interrupted this build-up to the juggling nun. One hand was telling him that that particular act was off the menu. With the other hand he mimicked a shaking glass being raised and lowered to the lips repeatedly. The dumb show told its own story. Frank considered for a second letting her go on anyway, passing it off as a novelty act. The audience at home might be amused by the sight of a comic nun dropping her balls and trying to stay upright. Should he risk it? He caught the eye of Sister Ellen sitting not ten feet away in Row A and decided to let decorum prevail.

'We've just been informed, *a chairde*,' he indicated his ear piece, 'that the Sister isn't quite ready yet. So let us move swiftly and unflappably onwards to the next part of the show . . .'

He eased himself into the master-of-ceremonies chair, acknowledged with a slight inclination of the head their renewed applause, and made a show of shuffling his notes. This was the segment of the show he enjoyed most, where he invited the studio audience's views on matters of current interest. He scanned the auditorium, peering through the arc lights. 'Now let's hear from some of the people we have in tonight and who have got something to get off their chests. Yes,' he said, his finger suddenly pointing to someone in the back row, 'the lady up there in the blue hat!' A cheer went up as the cameras panned out and then focused on the chosen one.

It had become one of his most famous catch phrases, '*the lady in the blue hat*'. Nowadays there would be a whole clutch of them, all in blue, trying to catch his eye and air their views. The burning issues of the day didn't change much – abortion and contraception, marriage and divorce, revival of the fortunes of the Irish language or the GAA, itinerants and beggars. The stranger forces that were welling up in society, the threats from without and within, were rarely mentioned. There was a timelessness about their preoccupations, irrespective of the events outside the studio that threatened some day to engulf them. Week in and week out there was a predictability about these discussions; it was clearly what the viewers wanted. They liked to see how he handled his audience; he in turn liked the feeling of power it gave him. He knew he was good at it, that Schnozzle would never find better. He knew exactly when to intervene to stop a discussion growing libellous, how to encourage the shy and control the flamboyant. He had a sixth sense for the true maniac, of which there was never a shortage, and knew when to encourage them and when to draw the line. Down the years many different groups and individuals had tried to hijack 'Father Frank's Half Hour' to propagate their various causes, but none had yet got the better of him. The millions watching at home loved him for the way he could put down the smart-ass. They loved his catch phrases and corny jokes, his occasional irreverence ('though I'll say this of him,' they told each other, 'he'll never go too far'), above all they loved him for asking the common people their opinions and appearing to find them interesting.

The Tyrone man, despite repeated requests that he should buy his round, pocketed Peadar's fiver. 'He bottled out when it came to the bit!' he laughed. 'Don't tell me they don't stick together.'

'You'll take your custom elsewhere,' Eugene told him. 'Can't you see Mister MacBride is trying to watch the show.'

'I've never seen Father Frank looking better,' Peadar said, hoping for a drink from that quarter.

'I believe he's actually put some weight on at last,' the major-domo conceded. But he spoke with no real conviction. For he alone could detect, behind Frank's outward show of confidence and urbanity, a glimpse of a soul in distress.

'He's handling it like a pro,' Peadar went on. 'I'll say this for His Eminence, he knows how to pick a winner.'

But it hadn't always been plain sailing. There had been times in the show's early days – they had passed into folklore now – when its very survival had been touch and go. Little in the training had prepared Frank for the potential awfulness of a live audience. Tedious boys in UCD scarves who wouldn't shut up. Or a crowd in who couldn't take a joke, despite the best exertions of the warm-up man. There'd been other nights too when things had threatened to get out of hand. Spontaneous outbursts of loyalty to the Church. Impassioned pleas for the clergy to take over and run the spiritual, moral and economic affairs of the country. He could guess who had been behind that particular piece of orchestration. On another occasion a movement had got up demanding that he himself should lead the people back to their duties, and turn a part of his show over to a Rosary Crusade. To all these suggestions Frank was expected to play Devil's Advocate, picking holes in their logic, raising the odd laugh at the expense of the less articulate, arguing the contrary point of view tongue in cheek so as not to give too much offence. In the middle of this cut and thrust would sit Sister Ellen, ready to intervene with the official line if things were not to her liking.

And there had been the never-to-be-forgotten night with the fish-eye lens.

'Double or quits,' the Tyrone man said, 'he'll have Schnozzle on the show before the night's out.'

'You're definitely on, squire!' Peadar said.

'Here's a pound says you're off your head!' Eugene said, slapping one down on the counter. The Tyrone man took the bet.

'What makes you so confident?' Peadar asked.

'Use your loaf!' He jerked his thumb in the direction of the lavatory where the major-domo had scurried during the commercial break. 'Why do you think Snotters is out on shore leave tonight? Because the man himself is off in Dublin for the weekend. Throwing the ball in tomorrow at Croke Park. He'll not be able to resist sticking his nose into the show.'

'That's the easiest money I've ever made. It'll be a long time before we see him on the screen again.'

Back in the beginning it had been part of the understanding, made clear to Frank when he'd been summoned to Ara Coeli and his duties outlined, that Schnozzle wanted a show that would highlight true family virtues. A show that would counteract the stream of pagan propaganda from across the water. It went without saying that His Eminence would be making a regular appearance. Week after week Schnozzle was chauffeured down to Dublin in time for a guest spot on the fledgling programme. His intervention was the kiss of death. The ratings plummeted. The punters in the bars turned their backs on the set and ordered fresh pints. The women of Ireland, bent over the ironing board, switched on the wireless instead, searching for something soothing. Even the nuns in the convents, allowed to stay up for this one treat, found themselves, when confronted by His Eminence in full flow, stifling a yawn and talking of turning in.

Schnozzle's voice, its timbre exaggerated by the microphone, grated on the ear. His nervous, close-set eyes invariably fixed on the wrong camera with a stoat-like stare. His adam's apple jogged with every syllable. Rivulets of sweat formed on his forehead and trickled down his cheeks. And the nose! The nose wobbled and twitched and dribbled and suppurated. Frank, watching his ratings plummet, tried to put it to him gently that he was not a

167

television natural. But personal vanity would not deter Schnozzle from his task.

Week in and week out he claimed his place on the studio sofa, and week in and week out he harangued the dwindling viewers on the intricacies of theological jurisprudence. He thought nothing either of interrupting a guest if he disagreed with the tenor of his thesis. He thought even less of interrupting his host if he detected any uncalled-for levity in his presentation. Not even the aspiring amateur talent that the show attracted in its early days was safe from him. At the first perceived threat to Irish values he would personally leap to his feet, pulling the microphone plug on them before treating the audience to a sermon on the evils of popular music and modern dancing, and their softening effects on the moral fibre of the young. It was clear that something had to be done.

One infamous New Year's Eve the medium had struck back.

Even under the third degree the cameraman had stuck to his original story. It had been his idea and his alone. He'd done it for a bit of a laugh, he claimed. No one had put him up to it. He thought there'd be no harm in it! No harm in fitting a fish-eye lens to his camera and waiting for Schnozzle to swim into close-up! The nose alone had filled the screen, glistening and throbbing under the studio lights. The best endeavours of the make-up girls with their powder puffs had only succeeded in highlighting its engorged contours. It had a life of its own. Full frontal or in profile it called for attention. The nuns watching in the convents fiddled with the horizontal hold and crossed themselves piously at the enormity of the affliction. The drinkers in the snugs put down their glasses and gave the apparition their full attention. The women at home let the iron burn through their men's collars as they permitted themselves a seditious chuckle.

The vision of the schnozz had lasted a few seconds at best before the producer, realizing his predicament, had switched cameras and gone off to throw himself into the Liffey. But the damage was done. Next day, in every one of the twenty-six counties, and those of the six which could get a signal, it was the only talking point. Graffiti appeared overnight, a crudely drawn cartoon character in a dog collar with a long nose looking over a brick wall.

Greengrocers, Peadar among them, held their cucumbers sugges-
tively and cracked cryptic comments to ould ones if the coast was
clear. Even the schoolchildren fashioned false noses from their
jotters and ran screeching with them into the playground. The
Cardinal had never appeared on the 'Half Hour' since. The insult
had cut deep. So too had the suspicion that there was a conspiracy.
And though the ratings rose from that point on, Frank knew that
he would have to watch his step for the rest of his days.

The microphone boom had located the woman at the back and
they could now hear what she was saying. He was relieved to
hear she had a bee in her bonnet about contraception. Everybody's favourite topic, a vicarious way to talk dirty while pretending social concern. If they could stick to this all night he'd
have no worries. He settled back with a concerned expression on
his face, the glimmer of a smile playing round his lips, as the old
familiar arguments began their inexorable dialectic.

It was two in the morning when Frank got home to Adam and
Eve's. Though the furniture in the Parochial House had faded
since the heyday of Canon Tom and limescale had blunted the
jacuzzi's effervescence, the house was still the pride of the parish
and the cellar was as well stocked as ever. He was, on paper,
chaplain to the flock, but ever since the Canon's day, when things
had been allowed to get out of hand, the parish was under occupation by the Sisters of the True Faith, and Frank's duties were
minimal. He had everything a young man in his position could
ask for. All was quiet in Adam and Eve's. The middle classes were
sleeping the sleep of the righteous secure in their fine houses.
Even in the turbulent city below they were sleeping at last, in the
tenements and in the shanty towns and the cardboard squatter
camps along the canals. Frank stood at the door and listened to
the silence, envying them their peace.

For there would be no sleep for Ireland's golden boy. The show
might be full of light-hearted banter, but Frank's heart was heavy
and troubled. A deep unhappiness had settled on him that he

couldn't shake, a feeling that the world was passing him by and that he was doomed to eke out his days, a performing puppet at the whim of those he had come to despise. Others might envy him his worldly possessions, but he would have gladly swapped everything he had for one day of true freedom.

He was troubled by the memory of the girl he had left behind in the wilds of Donegal. If he were half a man he would go and rescue her from the living death that had become her fate. If he were a man at all he would defy the Cardinal, refuse any longer to be his amanuensis, walk out on the job and the mockery of his vocation. But had he the nerve to defy the forces ranged against him? Was he willing to throw it all away, to risk everything, for her?

And there was something else eating away at his confidence. His show might deal with the public face of morality, packaging its awkward questions into ninety-minute segments, all the loose ends tied up. But Frank had begun to learn that real life was not so neat. The people told a different story, a story of confusion and despair.

He knew it from his postbag. Ever since the show had started the letters had been pouring in, from every corner of the land, even from areas where the reception was poor. They needed his guidance. They needed his reassurance. Many were anonymous, the writers fearful of the letter falling into the wrong hands. But the stories they told were the same. They spoke of a people trodden down by their own customs. They spoke of the darker side of Irish life, the narrowness of the country and the bigotry of the small towns. Where you could be ostracized for the slightest peccadillo, where life could come to a halt after one mistake. As he read them, he could feel the anger welling up inside him, knowing that he was part of all this, a cog in a machine that smiled as it subjugated.

There was a backlog of unopened letters in a box at the bottom of the bed. If he didn't keep up with them, they would pile up on him. Schnozzle was in town and would be expecting a report in the morning. He reached down and pulled a sheaf of them towards him. They each contained a cash donation for his special intentions. He could feel the coins through the cheap envelopes.

Was there one from Fidelma, he wondered? It was more than a month since she had written. One was due by now. Sure enough, there was the familiar violet envelope and the familiar handwriting. He left it carefully to one side, unopened. His Eminence could have that pleasure himself. He could send for Fidelma's file and add it to the rest. There were few correspondents as faithful as Fidelma. Though she aspired to anonymity, it hadn't taken Schnozzle long to tumble to the fact that the correspondent with the fancy writing paper and the marital problems was none other than Mrs John Joe Sharkey. Her letters ached with the disillusionment of marriage, charting its ups and downs, its myriad infidelities and disappointments. It might have been the story of any marriage in its catalogue of frustrated hopes and broken dreams. What made it special was that the man in Fidelma's life, the man who had given her such a shoddy time over the years, was once again (by the skin of his teeth and a shaky coalition) the Taoiseach. Little wonder that Schnozzle had it, every word, on the hard disk.

There was another handwriting that he recognized, too. He cursed when he saw it. Inspector O'Malley again! He didn't get the time to write as often as he used to, with his new duties and responsibilities, but it was still too often for Frank. He didn't need to open it to know what it contained, a screed of filth and frustration parading as civic concern. He lifted it between finger and thumb and with a small sense of triumph tossed it, unopened, into the wastepaper basket.

With the paperknife that lay on the bedside table he began to slit the others open, one by one. Letters from middle-aged men tied to the dying countryside, condemned to a lifetime of guilty self-abuse and internecine warfare. He read of the fears of women in the North, watching their sons go out at night, knowing that each time they saw them might be the last. Or wives who feared for the knock on the door that would tell them they were widows. He read of the despair of women, fleeing alone to England burdened with unwanted pregnancies. He read of girls giving birth in the ditches. He read of incest and abuse and drunkenness and drugs and violence and poverty and sickness and death.

171

He sorted them into two separate piles on the bed. There was a pile of letters that could be left to Sister Mary (was the title medical or religious? he was never quite sure) to sort out and answer. There was a larger pile from anguished souls who had turned to him in person for help. Somehow he would have to find answers for them. Spilling off the bed was a heap of scapulars, medals, sacred bookmarks, holy pictures and relics, in paper and cloth and metal, which had touched unmentionable parts of saints long dead. Many bore the stains of injudicious immersion in holy water, or Knock water, or Fatima water. These he would in due course consign to the dustbin, double bagged in heavy plastic lest the binmen one day discover his secret and denounce him to the authorities. And nestling safely beside the pillow, was a pile of money. It had begun to intrigue him how the Irish housewife, isolated and powerless as the letters made all too clear, yet agreed with uncanny accuracy the price of the service for which they were paying. Few if any insulted him with the single punt. Fewer still stretched to the fiver. As if by telepathy they each enclosed two pounds with each letter, adding a ritualistic paragraph apologizing for its inadequacy.

What need had he of their money! Tomorrow he would hand it over to the Vincent de Paul. Some of it would find its way back to those who had sent it. He said his prayers and tried to sleep. From across the bay a boat hooted forlornly and a monastery bell tinkled for matins. There would be no sleep for him tonight. He sat up and read through the letters again, hoping for some form of words that would ease the pain they expressed. But no glib words of his could pour balm on these wounds.

Inspector O'Malley stepped out of the garda station and inspected the scene from the steps. Though it was still dark, bells were ringing and sirens screaming from all over the city. It hadn't been like this even a few years back, he thought. Lately it seemed things had got out of hand entirely. When he'd first moved to Dublin with the promotion you'd have four or at most five Masses to supervise on a Sunday morning with a breather in between; short

172

seven for the man lucky enough to have work to go to, a big sermon at the ten o'clock, maybe a Missa Cantata at half-eleven. That was the one he liked best. How did it go again? *Credo in unum De-e-um*. How things had changed in even a few years! The old fanaticism was rearing its head once more, he mused. Making more work for the Guards when all was said and done. Today's do would be a bit of a show, of course, with it being Easter Sunday and Cardinal Schnozzle in attendance. But the rest of the time it was more like a production line. Mass after Mass all day from morning till night. And the Dublin ones running from one church to another in case they'd miss something; trying to catch the tail end of another when their own was hardly over. Where was it those children had been trampled last year? Not far up from here. The crowd from half past ten at Saint Bridget's running into a crowd who'd been short-changed at eleven in the Holy Rosary, both of them trying to get to the half-eleven and Exposition down in the Monastery.

He'd been glad of the Sisters that day. If it hadn't been for them he'd have had a right riot on his hands and only half a dozen gobshites of trainees for assistance. Just as well when you came down to it that there was so much church property around. 'Outside my jurisdiction,' had become his defence. He loved that phrase. But Jesus, those Sisters didn't half get stuck in! Took no prisoners, that lot! In the old days you'd hardly need an usher in the chapel. Now the Sisters were patrolling with sticks and walkie-talkies, not to mention the big one in the organ loft with the semi-automatic. O'Malley chuckled. Not really supposed to know about that, turn a blind eye. Not within my jurisdiction.

He left the Green and headed down Grafton Street. Would you look at the streets at this hour? Don't tell me they're all up for the hurley final. Dublin full of riff-raff this weather. Where in God's name are they all coming from? Far too many people nowadays. Too much shagging at the bottom of it all, half the country must be at it night after night. To look at them the next morning you'd think butter wouldn't melt in their mouths. Secretaries round the station, smiling at you one minute, they'd have the drawers off you the next if you gave them any

173

encouragement. Dropping babies right left and centre, it'll be standing room only soon. Mind you it might be indiscreet to point any of this out to our long-nosed leader. Have your head on a plate for thoughts like those. No contraception, no abortion, no divorce. That was the law of the land, and his duty to uphold it. Breeding like fleas in those shanty towns out by the airport and beyond in Tallaght. Dun Laoghaire's overrun as well, that used to be so nice. It seems the whole country won't be satisfied till they've all come to Dublin. Pouring in every day, swelling the tenements. Camping in trailers and tents, sleeping in paper bags. Cardboard huts the length of O'Connell Street. It's no wonder food's getting scarce, no farmers left. All we need now is cholera or some such. Look how long it took us to get over the last outbreak. What's got into the people altogether?

Progress was slow. He elbowed his way through the crowds that swirled aimlessly between the chapels. Some ran barefooted, either through poverty or penance, maybe both. Here and there a penitent would be crawling on his knees, in reparation for some past sin or in the hope of some preferment in the race for salvation. O'Malley's uniform and his girth were some help in making his way through the throng, but he was panting and red-faced by the time he reached College Green. Hasn't respect for everything gone to the dogs, he thought. It's as if they can hardly see what's in front of their eyes. By O'Connell Bridge the crowd was densest and he decided against trying to get across the river at that point. Law and order of a sort was being kept by a truckload of young curates with cudgels. Don't get involved, he told himself. Maybe cop a clout from one of those young buckoes myself! Sunday was the priests' day, they were never done preaching it. Let them take care of business if they're so keen.

In the middle of the bridge a commotion erupted. There was a flash of black serge and the sound of shillelaghs on skullbones. A great shout went up from the crowd. 'A miracle! The stigmata!' A young man was handed over the heads of the crowd and thrown into the back of the truck. His head was wreathed in blood. Before they carted him away, O'Malley noticed the gaping wounds in his hands and feet and the blood oozing from his side. My God

174

but aren't they mad for miracles! The rumour had gone the rounds that there would be great signs and portents before the year was out. Apparitions too. Half the country telling the other half that the prophesies of Saint Malachy were about to come true, the signs were all there. He took that sort of thing with more than a pinch of salt. If the end of the world really was coming he wouldn't be hanging round Dublin, punching in time till he drew the pension. He'd be off doing a bit of fishing, round the lakes of Leitrim. For I shall have some peace there, for peace comes dropping slow. If things were a bit quieter he could have booked a week's leave. Not much hope of that at the moment. He'd heard the fishing had gone to blazes anyhow. They blamed the snakes. There were never any snakes round Sligo or Leitrim when he was a boy; or if there were he'd never seen them. Wasn't Saint Patrick supposed to have sent them packing when he converted the country? Probably just another pishrogue. There were enough of them nowadays by all accounts. He'd seen them himself, near the lakes. Would take the arm off you some of them. No wonder the local people took it as an omen.

Mind you, a real apparition would be the quare thing. The Blessed Virgin in her full regalia. Queen of Ireland. He'd never breathed a word about the night McCoy slipped through his fingers. Not to a soul! He had been on border duty the night of McCoy's raid. He could have challenged him. He could have rescued Her. Instead a native caution had counselled him against taking action. But the guilty memory of the ice-cream van splutt-ering over the border with the Madonna lashed to its roof was never far from his mind. He had done nothing, been too cautious to act. That had been the start of the present trouble. Downhill all the way since then. If a thing like that got out you could be facing a show trial. It was a great mystery what had happened afterwards; not a sighting of Her since that day. O'Malley had hoped that down the years they'd have forgotten Her, but there seemed to be more talk about Her these days than ever before. A bit of a cult building up round Her and the priests doing damn all to put a stop to it. Shrines with empty niches to tempt the Dancing Madonna out of retirement. He knew only too well the latest rumour that had sprung up. If She ever reappeared there'd be a united Ireland! A nation once again. He smiled to himself. That would be a miracle and no mistake.

❖

As befitted its elevated status, in Adam and Eve's the dawning of the Sabbath was altogether more refined. Outside Frank's bedroom the first bells of the new morning began to toll. The sweet, muffled sound of the Adam and Eve's bell from the nearby church, almost drowning out the harsher clangings from lower down in the city. But Frank knew that before nine o'clock the klaxons in the dockside parishes would start up their urgent wailing, ordering the faithful to their duties, and no one could for long ignore their urgent summons. He lay in bed, smoking the first cigarette of the day and taking stock of his life. And for the first time in many years, he discovered that he was not unhappy. The black dog of despair that had been hanging over him for so long seemed to have lifted during the night. In its place he felt a new contentment, an optimism almost, even the first stirring of hope for the future.

Frank finished his cigarette and closed his eyes once more. He was afraid to explore these feelings too closely in case this new mood turned out to be merely ephemeral, disappearing the moment his foot hit the floor and he had to face the day ahead. But the longer he lay on, the more convinced he became that his new-founded contentment was here to stay. He had told himself a thousand times that he should count his blessings, give thanks for the easy life he had. Dublin swarmed with a hundred thousand stunted lives, its slums and shanties crawling with abandoned kids any one of which, but for the grace of God, could have been him. But his present state of mind owed nothing to such sophistry. He had a premonition that his life was about to take a new turning.

He rose at last and braced himself for the world. It was a special day, the All Ireland final, and Schnozzle was back in town on a tour of inspection, checking that everything was hunky-dory. Thoughtfully he opened the wardrobe door and turned his mind to what outfit might be appropriate for the occasion. He was aware how late he was; already the wail of the sirens had died away and he knew that soon the Sisters would be patrolling the streets, looking for stragglers. They wouldn't venture up as far as Adam and Eve's; they had their informants for that. What did he care? No one was going to bother a man in his position. The right sartorial look would be all-important. Something casual, he mused? He riffled through a rack of jackets he used for the show, rejecting them all. Too frivolous for the occasion. Today called for something more formal, something that would make a statement.

At the back of the wardrobe, unused since his ordination day, his best clerical suit hung neatly folded, as good as the day he had bought it. He remembered the last time he had worn it, on that trip to Ballychondom, and the last time he had seen Noreen. For a moment he felt the awful despair creep up on him again ... He fingered the material. Squeaky had been right, you couldn't get cloth like that nowadays for love or money. He pulled out the hanger and removed the mothballs. Should he try it on? He had filled out a bit since those lean years back in Maynooth – too many vol-au-vents and brandy snaps backstage. It was tight at the waist, even when he pulled himself in. All the same he thought, admiring himself in the full-length mirror, you had to admit he was still in good shape. A suit like that never went out of fashion. He tried on the clerical collar and stood back to admire the finished look. He could nearly pass for a country curate, up in town for the GAA final. It was a look that spoke of quiet, unquestioned authority, the authority of the cloth.

All he needed now was the hat.

O'Malley was approaching Saint Enoch's. The crowd was thick behind the crush barriers. He shoved his way through to the first checkpoint. Reserved Mass, ticket only, not for the hoi polloi. A burly Christian Brother looked him over carefully, despite the uniform, and told him to turn out his pockets. O'Malley submitted without demur. There would be further indignities, no doubt, before he was ushered to his seat.

He genuflected in the aisle and edged his bulk into the narrow pew. Knelt, blessed himself, said a few prayers. Just enough for the sake of decency. You wouldn't want to draw too much attention to yourself in front of this crowd. He cradled his head in his hands and smelt his breath. Our Father, Hail Mary, Glory be to the Father. The preliminaries over he eased his backside up on to the bench and took a look round at the rest of the congregation. The church was filling up with the cream of Irish society. Rich and thick. Invitation only. Tickets sometimes sold on the black market. Everyone in their best bib and tucker. He scrutinized the red necks in the seat in front of his. Sam 'Have you got a statement?' O'Dowd and the missus out for an airing. Our fearless editor-in-chief. Will print anything he's told to, verbatim, if it comes from the parochial house. They say Schnozzle has only to get on the mobile phone should it be midnight and Sam will hold the front page. Here for his orders like the rest of us.

There was a rustle of silk and the smell of rich perfume. Fidelma, flustered, ushered to the front. Counting the children into the pew in case one of them's done a runner. One a year to keep the voters happy. Heard she was thinking of leaving him, to join the sister in Canada. No way, José! John Joe Sharkey would never stand for it. You couldn't blame the girl after what she's had to put up with. Look at the arse she's getting on her. No wonder John Joe's spreading it around. All the same you wouldn't kick her out of bed if you had the chance! No harm done in looking, he told himself. But not the right place to be getting a hard on. She can carry the extra weight the best. All done up like the dog's dinner on account of Schnozzle Durante. Going through an elaborate ritual of piety for the benefit of the gathering congregation. He shuffled his position to get a better look at her, to study her slowly and thoroughly. The ankles, the thighs, the contours of her breasts under the fox fur. Like a Mullingar man assessing a heifer.

Heeere's Johnny! John Joe looking somewhat the worse for wear. The Taoiseach and his cronies, all smiles and aftershave. A big GAA man in his time. A right tough boy on and off the field by all accounts. Fair play to him, he's always seen the Guards right. Well he might, too, the number of wee favours we've done him down the years. Turning the blind eye. Can't leave the women alone. And to hear him on his hind legs in the Dáil upholding family values you'd think he was some class of a virgin still.

Who's this they're all rubbernecking to see now? If it isn't Father Frank, the matinee idol in the flesh. There's a boy who's made a name for himself. Schnozzle's alter ego, the man he never was himself. Maybe the last letter I sent him made him sit up! Wouldn't be surprised. Don't give a fuck. Only telling the truth as I see it. Hear they all get back to Schnozzle in the long run. Sentiments like that bound to do the promotion prospects no harm.

O'Malley swivelled slowly, taking in the congregation behind him. A few smiles of recognition, cautious ones reserved for the Garda. All the women dressed to the nines. Not one for the ladies himself. Thank God he'd never been afflicted that way. Much too careful to get hooked. There'd been that landlady once, years ago now. Marriage had never been mentioned. Nothing had come of it, just as well. A man had enough with his work, maybe a bit of fishing in his spare time, better off not getting involved in the woman business.

The organ blared and the congregation rose to its feet. Up the central aisle filed the procession, led by three altarboys with crucifix and candles. Following them, a plump priest with a steaming thurible, walking backwards and shaking it in Schnozzle's face. Two deacons were holding the hems of his cassock, and he had his hands joined and face elevated in an attitude of prayer. They stopped at the foot of the altar. Paused, then genuflected in unison. The priest sent up clouds of incense which curled upwards to the high roof beams. Schnozzle walked slowly to the prie-dieu which had been set out for him; the thurifer walked over and clicked the censer three times in front of him. He prayed for a moment, then rose and mounted the steps. He bent to kiss the stone, stretched out his arms and began to intone the familiar words of the Mass.

'*Introibo ad altare Dei.*'
'*Ad Deum qui letivicat juventutum meum.*'
'*Dominus vobiscum.*'
'*Et cum spiritu tuo.*'
'*Oremus . . .*'

❖

179

There were more letters waiting for Frank when he got back at midnight. The producer had sent over another sack. He kicked off his shoes before he scanned them. Many of them bore familiar handwriting; they could wait till the morning. A few looked unusual, or carried strange postmarks. It was among these that he noticed the letter from Donegal.

Letters from anywhere in the north were rare since the trouble, and those from Donegal rarer still. He turned it over in his hand before he opened it. There was something about it that suddenly excited him. His heart skipped a beat. The envelope was dirty and torn, and had evidently lain for long in a series of disused sub post-offices as it travelled down the country. With a trembling hand he tore it open.

He didn't need to read more than a sentence or two to know that Noreen was calling for help from her exile at the end of the Yellow Meal Road.

Eight

Old Tobias Sharkey had buried Cornelius in the grave beside Noreen's mother, and already the weeds straggled over the thin topsoil. Frank took off his hat and gave out a decade of the rosary, while Noreen in a faltering voice made the responses.

'Eternal rest grant unto him, O Lord.'

'And may perpetual light shine upon him.'

'May he rest in peace.'

She was crying again, the tears on her face mingling with the rain that was falling softly on the graveyard. She looked older than the last time he had seen her, as if each year in this dreadful place of exile had counted a decade. Frank took her gently by the arm and led her away from the graveside.

'Go in and make the Canon his tea,' he told her gently. 'You can't blame him for being peeved.'

'He could at least have had the decency to speak to you in a civil fashion.'

'It's hard for him. Doubly hard now that his only companion is gone. When I mentioned Adam and Eve's it must have been the last straw!'

'He's always been a grouse. You'd think he could be gracious just for once.'

He looked at her again, this pale woman whom he'd abandoned. 'I'm sorry,' he said softly. 'I could have made the effort to get up.'

'Didn't you have your work? You got here as soon as you got the letter.'

He took her suddenly in his arms. She didn't struggle. 'Come away from here for the love of God. Come away from this

181

accursed place. Your duty here is done!' She looked at him sadly, then pushed him gently away from her.

'How could I ever leave?' she said with resignation. 'The Canon is still here. My duty is to him now.'

'If you could read the letters I'm getting every day, hundreds of them, you'd know where your duty lay! Your place is with me.'

'He can never leave, any more than my father could. I can't abandon him here to die.'

'Then we'll take him with us,' Frank said suddenly. She pulled away from him, her eyes open wide with disbelief.

'You're not thinking what you're saying,' she said. 'How in God's name could you conceive of such a thing? They'd never stand for it.'

'We'll tell no one! He can live with me in the old house. No one need ever know!'

'I can't let you go on with this madness! What would happen if His Eminence finds out you have defied him?'

'It's a risk I'll take. The Canon deserves a little comfort in his fading years.'

'But who'll look after him?'

'The pair of us together. It'll be our secret.'

'You're talking pie in the sky,' she said. 'None of this can happen.'

'But I need you. The people need you. I'm out of my depth. And besides . . .'

She put her fingers on his lips to silence him. 'I'll go in and tend to him now. He's feeling the loss more than he's prepared to let on. Stroll around for a while. And don't go off without saying goodbye.' But as she moved back over the rocks towards the house he noticed that her step was lighter. She had become a girl again. He had seen a flicker of hope in her eyes. And though he wasn't ready yet to face the consequences of what he was proposing, he knew one thing for certain. He would not leave Ballychondom without her.

He stood on the lonely road and looked at the old place. All was silent. The track beyond the graveyard led down to the bottom of the glen, where the houses of the native speakers still stood. He followed it down. The area was overgrown, the cabins deserted. Weeds sprouted from the thatch. No sound of the bodhrán now, no echo of the fiddle or the squeeze box; the voice of the *seanchaí* was stilled for ever. He kicked open the rotting door of one of the low houses and looked at the remnants of their civilization, feeling as intrusive as an archeologist surveying a burial mound. The settle bed, its straw plundered by the mice, the fiddle hanging on the wall, its strings rent asunder. Above the door the faded triptych of JFK, Padraig Pearse and old Pope John. The iron pot on the hearth where the fire once glowed. The scene was eerily undisturbed. No grave robbers hungry for gold had ransacked these remains. It could have been a year or it could have been ten since the last of them had walked these earthen floors, eaten off the oilcloth, tilted themselves back in those sugan chairs. It was like the *Marie Celeste*. The last remnants of old Ireland had folded their tents in the night and quietly stolen away.

In the workshop the benches were idle and the machinery rusted. Half-empty boxes piled in a corner had fallen unnoticed on the floor. He was turning to leave when he heard a noise. A scuttling noise. Was it a rat? He heard it again and recognized it as the irregular rasp of someone breathing. He lifted some of the boxes nervously and saw the outline of an ancient figure lying there. A bottle, almost empty, lay on the floor. Frank lifted him – he presumed it was a man but he couldn't yet be sure – by the shoulder and tried to get a better look at the face. It was the face of age, incredible age, gnarled and blackened by the years and the weather, by winters spent in the smoke of turf fires and summers spent cutting it on the bogs. The old man coughed, opened his eyes slowly, coughed again, reached out for his bottle and, realizing perhaps that he was not alone, tried to focus on Frank. Then noticing the collar and the suit, and perhaps the concerned look on Frank's face, he struggled to his feet and saluted the man of the cloth, as he had been taught to do a century before.

'What are you doing here?' Frank asked as clearly as he could.

The old man thought for a long time before he spoke. His Irish was the purest Frank had ever heard, untainted by *Béarla*, the English usages that had crept in elsewhere during the last days. In the man's mouth it sounded sweet, like the humming of bees in the summer, or a maiden's laughter at dawn, or any of the thousand other metaphors that the old poets employed to describe the uniqueness of their tongue. Frank caught the word *sagart* – priest – and the words *ag obair*, working. '*Tá tú ag obair anseo?*' he asked. You work here?

The old man spoke again, nodding vigorously. This time his speech was like the wind in the oak trees over the grave of Oisin, or like the water cascading over the great falls into the Poisoned Glen from the side of Errigal itself, or like the music of a thousand harpists at the court of Setanta, the hound of Ulster. Frank couldn't catch any of it. The man had no teeth, and the mouthful of gums seemed to add to the mellifluence of his diction. He ended his flow on an interrogative, waiting for Father Frank.

A Derry-educated man like Frank prided himself on his Irish. Hadn't he been the first in the Seminary to flaunt the fáinne, the band of gold the size of a wedding ring worn in the lapel beside the Pioneer Pin, that signified to any passer-by that they could stop you and have a conversation with you in Irish, you were so fluent in it? But devil the bit of use the fáinne was to him now, he thought, when faced with the real thing. The old boy was on his feet now and his talk was becoming animated. He pressed the poteen bottle on Frank, wiping it with his sleeve and inviting him to drink. Frank declined. The old man insisted, loquaciously, poetically. He was clearly outlining its benefits, extolling its special purity, eulogizing its pedigree. This time Frank accepted and took a tentative slug. The liquid hit the back of his throat like a premature Mills bomb and torpedoed down his gullet and into his intestines. He felt his stomach contract and his ass tighten. It was good stuff all right. The *cainteoir dúchais* cackled gaelically and pressed him to try again.

'Why the hell not?' he thought, and took another mouthful.

The late Sagart de Bhaldraithe, he had once read, held the theory that prolonged use of the English language, as well as debasing the higher areas of the brain, would so atrophy the vocal chords that the production of fine Gaelic would in time become impossible. The tongue grew distorted and the teeth got in the way. He now recognized the validity of the professor's hypothesis. The poteen seemed to be rearranging his tonsils as it hit them, and straightening out his epiglottis. Another wallop of this stuff he told himself, and he'd be on all fours with your man here in the matter of *blas*. Sensing the danger, the old man retrieved the bottle, and with a peasant cunning bred of generations gave himself another relaxer of the fluid that as good as finished it.

With an elaborate show of caution, he started to rummage among the rusting remains of what had once been a machine of sorts and produced another bottle. He uncorked it with his teeth and took a swig. '*Caidé tá ann?*' asked Frank. What is it? The old man said nothing, but tapped his nose instead. That would be telling, he implied. His lips were sealed. Frank felt in his pocket for his cigarette case and formally offered him one.

'You can tell me,' he said. The man looked around cautiously to see if the Canon were about. Then he pulled Frank's ear close to his mouth. He could smell the poteen on his breath and the smell of the sea from his rags. He was trying to put English on what he was saying.

'Secret Formula,' he said at last.

Frank took the bottle from him and held it up to the light. The lettering was faded but he could still make out the crude drawing of the Madonna on the label. Years earlier, he recalled his father telling, when Cornelius had first been hounded to this place, he had tried bottling the local fire-water and selling it to Sharkey. There hadn't been many takers then or since, for by the look of things there were enough bottles left to do the native speaker his time. But as the old man started talking again, the Irish pouring out of him like the flood waters of the mighty Shannon itself, a mad idea was forming in his mind. It was dawning on him that he had found the one ingredient that the show had been lacking all along.

'You can't possibly take all three of us with you,' Noreen said when he told her what he had decided. He no longer doubted that Noreen would go with him. He had thrown her a lifeline and despite her fears he knew she was prepared to take her chances with him. But she was right. He might just have got through

185

Annagery with one fugitive in the car without being spotted, but taking the native speaker as well as the Canon was courting disaster. Besides, the Canon's reaction when Frank tried to bring up the fate of the last of the Irish speakers, was downright hostile.

'You've no more sense than your father had! Leave the bucko where he belongs and let's hit the road.'

'Will you hold your whisht a minute till I outline the plan to you?' Frank pleaded. 'This boyo is a goldmine. He's the very thing I need.'

'It's Páidi Mhici Óig you're talking about. Nothing but a dirty old culchie, and if he's going I'm not coming in the car!'

'Now listen, will you, for the love of God! You see here before you not just any old native speaker but the very last of the native speakers. A living fossil, no less. By rights he should be a national monument. He should be living in luxury up in the Phoenix Park, with the top doctors in the land trying to keep him alive, instead of scratching a living round a place like this.'

'What do you propose doing with him?' Noreen asked.

'I'll sign him up for the show! He's just what it needs. The Cainteoir Dúchais Spot. They'll hang on his every word. I'll put him on the panel and he can contribute his twopence worth like everybody else. When he dies, a little bit of our soul dies. Think of the lads with the tape recorders. They'll be queuing up to get a record of that *fíor blas* before it's too late. We could charge admission to the dressing-room afterwards . . .'

'What makes you think he'll talk if you get him to Dublin?'

'He'll talk all right. I could hardly get a word in edgeways.'

'But he'd be like a fish out of water,' Noreen protested.

'Not a bit of it. A couple of bottles of poteen a day and he'll be as right as rain. When you clean him up a bit you'll not know him.'

'I'm not touching him,' the Canon shouted hotly. 'And that's another thing. Where, as a matter of interest, do you propose putting him while you're waiting to get him this grand home in the Phoenix Park? I can tell you now, I'll not have him under the same roof as me!'

'Isn't that the best part of it,' Frank said, ignoring the Canon and turning to Noreen. 'This is where the Sharkey connection

186

comes in handy. You remember I told you about Fidelma? How she has my heart scalded with her letters? Take a guess what she was on about only the other week? What a pity it was she couldn't get her hands on a live-in Irish speaker to civilize the kids, instead of the Filipino au pair. He's an answer to her prayers! Your man is just what the doctor ordered. Her ladyship will love him.'

'Will you go to hell,' Canon Tom said. 'John Joe Sharkey will never have him about the house!'

'That's where you're wrong. John Joe will see the sense of it. I can see it in the papers: Taoiseach rescues last of the Mohicans. One of the family, says Sharkey.'

'Easy for him. He's never there.'

'It'll only be during the week. The studios will take him off Fidelma's hands at weekends. I'll have him under exclusive contract to the show. No other bugger will get near him.'

'I suppose this Fidelma would have to pay a handling fee,' said the Canon grudgingly at last.

'And expenses. She'll be honoured to pay,' Frank said. 'Now let's get him into the car before the poteen wears off.'

The Canon disappeared to pack his few belongings while Noreen and Frank manhandled the native speaker into the back seat and covered him with the car rug. In spite of the cold wind they opened the windows full.

'I don't suppose there are any more like him left round here?' Frank asked.

'What were you hoping for?' Noreen said, laughing for the first time. 'A breeding pair?'

Though the road was treacherous after dark, they waited till nightfall before daring to make a move. There was only the one way out of Ballychondom and the Sharkey clan would be monitoring his coming and his going. He had his papers giving him permission to visit the area, grudgingly signed by Sister Ellen. But if they suspected that he was leaving with a carful of assorted renegades the word would be in Dublin before him.

It was a chance he had to take.

They drove through the night and all the next day, the Canon and Noreen lying on the floor till they had cleared the first fifty miles. They travelled slowly through the seemingly endless mountains of Donegal, range after range rising up before them. Through Gweedore and Gweebarra, and the Blue Stacks. At dawn the mountains were behind them and the lakelands were laid out below them. The *cainteoir dúchais* woke as they came down through the mists of the Barnsmore Gap. The countryside was deserted; no animals in the fields, no smoke from the empty farmhouses. Frank and Noreen sat silently in the front, viewing the lonely landscape; but the *cainteoir dúchais* began to enjoy himself. He perked up like an excited child at his first view of the marvels of the Galltacht.

He was too moved for prose; the lonely beauty of the passing scene moved him to verse. He slugged at the bottle Frank had provided, taking in the details of abandoned farms, derelict towns and rivers in sullen, perpetual flood. Silently they passed through deserted roadblocks that told of the unrest that had once gripped the area, and deserted villages that spoke of the exodus of the people, some to Belfast, some to Dublin. They passed through Marble Arch, where the rivers ran underground through great limestone caverns; through bleak Boho and the ruins of Kinawley.

Frank slowed the car as they approached Cavan, for there was sign of life in the fields at last and smoke was rising from the occasional chimney. 'Maybe we could get a cup of tea,' he said.

'Watch yourself,' Noreen cautioned. Cavan never had a reputation for hospitality, and she had heard stories of the desperation of the people.

'Amn't I a priest?' he reminded her. No one would lift a hand against God's anointed. He parked the car in the bleak main square of the town and began to knock on the surrounding shops. But cleric or not, the natives huddled together indoors, suspicious of the strange car on the deserted streets. His knocking echoed through the houses, and though he heard scurrying inside, the doors remained firmly bolted against him. The *cainteoir dúchais* saw the irony of it and wasn't long in finding a poetic sentiment to fit the occasion. '*Uaigneach sin, tithe Chorr an Chait, is uaigneach a bhfir is a mná,*' he declaimed, till the Canon, whose stomach was beginning to rumble alarmingly, told him to put a sock in it.

'We'll try somewhere else,' Frank said. 'Maybe the next town will prove friendlier.' A broken fingerpost pointed to Ballyjamesduff, and without preliminaries the old man in the back began crooning in English. 'Come back Paddy Riley, to Ballyjamesduff.'

'For Christ's sake!' the Canon shouted. But Frank and Noreen laughed. 'You have very good English. *Tá Béarla maith agat*,' he shouted over his shoulder. The old man laughed as he sang, tapping the side of his nose with a finger.

They found a shop at Navan and bought fresh bread and milk. The dereliction of the North was behind them at last and the towns were crowded and the fields under cultivation. The Canon was more cheerful now that they were back in the Pale. The smell of the bread reminded him of the pleasures so long denied him.

'Let's take it up to Tara,' Frank announced, indicating the hill that stood sentinel over the town. 'Do you know in all these years I've never once visited the place. We'll have a picnic before it gets dark.'

The old man gathered his shawl round him and, taking Noreen's arm, began hobbling up the well-trodden track that led to the summit. Canon Tom refused to budge. Frank left him guarding the motor with orders to speak to nobody, and set out after the others.

'The Hill of Tara,' Frank said slowly when he had caught up with them. He wasn't sure how much the native speaker understood, but there was something about the place, some quality that he couldn't quite describe, that filled him with a sense of awe and a sense of doom. This was the spot where the High Kings had once ruled. It was said that Dan O'Connell, the uncrowned king, had once gathered over a million people here to hear him speak.

'That must have been every sinner in the country near enough in those days,' Frank suggested.

'Gather a crowd like that round you today and you could do anything,' Noreen said softly.

The fields were quiet all around, the silence broken only by the lowing of a herd of distant cattle and the sounds of children squealing in the houses below. The hillside had seen, down the

189

centuries, the passing panorama of his country's history, but what did that signify any more? Who knew or cared any more what had happened in the past? Did it mean anything, or should it mean anything? John Joe and his cronies, like their ilk before him, would be quick enough to coin a phrase that invoked the glory or the ignominy of the past, careless of whether their allusions had even the seed of accuracy or meaning. Kings and heroes, real or mythical, would serve their purpose just as well. Maybe that was all there was to it, this ragbag of history from Derry to Tara, Armagh to the Blaskets. Nothing but a palimpsest to be used by whoever came along.

'Tara! The High Kings of Ireland!' he said again, enunciating slowly for the old man's benefit. But the ancient knew well enough where he was, and had a quotation to match the mood and the occasion.

'Do threascair an soal is shéid an ghaoth mar smál
Alastrann, Caesar, 's an méid sin a bhí 'na bpáirt;
tá an Teamhair 'na féar, is féach an Traoi mar tá,
is na Sasanaigh féin do b'féidir go bhfaighidís bás!'

The poem transported Frank back to a dusty schoolroom of his youth. He heard once more the drone of the class as they read aloud from the *Duanáire*, the whispered voice of Bosco Doherty at the back distracting them with obscenities, and the distant raucous sounds of Derry beyond the open window. The quatrain had been a favourite of old Father Ó Dochartaigh; he had made them learn it by heart from the first day. It was his answer to all questions. The wind of time has blown away like so much dust, Alexander and Caesar and the rest of them. Tara is under grass; what remains now of Troy? Even the English will meet their deaths in time! Father Ó Dochartaigh had recited it with triumph sometimes, other times with bitterness, inviting them to contemplate what the English had done to their country. Sometimes he had hammered his desk, or the blackboard (or Bosco Doherty's head) as he intoned the word *bás* – death. But the *cainteoir dúchais* recited the verse passively and with resignation. There was no bitterness in his voice, only the realization that everything would pass away in time, stealing with it all meaning.

They could smell Dublin from five miles out, even before they hit the first of the shanty towns. Frank turned off the road and on to a potholed track, deciding to risk the shortcut that would take him to the North Circular Road. He wasn't expecting trouble; the only men driving cars these days were the priests, and the people still retained a residual respect for the clergy. Nevertheless there had been incidents, stones thrown, cars over-turned and set alight, the odd atrocity that he didn't care to dwell on. But it was still light and would be for an hour more. They hadn't started to gather at the corners yet. He locked the driver's door and turned on the lights. Half an hour would get him to the Park, then he would be as good as home. In the back seat the native speaker, sensing trouble, had got his head down with-out having to be told.

As the car headed up from the city and into Adam and Eve's the Canon became noticeably agitated. With his first glimpse of his old parish some deep memory, a memory of unfinished business, began to stir in his breast. No number of threats, no amount of persuasion could convince him to keep his head below the dashboard until they were off the street. And as Frank finally pulled into the drive in front of the parochial house, he was tumbling out of the door before the car had stopped moving. He knelt to kiss the gravel like a pontiff laying claim to a continent, then rose and strode towards the porch with a decidedly pro-prietorial air. With one hand on the doorknob he turned to face the other three.

'He's not sleeping in my house!' he shouted. 'That's definite! You can put him up in the garage for now. But I'm not having him in the house.'

'Will you shut up!' Frank whispered. 'You're not in the wilds any more! I told you it was only for one night. Besides you could kill him putting him in the garage.'

'I don't care. I'll not have him in my house!'

'I'll not tell you again, it's my house now! Any more nonsense and you're heading straight back to where you came from.' He

191

already had a sinking feeling that the Canon was going to be big trouble.

'Not in the house!' the Canon said, digging his heels in.

'He just needs a bit of a clean-up.'

Frank knew he was getting nowhere. Besides, Canon Tom had a point. It would take more than a squirt of air freshener before the wild man was ready to pass in mixed company. He dreaded to think of the effect of soap and water on the aged body in the back seat. '*Agus féach an Traoi mar tá . . .*' opined the *cainteoir dúchais*.

'For Christ's sake play another record!' screamed the Canon.

'Easy on,' Frank pleaded, feeling his control over the situation slipping away. 'I'll tell you what,' he suggested. 'I'll run himself and Noreen over to Fidelma's this very minute.'

'You told us there was a curfew after dark!' Noreen warned, with real concern in her voice.

'I'll put the blue light on.'

'She's not expecting us.'

'Besides we haven't agreed a price yet,' said the Canon. 'Remember I have a half share in this bucko!'

'Leave all that till the morning. I'll just deliver him to the door with a note. Fidelma'll be delighted to see you!'

'John Joe will put the Guards on them,' the Canon said, 'coming round his place at this hour of the night.'

'Isn't John Joe in Cork with a certain party,' Frank assured them both. 'Put the kettle on,' he told the Canon, 'keep the curtains drawn, don't let anyone in, don't answer the phone and for Christ's sake stay away from the jacuzzi! I'll be back in under an hour.'

Inspector O'Malley flagged down the car as it pulled into the drive and Frank wound the window down.

'Is it yourself Father Frank?' said O'Malley. 'I just thought there I recognized you from the TV.'

'In the flesh,' joked Frank. He never felt completely comfortable in the company of the police.

'And what brings you calling on his nibs at this unmerciful hour of the night?' inquired the Guard casually.

'I've a wee bit of business with his wife.'

'Nothing wrong there, I hope?' O'Malley could see the EMERGENCY: PRIEST ON CALL sign in the windscreen.

'Nothing wrong at all. I've brought her a wee something back from the country.'

O'Malley shone his torch into the back seat. Something was snoring quietly under an old blanket. He let the light play on the bundle for a minute, then turned and shone it into Noreen's eyes. Hers was the face of a shy girl, a country girl, a girl as yet uncorrupted by the city and its ways. O'Malley felt a sudden rush of interest.

'Would you mind me asking you now what you have there?' he asked, indicating the blanket, 'and while you're at it maybe the young lady would care to introduce herself.'

Frank lowered his voice to a conspiratorial whisper.

'Tell me,' he said,' do you ever get to watch the show at all these days?'

'I do, Father. When I get the chance.'

'Well I'll tell you what,' said Frank, reaching into his pocket and producing a couple of complimentary tickets, 'maybe you'd do me the honour of joining the guests on the sofa next Sunday night if you can get off duty. We're having a bit of a barney about the moral state of the nation, what with this free love business and so forth. Your contribution will be appreciated.'

O'Malley took the tickets and pocketed them. It was the opportunity of a lifetime and he knew it. A chance to put the country right once and for all. It was the break he had been hoping for, praying for since his promotion to the capital.

'The gentleman in the back seat is none other than next week's mystery guest,' whispered Frank.

'And the young lady?'

'His personal assistant.'

O'Malley hesitated for a minute, then winked at Frank. 'You're a terrible man, Father. I'll take your word for it. On you go now,' he waved him forward, 'and don't make too much noise. The neighbours hereabouts can be wild nosey.'

He parked outside the front door. The house was in darkness. Far away in the north of the city a bell chimed the hour. He lifted the *cainteoir dúchais* out of the car and carried him round the back. An engraved notice informed him that this was the appropriate entrance for tradesmen and hawkers. Frank propped him up against the back door and wrote a hasty note of introduction.

'You'll be on the pig's back here!' he whispered to the old man. 'The Taoiseach's house. *Teach an* . . .' He wracked his brain for the genitive case of taoiseach – the chief of the clan – but the word eluded him. The native speaker by now was half awake. He went to say something of profound importance, thought better of it, and relapsed into slumber. He slithered down on to the doorstep. Noreen bent over and wrapped the rug round his shoulders. There was another bottle of firewater in the car. Frank fetched it and placed it carefully in the old man's hand.

'It will all work out, trust me,' he said, seeing the look of terror on Noreen's face. 'I'll send a car for you in the morning.'

He wanted to take her in his arms and kiss her but as he reached out to her the beam of a torchlight wavered round them and he heard O'Malley breathing heavily in the bushes.

'Go now!' she said. 'I'll be right as rain.'

She drew away from him and rang the bell. It echoed through the house. Frank tiptoed back to the car.

One by one he heard the children wake up and start to cry. He was down the drive, saluting O'Malley, and out on to the street before the lights began to come on in the big house.

Nine

Since the day John Joe first hit the big time, Fidelma Sharkey had grown used to the sight of good-looking young women hanging round her house. Secretaries, personal assistants, research assistants, foreign journalists, postgraduate students from Queen's. Young women smoking in the sitting-room, tossing their long, healthy hair over their shoulders and showing perfect teeth. Young women sitting crosslegged on the kitchen stools drinking coffee with their tight skirts riding up their thighs and smiles of complicity on their faces. There was a spare room at the top of the house always made up for them to stay. The girl standing shivering at the back door didn't look her husband's type, but *Bean* Sharkey had learned the hard way not to question her husband's taste. The old boy with the letter from Father Frank was a bit of a puzzle too, but then Fidelma sometimes thought that life in the fast lane was itself one big puzzle. She admitted her unexpected guests without a word and took herself off to bed with a Valium, locking the door behind her.

Fidelma's bleary-eyed brood, gathering in the kitchen to assess the strangers, ranged in age from surly nineteen-year-old twins to a mewling babe in arms. Noreen did her best to introduce herself and to explain the proposed role of the native speaker in their lives. The teenagers drifted away before she had finished and the baby started to wail. Nothing that the nuns in Caherciveen had taught her had prepared her for a challenge such as this.

She looked in despair at the state of the place and started to tidy up. But a bit of squalor never bothered the man from the Rosses. Admitted to the halls of power, the native speaker seemed as happy as Larry with the arrangements. He soothed the baby with a snatch of an ancient lullaby. He made himself at home in the rocking chair while the younger ones squealed round his feet for a while, smiling at them indulgently. When they had tired themselves out he ordered them upstairs in broken English. Noreen made a pot of tea. She was exhausted and apprehensive, but at the same time so exhilarated that she knew she would never sleep. Tomorrow she would get to grips with Dublin and her new life, whatever it might hold! She poured two mugs, but the native speaker's keen sensibilities had detected the presence of stronger palliatives under the Taoiseach's roof. He nosed around till he came upon the teenagers in John Joe's study, sniffing glue. Never one to miss the crack if crack was going he stuck with them till dawn.

'I'll rescue her at the first opportunity,' Frank told himself as he drove quickly home. No harm would come to her for a night or two, and when he got a moment he would drop round and explain everything to Fidelma. In the meantime he would inquire after a discreet boarding house where Noreen could be put up. He needed to keep the native speaker under wraps too till he made his debut at the weekend . . .

The Canon had fallen asleep when he got back to Adam and Eve's, but he woke him roughly to give him his orders. He showed him up to the granny flat, with its self-contained wc and black and white television, handed him a few bottles of the Mouton Cadet from the cellar and intimated to him that he should be grateful for this second bite at the good life. All Frank expected from him was that he keep his head down and didn't rock the boat. But his own head had no sooner hit the pillow than he knew he had trouble on his hands.

All that night he could hear Canon Tom pacing to and fro on the floorboards above, talking to himself in a loud, disjointed voice. What had seemed a good idea in the wilds of Donegal was turning in retrospect into what seemed like a very bad idea indeed. It was clear that the proximity of his former parishioners was beginning to unhinge him. Frank resolved that as soon as he got the next show out of the way he would have the old man smuggled out, in civvies, to some nursing home on the south coast where he could end his days incognito and where he would give him and the parish no further trouble.

It was mid-morning before he was sure the Canon had settled at last and that all was quiet upstairs. Frank checked that the door to the flat was firmly locked before heading out. He had a date with the King of Rock 'n' Roll which he couldn't break.

O'Malley got little sleep that night, either. His great opportunity had arrived and he intended to do it justice. He burned the midnight oil, practising for his moment in the limelight. He filled notebook after notebook with his reminiscences of patrolling with the nightstick round the hedgerows of the borderlands, redoubling his efforts to find the right anecdote that would show the kind of a man he was. When his prurient imagination flagged he thought again of the young lady he had seen in the back of the priest's car, finding himself aroused at the thought of her virginity.

But Fate was poised to frustrate the best-laid plans. The television debut of the last living *fíor gael* was to be summarily postponed. O'Malley's precious tickets were to be suddenly worthless. And for the first time since he opened, 'Father Frank's Half Hour' would be off the air.

The Elvis Presley lookalikes had been queuing round the block an hour before Frank arrived in Skerries. They were drawn there in their hundreds by the lure of the first prize, a three-minute spot on his show. He sat through them all, each worse than the last, a fixed smile on his face and his heart sinking with every wavering bar of 'Hound Dog' he heard. When he finally stumbled out of the hall darkness was falling. What he needed badly was a drink.

He headed for Haughey Street. The place was unnaturally quiet. Not a soul about. McArdles was in darkness; he rattled the door but it was firmly locked and there was no sound of muffled afters. Strange, he thought. The place was like a ghost town. Something was up. He returned to the car and twiddled with the radio. Nothing but Handel's Largo on all stations.

The lights were on in the Parochial House when he arrived home. And Noreen, flushed with excitement, was standing in the hall beckoning him inside.

'Who's dead?' he asked.

'The old Pope, God rest him. I'm just watching it on the television.'

'Natural causes?'

'God forgive you, Frank Feely!' she said, but she laughed.

'I thought it must be something of that order. The pubs are closed. There isn't a sinner about.' He poured two drinks from the decanter on the sideboard and offered her one. Noreen shook her head.

'Go on! Join me in one like a good girl,' he said. 'A small drop will do you no harm. I need to get the sound of Elvis out of my ears before I go crazy altogether.'

He kicked off his shoes, tore off his collar and threw himself down on the sofa to watch the news.

'Just a wee drop then,' she said, taking a sip. 'I can't be staying long. Schnozzle's ordered a week's official mourning, and the curfew's been brought forward. I'll need to be moving soon if I'm not to get shot.'

'Speak of the devil,' Frank said, indicating the television screen, 'there's the man himself!'

From upstairs there came the sound of a bottle breaking.

'It sounds like the Canon has the portable on too,' Frank laughed. 'I'd say he's just caught sight of his old tormentor.'

'Shouldn't we invite him down?' Noreen asked. 'I'd have gone up, but I couldn't find the key.'

'Leave him up there out of harm's way for a while,' Frank said, 'and come and sit beside me till we watch this.'

Schnozzle was standing on the steps of the chartered Aer Lingus plane in his full canonicals, solemnly blessing the cabin crew.

'He's not letting the grass grow under his feet,' Frank remarked. 'He'd want to be one of the first to Rome. I'm told himself and the old man were very close.'

'God rest him,' Noreen said.

'God rest him,' Frank agreed.

198

'John Joe's going with him too, by the looks of it,' Noreen said, as the stocky figure of the Taoiseach detached itself from the official party on the tarmac and lumbered up the steps after Schnozzle.

'The same boy never likes to miss a free trip. It's a pound to a penny that a certain female RTE newscaster will be covering the story too.'

'Are you codding or what?' Noreen said.

'It's well seen you've been in the convent too long. Sure it's common knowledge about John Joe and his fancy women.'

'No wonder Fidelma's been giving me funny looks all morning. I couldn't get out of the house fast enough, I was that embarrassed!'

Noreen blushed and Frank laughed.

'This calls for another wee drinkie, I think. The pair of them won't be back for a couple of weeks. Who has His Eminence put in charge of the country in his absence?'

'I haven't heard, but I doubt if it's yourself! I'd say if you step over the mark you'd find out soon enough. Your friend the big Garda gave me a lift over. He says the Sisters will have their orders.'

'O'Malley? Stuff him! And stuff the Sisters!' Frank declared. 'There's a bottle of Dom Perignon in the cellar just crying out for a special occasion like this.'

'God forgive you,' she said still laughing. 'You shouldn't be drinking at a time like this. Besides I need you sober to give me a ride home. With the blue light on you should be safe.'

'There's no hurry,' he said, reappearing with the champagne and popping the cork. 'The Sisters will all be on special retreat tonight, praying for the repose of His Holiness's soul. The streets will be clear.'

'Well just the one glass,' she said. 'I don't want to go doing anything silly.'

But who ever stopped at one glass? They knew what was going to happen, and though they were suddenly as shy as two birds they poured the wine and drank it till the bottle was empty, knowing that neither of them wanted to stop. Then she took him in her arms and kissed him, and he kissed her, feeling her hot breath on his neck and the strange, forbidden excitement rising in him. Elvis was pounding inexorably in his head. He moved his hand on to her breasts and slid it under her blouse, feeling the smoothness of her skin.

'We should stop,' she said.

'I know,' he said.

'We should stop now,' she said a minute later when he could feel the roundness of her breasts cupped in the palm of his hand, and she could feel the stiffness of his prick straining against her thighs. But they didn't stop, but clumsily undressed each other, tearing their clothes off, their lips never leaving each other.

'We really should stop now,' she said for a third time, groaning softly as she guided him into her, feeling him strong and young and vigorous inside her, and he felt her warm and soft and willing, overpowering him. He began to move rhythmically within her, and she pulled him closer and closer to her, her own rhythm as urgent as his and together they eased their tortured souls. When it was over she lay beside him in the light of the flickering television and watched the jet plane climb laboriously into the sky, examining her conscience for the terrible guilt she had been taught to expect. She was relieved to find, before she dropped into the sleep of the initiated, that her conscience was untroubled.

Frank awoke to the sound of birdsong. Noreen was still beside him, sleeping gently. He looked at her face and knew that he could never leave her, that he would fight to keep her, no matter what they said or did. He gently eased his arm from under her and felt the warmth of her body as she snuggled closer into him. His hands moved slowly over her breasts and he felt his desire awaken again. He slid quietly down and rested his mouth on one of her nipples. They were soft and pink, but he could feel them stiffen as he let his tongue touch them in turn. This, he told himself, was a true sacramental.

Noreen stirred awake. Frank stopped. Would she disown the night before? Work herself into a terrible state about what she had done? Flee from his house in a panic of guilt and fear? She opened her eyes and smiled. She reached down and pulled his face up towards hers.

'Good morning, lover,' she said softly.

He knew now that he would go through hell itself for her if that was the price he had to pay.

Though there was a moratorium on the pubs for the duration, the off-licences were doing a roaring trade. When the cat's away the mice will play. Frank phoned out for a magnum of champagne, intending to mark the papal passing with due respect. He phoned his producer and confirmed that 'Father Frank's Half Hour' was on hold; with His Holiness lying in state in Saint Peter's it was not deemed seemly to have comics cavorting and secular music on the airwaves. The slot would be filled with solemn music and old documentaries of an uplifting nature. He cancelled all his other appointments, spiritual and temporal, disconnected the phone and took to his bed with the bottle, the television set and Noreen. It was his idea of a perfect honeymoon.

When they weren't making love, they watched the television, now given over night and day to the activities in the Eternal City, and were reassured by the sight of John Cardinal Augustus standing solemn guard of honour over his late friend in the nave of the great basilica. Together they witnessed the last rites solemnly performed. The Requiem, the tap on the head with the silver hammer, the slow march to the tomb in the crypt beneath. No Pharaoh was ever interred with more pomp. Without leaving the comfort of the bed, they watched the long, red line of cardinals file prayerfully into the Sistine Chapel, sealing the door behind them. He watched Honest Eddie tick-tacking the odds on possible winners, and sent Noreen round to the bookies to place a tenner on an ageing Italian on whom Honest Eddie was offering twenty to one. But this was to be no one-horse race. Daily the black smoke curled up from the chapel chimney, indicating to the world that they were still locked in deliberation. Daily Honest Eddie grew more animated, appearing every hour on the hour live from Vatican Square in a deerstalker hat and plus fours. It was no accident that Eddie was a millionaire. By the end of the first week he was confidently predicting the emergence of an outsider coming through on the rails and the smart money took him at his word.

Whiskey in hand, Frank sprawled on the counterpane, watching as the smoke turned white. And a sixth sense whispered to him, even before the Swiss Guards had flung open the sealed doors, that he had lost his money. A feeling in the pit of his stomach, half excitement and half terror, told him, even before he heard the cry of 'Habemus Papam!' that the man emerging from the shadows on to the sunlit balcony, sweating in the white rigout and the triple tiara, would be Pope Patrick the First.

❖

'Jesus, Mary and Joseph!' shouted the man from Tyrone.

Though the picture was almost indecipherable, there was no mistaking Schnozzle. There was pandemonium in the bar. A roar had gone up from the drinkers who were now crowding forwards and craning their necks at the screen, simultaneously berating Eugene for the poor reception and demanding free refills. Whether it were a roar of approval or a roar of pain it was hard to say. National pride, and local pride, that a man from the Shambles had been so elevated. And anguish at what might lie in store.

'Jesus, Mary and Joseph!' the Tyrone man shouted again above the noise. 'Tell me this! Where will it all end?'

'An Armagh man!' Peadar was shouting, flushed suddenly with Shambles chauvinism. 'That's put us on the map and no mistake.'

'It's a proud day for yourself, Mister MacBride,' Eugene said as he reached for the brandy bottle. And Snotters, the cynosure of so many eyes, did not demur.

'*Ciúnas!*' demanded the Patriot, suddenly speaking for the first time. Silence! Somehow he had discerned that Schnozzle was about to speak his first words as Pope.

'Whist and listen to the man for fuck's sake,' Peadar demanded. 'He'll likely give us a few words in Irish to kick off with.'

But whether or not Schnozzle raided his word store for a meagre phrase or two in the first national language to launch his pontificate the Patriot was never to know. For as he raised the Bernini crucifix, blew into the microphone on the balcony and began to address *urbi et orbi*, the picture on the television was skewered into a thousand jagged lines, and instead of the tuneful chanting of the castrati they heard the manic voice of McCoy screaming a rant of contumely against the new occupant of the chair of Peter.

'Turn that renegade off, for fuck's sake!' the Tyrone man demanded. 'It's a wonder no one was man enough to silence his warbling long ago!'

❖

An almighty crash from the floor above brought Frank to his feet.

'Holy Mother of God!' he shouted. 'That sounded like the wardrobe!' There was another crash and the sounds of splintering wood and shattering glass.

'Has he gone berserk altogether!' Noreen was screaming. And then they heard the voice of the Canon, declaiming at the top of his voice to the surrounding parish. Frank froze in terror, listening spellbound as the nightmare came true. The Canon had redis-covered the gift of tongues and was calling together the Children of Love in an exotic mixture of English and Aramaic. Adam and Eve's lay all before him and was filled with his prophesying.

Oblivious of his bare backside, Frank bounded up to the granny flat taking the stairs two at a time, Noreen on his heels, pulling his soutane round her nakedness. He kicked open the door in time to see the Canon's legs disappear through the skylight. He ran to the middle of the room, climbed on to the tumbled furni-ture and stuck his head out. Canon Tom was on the roof, his white hair flowing in the breeze, bellowing for all he was worth.

'For Christ's sake!' Frank shouted. He knew he was wasting his breath. The Canon was a man possessed, in the grip of an elemental force that had been unleashed once before in this same spot. Frank knew that he had to stop him at all costs. He hauled himself out of the skylight and on to the slates and began to inch forward to the apex of the roof where Canon Tom was standing, legs akimbo, staring out over Dublin. He could hear the slates creaking beneath him. He could feel the roof buckling under their combined weight. He was suddenly aware of how high off the ground he was, and how naked he was to boot.

'Let me talk to him,' Noreen cried, poking her head out.

'You can talk but I doubt if he's in any mood to listen,' Frank called back to her. 'I'm going to have to manhandle him down somehow.'

'Don't let any harm come to him,' she pleaded.

But Canon Tom, the Spirit moving more strongly in him with each passing minute, had become as nimble as a mountain goat. As Frank edged towards him he suddenly jumped down into the valley gutter, swung himself up on the other side and began inching towards the flat roof at the back of the house where the old jacuzzi stood. He swung down on to it, hauled himself up the party wall that separated the parochial house from the garage, leaped the divide between the garage and the adjoining property and was off, declaiming now in ancient Aztec and hopping from roof to roof, like mad Sweeney among the branches.

'Is everything all right there?' a voice said from below. Inspector O'Malley was standing on the gravel driveway, hands on hips, witnessing the scene. 'We've had a report of voices raised, disturbing the peace this glorious and joyful morning.'

'Only a cat,' Noreen said, her head still out of the skylight.

Under O'Malley's unflinching stare Frank tried to cover his private parts, but he quickly found that he needed both hands if he were to get back inside the house in one piece. He slithered down the roof, grabbing for Noreen's outstretched arm.

'Only the cat escaping,' he shouted lamely.

'The cat was it?' said O'Malley. 'If you ask me, that's one cat that's well and truly out of the bag! It's as well they have nine lives.'

'Everything's under control now,' Frank shouted, diving into the room head first and cursing O'Malley.

'I suddenly see it's yourself, Father!' O'Malley shouted, 'You'll forgive me for not recognizing you there for a minute without the collar. You're the very man I wanted to see.'

'Fuck off!' Frank screamed through clenched teeth as loudly as he dared.

'It's about the show . . .'

'I'll be in touch,' Frank screamed down to him. 'Fuck him!' he whispered to Noreen, 'he's seen everything.'

'And you really mean everything,' she laughed, playfully reaching for his balls.

'Jesus, Noreen, this is no time for levity. You can't trust the Guards.'

'With the great news from Rome and all, I thought . . .' O'Malley persisted.

Frank closed the skylight with a crash.

'Whatever you say, Father,' O'Malley said, still showing no inclination to move.

All over the city, all over the country, the bells began to ring. The people of Ireland poured from their houses on to the streets ignoring the curfew. The pubs opened and refused to close. On every street corner there was music, and dancing, and praying. The rosary was heard in every home. The news swept across the country, from the cottages of the west to the farms of the south. It travelled up north, to Fermanagh and wild, lonely Donegal. It even reached the gates of Portadown itself, spreading in hushed whispers down the backstreets and alleys.

But if there was fear and loathing in Portadown, there was an outbreak of mad joy everywhere else. An Irish Pope! Who ever thought, they asked each other, that we would live to see this day? Why not, others said, aren't we as good as anyone else? Italians, Poles, Filipinos. The convents were bedecked with flowers, the churches threw open their doors. Who could think of work at a time like this? A new, delirious spirit was everywhere. Men who had not seen the inside of a chapel for years were suddenly back in the fold, the past behind them, forgiven and forgotten. The confession boxes metered record returns. Young priests were everywhere, sweating with excitement and extra work, calling to each other from their cars that they couldn't stop, they were in such a rush, they'd never known anything like it. The queues for communion were out the chapel door and halfway down the street on weekdays, never mind Sunday. It was a new birth.

Nor was it long before the miracles started. Statues that hadn't moved a muscle in fifty years began to twitch. Holy wells, dried up for generations, suddenly overflowed. The papers were nervous about reporting such things at first, fearing the wrath of Immaculata and the hierarchy; but rumour was so widespread that Sam O'Dowd could hold back no longer. Everywhere was in a turmoil of excitement. A priest in Limerick preached from the pulpit that the time had come for a *coup d'état*, and the local council had taken to the streets behind him, waving their resignations in the air and demanding firm church leadership. Seventh sons of seventh sons, boys who had been keeping a low profile for some time for fear of attracting the wrong sort of attention, now inserted bold advertisements in the local papers offering their unique services. Openly the prophesies of Saint Malachy were discussed and dissected. The streets of Dublin swarmed with penitents and celebrants; they poured in daily from the outlying countryside, wanting to be where the action was. The Legion of Mary set up a Perpetual Novena in O'Connell Street, blocking the thoroughfare round the clock.

So it was only a matter of time before the whereabouts of the Missing Madonna of Ballychondom, for long the subject of private piety, became a question of popular conjecture.

❖

The remnants of the Children of Love had gathered in an upper room in a state of mounting anticipation. The doors and windows were locked, for they feared the anger of the Sisters. They huddled together on the floor, waiting and watching, watching and praying. All night long they had heard him calling to them, from somewhere among the chimney pots, summoning them together again in a thousand tongues. But could they believe their ears? Or was it all a cruel trick? For surely Canon Tom was dead these years and with him the Charismatic Movement he had inspired? But as the night wore on each of them had heard him calling them by name and they knew that their lost leader had somehow returned . . .

There was the sound of footsteps on the roof. The casement burst open. Canon Tom was suddenly among them, his face flushed, his eyes bulging with anticipation, his voice loud with urgency. He was addressing them in the language of our first parents, but they could understand his every word. The women began to ululate and the men to bear witness, each in his own tongue. They crept forward to where he stood, silhouetted against the shattered window. Cautiously at first, as if fearful that the vision might fade away at any moment. They reached out to touch him, to stroke him, to feel for themselves that he was indeed among them again. Then, satisfied that he was truly their leader, they threw themselves on him, smothering him with their collective love.

Frank knew he could spend all day trying to round them up, probably to no avail, and maybe get a black eye or worse for his pains. What were a few hundred more head-the-balls on the streets anyway? By all accounts there were more than enough out there already. No, he decided, his responsibility was elsewhere. He dropped a couple of Alka Seltzer into a glass of Lourdes water and ran the electric razor over his jowls. His place was in the studio. 'Father Frank's Open House' would run till the emergency was over or till he dropped. He phoned Montrose and told them to cancel their schedules, such as they were, and to contact his regulars. He phoned Fidelma's and left a message with one of the twins to get the *cainteoir dúchais* scrubbed and dressed and down to the station post haste. He phoned Dublin Castle and left a message on Immaculata's ansaphone inviting her contribution on the show. He briefed Sam O'Dowd and dictated the editorial. He showed Noreen his bulging mailbag, invited her to pick half a dozen at random and work them up into a fifteen-minute spot to be aired round midnight. It was all taking shape in his mind. It would be the show to end all shows.

It would be open-ended, running through the day and night; guests dropping in, celebrities making appearances, glad of the publicity, everyone wanting to be associated with the great spirit sweeping the nation. It would be open house for talent of all kinds; he'd fill the studio with céilí bands and musical families,

207

and have them standing by to fill any awkward pauses. He'd have one of the outside broadcast units permanently in the Pro-Cathedral; and when he needed a few hours' rest he would nip backstage and have a lie down while they relayed one of the Masses from the high altar. He'd have another unit in O'Connell Street, sending back reports and vox pops of the carry-on there. He'd have the newsroom boys sweating away in a corner of the studio, trying to keep the viewers up to date with developments round the country as they happened. It would be chaos, but it would be great! He pictured himself, mug of coffee in hand, tired but unflappable, maybe slipping into a pullover during the wee small hours to add a casual touch, the unruffled anchorman at the centre of this great storm of activity. He knew that in years to come, when their children asked them about those heady days, it would be Father Frank's show they would recall as much as anything else.

'I dreamt that I dwelt in marble halls!' he hummed to himself an hour later as he sat back in his master-of-ceremonies chair and thought about Pope Patrick. The show was on the road and going well, gathering a momentum of its own; everyone was loquaciously asserting that this was the greatest day of their lives, and he was giving them their head, giving them all day if they wanted it. O'Malley, drafted in to oversee security, was run off his feet showing minor celebrities into the seats and finding room for the performers who were swarming round the place, tuning up goatskin bodhráns and smoking illicit substances in the lavatories. The *cainteoir dúchais* had been wheeled on to thunderous approval and had so far acquitted himself well if enigmatically with some apt and cryptic verse. Frank was pacing himself for the long night and day ahead, taking only the odd hair of the dog and resting his voice between turns. A buxom soprano was warbling centre stage, accompanied by the boys in the band.

Marble halls, thought Frank. The corridors of the Vatican were wide indeed, and from every window there were vistas of the Eternal City below. The marbles of Bernini and the frescoes of Michelangelo might not be Schnozzle's cup of tea, but the temptation to meddle in world affairs would be one he couldn't resist. The problems of the world cried out for his caring attention!

From his apartments over the Tiber he could mediate in the problems of South East Asia, the Americas (Latin, Anglophone and Francophone), Europe east and west. Surely the problems of one small island on the edge of the world would hardly concern him again? Nothing, Frank told himself, would draw Schnozzle back from the fragrant salons of Rome to the draughty Mansion of Heaven on the wet hilltop in Armagh. In his enthusiasm he had already taken out a small wager with Honest Eddie on Schnozzle's successor, and had been flattered to see his own name included in his list of runners for the Primatial See of Armagh, albeit as an outsider at a hundred to one.

He might have felt less sanguine had he known that not half a mile away the Inner *Cumann* of the Sisters for Church Security were coming to order and that he was high on their agenda. In the corner of the room a portable television set flickered silently; Sister Immaculata eyed the grinning face that filled the screen with mounting distaste. The opening prayer came to a close and she got down to business. Reports coming in from all over the country revealed the same pattern, statues weeping miraculously, strange silent apparitions on church gables, restlessness among the faithful.

'The Holy Man of Ballyporeen is loose again,' reported one of the Sisters. 'They say he is gathering great crowds behind him this time.'

'That's impossible,' flared Sister Philomena. 'Didn't I personally give him the treatment last time!'

'Nevertheless,' she persisted, 'it seems he has reappeared. Some of them are claiming he's risen from the dead. If it's not him, someone else has jumped into his shoes pretty quick.'

Philomena was on her feet now, shouting. Immaculata reached under her habit and produced the whip which all the Sisters carried for ritual chastisement. She reached across and struck Philomena firmly across the backside.

'Decorum, Sister!' she admonished. Philomena subsided resentfully. 'We can't possibly risk another failure in that part of the world,' she continued in her unruffled voice. She turned to the bottom of the table where Sister Pat was busily rolling a cigarette, sprinkling the pungent tobacco from a crucifix that dangled between her breasts.

'Sister Pat,' she said quietly. Sister Pat looked up. 'Sister Pat will go to Ballyporeen,' she said. The nun's face split into a grin of pleasure. She rose to go. The Church would have nothing more to fear from Ballyporeen.

One by one they were allotted their duties. In Athlone an old priest had taken to walking the streets naked as a monkey, claiming he was the Second Coming. That was the sort of behaviour that could give the clergy a bad name and needed to be stamped out. There was a new outbreak of feverish dancing mania in Derry. Sister Columba was dispatched north to silence the fiddles. An old woman in Drumshanbo was claiming to have discovered the Holy Shroud, miraculously preserved, in an outhouse on her smallholding. She had invited the Yanks over with their computer enhancers and laser scanners to prove its authenticity. Sister Bernadette didn't know much about gadgets like that, but she had other skills, and she was on her way.

The *cumann* had almost all dispersed when Immaculata turned to the matter of Father Frank. She held up the morning's *Irish Press* gingerly between finger and thumb. 'FATHER FRANK'S POPEATHON!!' screamed the headline. 'This,' she announced with palpable disgust, 'appeared this morning on the news stands. I look in vain for the nihil obstat that assures me this has been cleared by the bishops as fit for Catholic consumption. It would appear that Father Feely . . .'

Sister Ellen's eyes had lit up at the mention of Father Frank. Sister Ellen was a pale and pasty little creature from the west of Galway, whose looks belied her potential. No one had followed Frank's career as obsessively as Sister Ellen. And none of the Little Sisters had nurtured such a deep hatred of him. It grew and fed on itself. She tortured herself day and night thinking about him. She followed his career attentively, ranting at the screen every time he appeared. She had his photograph on the wall beside the Little Flower, and a secret scrapbook with every column inch ever written about him. Even Immaculata understood that she was quite mad, compulsively crazy, cunningly vicious in a way that only Galway ones could be.

'Father Feely, I see, took a trip down memory lane recently. To Ballychondom, no less.'

'It was cleared by the Palace. I did the paperwork myself.'

'Be that as it may, it would appear that Father Feely's vow of holy chastity has been put to the test since he got back. O'Malley himself reported a disturbing instance.'

'Perhaps I could do what is necessary,' Sister Ellen offered, her eyes glinting at the mention of this rival in Father Frank's life. 'Eliminate the occasion of sin.'

'Not just yet, Sister, I'm afraid. I spoke to His Holiness this very morning about the matter. There is another dimension to this affair that complicates matters. A more serious development. It would appear that when Father Frank visited the wilderness recently he may have brought back something more than a fancy woman! A virus has been unleashed that is threatening us all!'

Her senior colleagues nodded but said nothing. There had been no definite sightings of Canon Tom as yet, and it was possible that the whole thing was hysteria and rumour. But if it proved to be true, decisions would have to be taken at the highest level.

'As for the so-called Popeathon, it is His Holiness's wish that the thing should be allowed to continue, as long as it gives no offence. But in the meantime there is plenty for you to do. Get down to the studios and stay there. Keep an eye on Father Feely, day and night. Report back to me personally every hour. Surveillance only, for the moment at least; His Holiness was quite clear. We want no martyrs just yet!'

'Thank you, Sister,' muttered Ellen, hurrying from the room. She knew where to find him, and when she did she would stick to him, day and night, like a limpet.

Immaculata turned the sound up and listened for a while. Nothing but the usual rubbish, she assured herself. Nevertheless, she wasn't going to take any chances. With His Holiness gone, she was aware that responsibility for Church Security lay with her. Security meant having eyes and ears in the back of your head, pre-empting developments before they reached danger point.

There was something about the anarchy of it all that made her uneasy. Live, open-ended, public access television was a very powerful weapon, one that could easily turn the tide of events in an unforeseen direction. It had happened elsewhere. She listened to the panel for a while and was reassured that it was still the same old shite. As long as the Irish people were happy with this sort of thing, there would be no harm in it. There would be time enough to deal with Feely when things had calmed down.

The audience had dropped to their knees and produced their beads while Frank led them in a decade of the rosary. Under normal circumstances this sort of carry-on might have embarrassed him, but today was no time for standing on your dignity. His audience, a sea of blue hats and brown suits, were wedged uncomfortably between the high-tech chairs in the auditorium, but far from causing the viewers to turn off, the rosary slot was proving to be a popular item. The ratings were sky-high. Every half-hour he jumped to his feet and they scrabbled to their knees, special guests and all, to bow their heads and pray for the new pontiff's intentions. His only worry was the insistent chorus clamouring for Schnozzle's imminent return to the Emerald Isle.

Frank saw no hurry on the return visit, a point he put to his panel when the advertisements were over and the audience had got back on to their chairs. There would have to be a return visit of course, with the crowds out and His Holiness showing off the new white outfit. But what was the hurry, let the new man find his feet.

'I suppose you're right,' opined the Greatest Living Irishman. 'Aren't we all exiles of a sort?'

'He may visit us from time to time,' said Frank, trying to keep a note of mirth from creeping into his voice, 'but by accepting the ring of Saint Peter he has become a permanent exile from the land of his birth. Am I right there, do you think . . . ?'

He turned to the novelist. 'You've known the pain of exile, Maire . . .'

The Romantic Lady Novelist not only knew the pain of exile, she had made her fame and fortune writing about it. She was willing once more to share with the viewers the pain of separation

212

from one's home and hearth. Striking a histrionic pose and sighing deeply in empathy with the plight of poor Schnozzle, she had launched herself into a monologue about the wild geese and the Flight of the Earls and the predilection of the brave to die young when the *cainteoir dúchais* woke up and the audience began to clap.

Though now confined to a wheelchair he was sprightly and dapper and in the best of fettle.

'I do believe that himself is trying to get a word in . . .' said Frank, interrupting the Lady Novelist, whom he'd heard in the same vein a thousand times before. It had rapidly become a convention that when the native speaker showed any inclination to join in the proceedings the floor was his.

'*Tiocfaidh do phardún ón bPápa is ón Róimh anoir is ní spáráilfear fíon Spáinneach ar mo Róisín Dubh,*' he intoned.

The Greatest Living Irishman tried to get in before the applause had fully died away.

'God, but isn't it great to hear the old language spoken so well,' he said.

'Give us a bit more,' Frank cajoled, speaking into the ear trumpet that John Joe had sponsored.

'Isn't that one of the Celtic languages?' the special guest interjected. He pronounced it as if he were talking about a football team and was mystified but gratified to get a laugh. He was a fresh-faced, sincere young priest from Chicago who had been marooned in transit at Shannon by the death of the Pope, and whom Frank had invited along to sit on the sofa and chew the rag with the others for an hour or two. So far he'd been a bit of a damp squib, lacking in wit and boring in his sincerity.

'*Beidh an Éirne 'na tuilte tréana is réabfar cnoic, beidh an fharraige 'na tonnta dearga is an spéir 'na fuil, beidh gach gleann sléibhe ar fud Éireann is móinte ar crith, lá éigen sul a n-éagfaidh mo Róisín Dubh.*'

The native speaker lapsed back into a coma after his prophecy, and his handlers, who had been waiting in the wings came forward and wheeled him off to continued applause.

'What was that all about?' queried the smooth young priest, misjudging the mood of the moment.

'A fine man, and fine sentiments, and a fine language,' said the Easter Week Boy Scout, who felt he had been rather upstaged all evening.

But the Yank persisted in putting his foot in it. 'Are you going to translate it for me, Father?' he asked, turning to Frank, notebook in hand.

'Well to be sure, we'll have to wait till the lads from UCD run it through the word processors. Didn't I tell you that every blessed syllable that man utters is automatically transcribed on to the machine back in Cardinal Newman House? A great gadget altogether . . .'

He thought he could divert his young guest with references to the latest technology, but the Yank was tenacious.

'Well,' said Frank, 'from my limited erudition . . .' he rolled the word around his mouth and winked at the nearest camera and the audience rewarded him with an outburst of mock jeering '. . . and attempting a very limited, nay facile, syntactical exegesis . . . There ye go again!' he shouted at them as they began to 'ooh' in unison. 'God but we've a terrible crowd in today, we must be scraping the bottom of the barrel!' and he winked at them from a dozen monitors to assure them he was only codding, wasn't that the way of him. '. . . but I would say that our old friend here was saying something very profound about the end of the world. The rivers in flood, the hills torn asunder, the ocean red and the sky filled with blood, every mountain and bog in Ireland shaking . . .'

'That sounds very ominous,' said the American. He had all the doggedness for which Beantown had become famous; it was clear he wasn't going to give up till he got to the bottom of it. Frank rolled his eyes and thought about a commercial break.

The Lady Novelist, upstaged by the turn of events, now assumed control again. She turned to the young man and laid one long, languorous arm on his knee as she stared into his eyes, fast dilating with fear.

'The note of melancholy runs deep in the Hibernian soul,' she said huskily. 'Imagery of death and destruction is never far beneath the surface. We are a very sad people.'

The young priest thought for a minute she was going to lay

her head on his lap and he tried politely to extricate himself from her grip.

'So you guys don't take that kind of soothsaying too seriously?' he stammered.

'It's mother's milk to us,' she said. Her long hands fumbled with the bone buttons of her peasant smock, and he had an image of her producing her breasts to drive home the simile. Frank too saw the danger. It wouldn't be the first time that she had gone too far after too long a sojourn in the hospitality suite.

'But to get back to His Holiness,' he interjected, hijacking a passing camera, 'do you ever think he'll be able to come back except as a celebrity?'

'As a tourist,' sighed the Greatest Living Irishman. 'An outsider among his own people. Oh, we'll show him a wonderful time, but we'll be speaking to him as we would to any returned exile who has had to turn his back on the land of his birth and who will one day lie buried in foreign soil. We'll show him the beauties of our country, the Cliffs of Moher . . .' there was a ripple of applause, quickly hushed as they saw the tears glistening in his eyes and realized that this was a solemn moment.

'. . . The Ring of Kerry,' Frank helped him along.

'. . . Connemara and the Burren and lovely Glendalough. He'll see once again the lovely lakes of Killarney, and hear the lilting voices of his people. We'll entertain him like a king, of course, the finest Irish dancers in the land, special hurling matches in his honour, the Kilfenora céilí band . . .'

'. . . Speaking of whom,' interrupted Frank, who had rehearsed this cue with the old codger earlier, 'aren't we delighted, nay honoured, to have the said ensemble,' he repeated it in a mock French accent to get them going, 'with us here this afternoon. They're going to start with a couple of jigs, or is it reels, do you know I can honestly never tell the difference. So put your hands together, *a dhaoine uaisle*, ladies and gentlemen, for the boys and girls from Kilfenora.'

The auditorium was filled with 'The Walls of Limerick'. The audience, like audiences everywhere began to clap off the beat. Father Frank switched off his lapel mike and, avoiding the eye of the American who was still trying to get to the heart of darkness, slipped out for a smoke under the watchful eye of Sister Ellen.

❖

Brother Murphy and the orphans returned to the Shambles at the weekend with what had been salvaged of the bunting. While the boys festooned the square, he retreated to the Patriot's to watch the show. The Patriot himself was seated behind the bar, saying nothing, his mere presence enough to guarantee good order. Since he had discovered the native speaker the Patriot's eyes had not left the screen, and though the picture danced and tumbled, and McCoy's and McGuffin's obscenities intruded every few minutes, and though he could understand but little of what the old man was saying when he did decide to hold forth, yet it was music to the Patriot's ears. Drink might be dispensed and matters of national importance settled during the country 'n' western interludes, but when the native speaker or Father Frank were centre stage, it would be a brave man indeed who would have broken the Patriot's concentration.

'There's a lad who's done us all proud,' Peadar ventured to Brother Murphy when the ads came on. Brother Murphy looked at him and thought about clipping his ear to be on the safe side.

'His poor father would have been as pleased as punch,' Eugene agreed, pouring a small one for the Brother and another for the major-domo whom he could see approaching across the Shambles, admiring the papal decorations.

'I've never seen him looking better and that's a fact,' Peadar said. 'I think he's maybe lost a bit of weight at last. Would you not agree, Mister MacBride?'

The major-domo said nothing. He was studying Frank, studying him with an experienced eye, recalling the ravenous boy forced to eat the scraps from Schnozzle's table.

'The man's worn out, any eejit can see that,' Eugene disagreed. 'He'll kill himself trying to keep it up day and night.'

The major-domo could see the lines under Frank's eyes and the droop of his shoulders. But he could see something else there too, something that the others had failed to read in the tired features of the host. The major-domo had been long enough in the service of the senior clergy to understand that discreet domestic arrangements, unsuspected by the parishioners, were the order of the day. One thing was clear, the boy needed his services now. He resolved there and then, despite the lumbago, to take the bus to Dublin in the morning to be at his side. He knew what was causing that jaded but buoyant glow.

Father Frank was in love!

❖

The foot patrol filed wearily into the station and the men began to divest themselves of their cumbersome gear.

'Well, Sister, I think all in all we did what we could under the circumstances,' O'Malley said, glancing furtively towards the bulky form of Sister Goretta.

'And I think all in all, Inspector, that it was a complete cock-up!'

O'Malley never took his eyes off her, the dishevelled hair, the face ringed with sweat from the night's business. Three nights they had been at it and though he would be the last to admit it in the present company, he was seriously worried. There hadn't been one confirmed sighting of the Canon or the Charismatics, but the city was all but out of control. Sporadic looting had given way to more consistent unrest; there was a craziness on the streets he had never known before. They were calling for John Joe to go and the priests to take over and he couldn't see any way he was going to hold on. Who would emerge as leader was anybody's guess, but O'Malley feared the worst. He had seen it happen elsewhere in the world, the mob turning to their spiritual leaders for guidance. There would be plenty only too happy to step in if the government fell.

'We did round up that crowd trying to crucify themselves outside the GPO,' he told her. 'Left to their own devices that lot would have done some damage.'

'Is it part of your job all of a sudden, O'Malley, to come between the faithful and their reward?'

'I was only thinking of the publicity, Sister. In my experience as a Guard with thirty years in the force, that sort of thing has a habit of catching on. All in all . . .'

'You've been too long in this job, it seems to me,' she spat out. Her eyes were ablaze with anger, for she recognized in O'Malley the sort of thick bastard who would try and stare her down. Men like that had their uses; she could see why His Holiness had taken such an interest in him for so long. He had the dourness, the doggedness and the cunning that made the perfect Guard. But the time had come to show O'Malley who was boss. If the change-over came, she had to be sure that O'Malley would come over too, and not try any heroics on his own.

'It's time you began to understand, Inspector,' she began, barely controlling herself, 'just what is at stake here. It isn't just law and order we're protecting here. Our Holy Mother the Church is under attack, in every parish from Donegal to Kerry, and your men are running round with batons and rubber bullets.'

'I suppose, Sister, you'd want me to start burning them at the stake or something.'

'You'd be well advised to take that note of sarcasm out of your voice, O'Malley. This country is at the mercy of heretics and heathens. Fanatics and wild men of every sort, setting themselves up as leaders of the people and usurping the authority of the Church. And you know why? Because the so-called politicians, the men you serve with such blind devotion, are weak and ineffective. They've watched as the tide of foreign filth has swept over us and they haven't lifted a finger. We were the last truly Christian state in the world, and look at us now, a mess of consumerism and greed! They have stood idly by while filth of every sort poured in from outside! They have connived at the enslavement of our people to the evils of modernism! They have sold us out! Sold out our Christian heritage, and for what? Do you think the people want to go on living like this? Listen to them, and you'll hear what they want. They want the priests to take a firm lead! They want the clergy to lead them back to the virtues and the customs that we once had. They have said so every time they've had a chance, and every time they have been ignored. But no longer! If the people want the clergy to step in and save them, you and your ilk will not stand in their way! Remember that.'

'I think you're being a bit unfair . . .' O'Malley protested.

'Unfair!' Her eyes were bulging with anger and the veins on her scraggy neck flared blue and swollen as she began the litany of the breakdown of the old order. 'Where were your precious Garda Síochána when the Holy Man of Ballyporeen was doing the rounds, openly defying the hierarchy and gathering a horde of eejits round him? Eh? Oh I'll tell you right away where you were; awaiting orders from the Taoiseach! Waiting for his nibs to get out of his bed, or somebody else's bed, and make up his mind to do something. Orders that never came.' She shoved her face into his. 'But let me tell you this, Inspector. The people have had their bellyful of weak government. They know what they want. Tonight and every night my sisters will be on the streets. Young women, pure in mind and body, willing to clean up the mess that you and yours have got us into. They won't be alone either. The seminaries are full of young lads just raring to be given the word. Lads up from Cork and Tipperary, lads who know how to hold a hurley stick and aren't afraid to break a few heads when they know that the spiritual survival of this country is at stake. And there are others too, the cream of the fraternities. They've been sitting round too long, wondering when someone would give them the lead. Their time has come. They've had it up to here . . .' her hand shot out and levelled on his adam's apple '. . . up to here with talk about divorce and abortion and filth of one sort or another. And they've had it up to here . . .' she poked him again in the throat till his eyes watered '. . . up to here with talk of contraception and free love and the charismatics and dancing in the aisles. They've had their bellyful . . .' with her free hand she dug the special issue baton she still carried into the soft flesh of his solar plexus till he almost cried out '. . . their bellyful of liberation theology and priests who behave like whoremasters. What these good people want, Inspector, is a return to the old values. If you can't provide that service, from tonight we'll be providing it ourselves. Only it won't be rubber bullets we'll be using . . .'

She turned suddenly to where the rest of the men were standing, half to attention, enjoying the Inspector's humiliation, but fearful that their own turn might be coming.

'My advice to the rest of you,' she barked, 'is to offer every assistance to the Church authorities if you hope one day to be drawing your pension.'

She flung the night stick on to the heap in the corner and strode towards the door. One of the younger men ran to open it.

O'Malley removed the riot helmet and scratched his head methodically. 'Perhaps, men,' he said, 'all in all it might be better if we took the Sister's advice. After all a bit of extra help never hurt, and this business might all blow over soon enough . . .'

His voice trailed off. They had already gone.

Since his years on the prison boat, the Patriot had been an insomniac. While the rest of the Shambles slept its fitful sleep, he kept a lonely vigil behind the bar, staring into the middle distance and dreaming of Caithleen ní Houlihan. Above his head the screen flickered erratically. Eugene had turned the sound down low before he retired upstairs, assured that the native speaker had been wheeled off for the night. The Shambles was quiet now, the only sound the background squawking of Born Again Radio, issuing from a dozen cheap receivers somewhere along Scotch Street.

But suddenly the wireless went dead. There was a commotion from across the square. Voices raised and the crack of wood shattering. A fight! The Patriot listened. The Shambles was no stranger to fights of one sort or another. But this was no run-of-the-mill domestic violence or sectarian brawling. This was a real humdinger! The Patriot strained his ears and stole over to the window, parting the shutters carefully.

Pastor McCoy was beating McGuffin, calling him for the renegade he was, threatening to kill him on the spot if he didn't raise the price of the rent before morning. He could hear McGuffin's wails from beneath the van and see the outline of McCoy, arm raised in fury, belting him for all he was worth. The Patriot grinned to himself and returned to his stool. Father Frank's show was coming through clearly now and he poured himself a double and sat down to watch. But he was no sooner settled than the radio came on again, louder than before, and the picture on the television screen went mad with distortion. He spat on the floor in disgust and reached up to turn it off altogether.

He was interrupted by a discreet rap on the window. He lumbered over and opened the side door. Peadar slipped in. The Patriot served him with a grunt.

'I couldn't sleep myself,' Peadar told him. 'What with the racket going on across the way.'

The Patriot said nothing, but it was clear he was listening.

'To tell you the truth, I couldn't resist tuning in to hear what the row was about. Talk about washing your dirty linen in public . . .'

The Patriot poured him another small one.

'The upshot is,' said Peadar lowering his voice, 'that McCoy's as good as bankrupt. He's had to pay the gorillas off! From what I could make out, they've already skedaddled back to Portadown.'

The Patriot refilled his glass. Eugene, alerted by the voice in the bar, slipped silently down the stairs to join them.

'If, and I'm only talking ifs mind you, but if a body were to volunteer to climb upon that scaffold high . . .' Peadar hesitated. Eugene nodded to him to contine with his line of thought. 'Have you seen the state of the eyesore recently? Half eaten with rust. It must be all the rain we've been getting. One good push would topple the lot.'

'I take it you're not putting yourself forward for this kamikaze mission, comrade?' Eugene said after a pause.

'If it weren't for the game leg I declare to God I'd nearly risk it. But if for instance, and I'm still talking ifs, someone had fallen foul of the Sacred Heart and needed a particular penance, a penance with a bit of punch to it, to buy their way back into that party's good books . . .'

'To cancel the debt . . . ?'

'Precisely! Or maybe even . . .' he lowered his voice '. . . have the Movement turn a blind eye to past misdemeanours . . .'

'That would be a matter for the Supreme Court,' Eugene said, looking towards the Patriot.

'Tiocfaidh ár lá,' His Honour declared, speaking for the first time. Our time will come. There was a glint in his eye.

And having thus done his bit for the national cause, Peadar let himself out.

It had been many years since Eugene had seen active service, but the prospect of imminent action thrilled him like a schoolboy. He knew there was a stick of weeping jelly in a pint pot somewhere in the back yard, waiting patiently its turn to play a part in Ireland's glorious history. He caught the Patriot's eye and taking his silence for aquiescence, slipped out in the darkness of the Shambles to break the good news of his redemption to Patrick Pearse McGuffin.

❖

The major-domo was waiting for him outside the dressing-room. He took him firmly by the elbow.

'Have you seen the cut of the place?' he asked. 'Jesus, Mary and Joseph, Father, they've gone too far this time.'

The lobby was full of statues. Hundreds of them. Large ones, small ones, miniatures, family sized and jumbo sized. Indoor models, outdoor models, in-car models. Statues that lit up at night. Statues incorporating alarm clocks and tea makers into their framework. Statues that played the Ave Maria when you wound them up. Statues that dispensed holy water from concealed stoppers. Statues with eyes that followed you everywhere. They crowded into every square inch of the reception area and were already stacked three abreast halfway up the stairs. Some were wrapped in jiffy bags, some were carefully labelled, some had their owners' details scratched on the blue plasterwork; others stood forlorn, arms outstretched, their name tags torn off in the confusion.

'They've been arriving all night,' Snotters said. 'The basement's worse. The cleaners have packed it in and who could blame them?'

'What in God's name is it all about?'

'A good question, Father. It's all down to your friend the Canon. As if things weren't bad enough, he's been putting it about that he wants his statue back! It seems the time has come to find the missing Madonna. The Charismatic crowd have gone mad altogether and they have the whole country as bad as themselves. Rooting round for retired statues and sending them to the studio in the hope that yourself or Miss Noreen will recognize one of them as the genuine article.'

'It's worse than a competition!'

'And have you heard what the prize is? They're all saying that as soon as the Missing Madonna of Ballychondom is found, we'll have a United Ireland and God knows what else into the bargain.'

'But none of these look even remotely like Her.'

'You're one of the few who can say that, Father.'

'She was unique. Nothing like this cheap junk.'

'What am I going to do with this lot in the meantime? I swear to God I've broken a dozen already, the way they get under your feet.'

'Chuck the lot of them out into the car park,' ordered Frank.

'Father I couldn't do that! That would be unnatural. There'd be ructions if it rained.'

'Outside! The lot of them! I'm not having them here. They're a fire hazard. These things are two a penny; every house in the country must have half a dozen. There's hardly a youngster hasn't seen them move at one time or other.'

'The landlady out in Howth tells me her sister had one could do the Rakes of Mallow,' said Mister MacBride, 'though I understand she never saw it herself, to be honest with you.'

Sister Ellen kicked at the embers with the heel of her boot. As the flames spurted, the kettle began to sing. She half-filled her glass with the scalding water and warmed it till it was almost too hot to hold. She emptied it on to the flagstones and ladled into the glass a spoonful of soft brown sugar. The lemon was already cut in segments, and she added a slice along with a stick of cinnamon and a few cloves. Then she carefully measured a double shot of whiskey into the glass, and reaching for the spurting kettle, topped it up with boiling water. She stirred it vigorously till the sugar had dissolved and the liquid was clear and pale gold. She lifted it to her lips and sipped, feeling it ease the ache in her bones and clear her mucus-clogged sinuses.

The familiar sounds of the Kilfenora Céilí Band, back by popular demand, filled the quiet room. Only a few of the older Sisters were about, for the younger element were all busy with their night-time duties. It was warm in the guard room and she knew she would not be disturbed. Father Frank's Popeathon might be compulsory viewing throughout the land, but after a week of it at close quarters even Sister Ellen was finding it a penance to be endured in the line of duty. But orders were orders. She had been told to stick to Feely and his show. As she had done, day and night, never leaving the studio, snatching a few hours' fretful sleep only when she was sure he himself was getting his head down backstage, forcing herself awake when he came jumping back on to the set to start another day. She had sat through a seemingly endless series of discussions and interviews. She had heard enough jigs and reels to do her a lifetime. The audience had come and gone, one group giving way to the next as Snotters MacBride ushered them to their seats, but Ellen had remained steadfast. There were special guests galore, and she had seen them come and go too. Old doting priests who'd published histories of god-forsaken parishes down the country with black and white photographs, wheeled on to a fanfare of hype; they would sit tongue-tied while Feely preened himself beside them. Or big bucks from the GAA talking about hurling in the west of Ireland. Or some poor nun back from the mission fields, and Feely prompting her to retell a few rehearsed stories from her days in the sun.

But tonight Sister Ellen was taking a night off. She hoisted up her habit and detaching a large linen handkerchief from her knickers blew her nose long and loud. She examined the results with interest. The cold had her slaughtered and no mistake. She couldn't remember when she had a worse one. That place must be alive with germs. The only cure was to stick by the fire and sweat it out. She poured herself another toddy, going easy on the water, and settled down to give the television her full attention. She was slightly guilty about what she was doing. By rights she should be down there still, sniffing and snorting in the front row. How could she explain it to Immaculata if anything went wrong? Sure what could go wrong, she told herself, wasn't she only taking a few hours' break? It wasn't as if she'd given him a free hand. Hadn't she left him in the care of two trainees, hot-headed country girls, who had strict instructions not to disrupt the proceedings but to phone her if they suspected anything unusual. There'd be no trouble tonight, please God. She thought about getting into bed for a few hours but then thought better of it. Wasn't she taking a big enough risk as it was! If Sister Immaculata ever heard she had deserted her post, she'd skin her alive.

The musicians began to fade and the set emerged from the shadows as the studio lights came up. There was a fanfare and the camera focused on the staircase down which Father Frank was expected to run to get the proceedings started again. There was no sign of him! The boys in the band tried again and the camera searched around the set, looking for the lost master of ceremonies. There was a ripple of consternation from the audience. Ellen gripped the arm of her chair. The camera panned round the audience. She noted with some relief the grim features of Sister Geraldine in the front row, middle seat, the script of the evening's entertainment resting on her knees, pencil in hand. There was another ragged fanfare; and then, coyly and boyishly, peeping round the wall of the backdrop, came Father Frank to uproarious applause.

'I had youse rightly codded there,' he joked, putting on a bit of a brogue to get round them, 'Did youse think I wasn't going to turn up?'

Ellen cursed loudly. Feely really was the pits. The fucker would do anything to get a laugh. She noticed with satisfaction that he was beginning to look jaded and haggard. In the studio he gave every appearance of being cool and collected, but on the box he looked slightly nervous. She rolled a little something to settle her nerves and ease the pain in her head, only half-listening to him blather on. What a sorry bunch they were when you looked at them. The Greatest Living Fossil in his tweed suit and green waistcoat, arguing the toss with the Boy Scout. 'Nothing but a pair of drunken old queens!' she shouted at the screen. She hooted with derision as the Lady Novelist tried to make a dramatic entrance to scrappy applause. They must be tired of that bitch by now, she thought. She only ever had the two stories, how she

225

dropped her drawers and how she didn't. And look at the cut of Noreen! Making her first appearance, letting on that butter wouldn't melt in her mouth. That's one lady would need to watch her step carefully. She's lucky that Schnozzle thinks of her as something special. One of the famous three that saw Our Lady dancing. Or so she says! I'll make the same lady dance before too long! Let her step out of line once too often . . . She took another sip of the hot whiskey and felt herself nodding off. What harm would there be in forty winks, and wouldn't she feel the better for it? She closed her eyes and let her weary mind relax.

She awoke with a jolt. How long had she slept? There was a voice in the room with her and her neck was stiff from the way she'd been lying. She remembered suddenly where she was and the risk she was taking. The voice came from the set in the corner; it was only Noreen droning on, she noted with relief. She looked up at the guard room clock. Almost midnight. The sleep had made her feel worse; what she needed was a proper night in bed. Her leg had gone numb under her and she needed to pee. She rose stiffly and rubbed the circulation back into her limbs. She made for the back door. She became aware of Noreen looking strangely at the camera which had moved into close-up. She lifted the latch on the door and the cold air flooded into the room, hitting her sinuses like needles and shrivelling up her bladder. Was something afoot? Why was Noreen apparently behaving so oddly? Was there something going on she should be aware of? But the cold air had already made up her mind for her. She was not going to piss herself on Noreen Moran's account.

With perverse ill timing, something that had dogged her all her life, Sister Ellen was about to miss the highlight of the show. The first miracle of the electronic age!

Noreen was sitting in a sugan rocking chair in a cardboard cut-out cottage, with ersatz rafters and inglenook, and a dresser lined with speckled delft. Her nervousness was palpable, but the audience were behind her, willing her to succeed with applause and cries of encouragement. She began to read from her postbag, a brace of letters that highlighted the inevitable shortcomings of married life, and Frank knew that she had them hooked. But as she set the sheaf aside and turned to camera three to deliver her rehearsed homily, a strange and unfamiliar presence entered the studio. The audience felt it and fell silent. The guests on the sofa felt it and crossed themselves. Noreen froze. Father Frank stood rooted to the spot and knew that he was no longer in control. Something very strange was happening!

Was it fatigue? Or was it a trick of the lights? Noreen felt her hands go cold and her voice falter. A strange feeling was stealing over her. Then she caught the spotlight's full beam and in that second she was transported back again to that young girl at her mother's grave, looking up into a halo of light and seeing there the face of the Dancing Madonna. She began to speak. The words that spilled from her lips were no longer the mundane obsessions of everyday life; Noreen was speaking now in the purest, sweetest Gaelic, retelling an urgent message that had been implanted there long, long ago.

Only one man among them could understand her. Only one could interpret the full implications of her stark message. The *cainteoir dúchais* was suddenly out of the wheelchair and hobbling towards the audience, shouting at the top of his voice, repeating over and over the words he had heard. There was a glint of triumph in his eyes and the words fell like a mantra from his tongue.

The mast above the Shambles swayed uneasily as McGuffin doggedly climbed aloft. Once, twice, three times. Like a drunken man it regained its balance each time. At its vertex the radio transmitter crackled with static. Now, slowly, it began to disintegrate. A rivet shattered and hurtled down to the roof of the chapel below. Another popped with the sound of a rifle. The fatigued joints in the girders holding it in place began to slip. Slowly at first, almost imperceptibly, the tower began to collapse. Then suddenly there was a flash that lit the town and a second later the crack of shearing metal. The crash broke every bottle behind the Patriot

Bar and every window in the Shambles, as ton upon ton of rusting metal cascaded to the ground below.

'Something's improved the picture,' Peadar said, not caring to allude to the shattered glass that littered the bar. The last bottle on the shelf, the elusive one that bore Sharkey's watercolour of the Yellow Meal Road, tottered and fell, disgorging its noisome contents on the earthen floor. There was a moment's silence from the square outside, then they heard the screams of McCoy emerging from the Boyne Tavern and coming face to face with his shattered dream.

Despite the diversion outside, all eyes in the Patriot's were on the television above the bar. They were watching Noreen, her face lit by a celestial light, her lips moving silently as she relayed the message that had been her secret for so long. The picture faded and the screen slowly filled with a triptych of children at the feet of the Madonna. The boy was recognizable as a youthful and gauche Frank. Noreen as a girl was weeping tears of fear and wonderment. But the dark, troubled features of the third child lingered longest. It was Chastity McCoy. The three children of the Dancing Madonna, united again.

It was quiet in the barracks yard. Sister Ellen squatted down beside the wall and eased herself. The night was calm. Here and there a few stars winked. Below her the houses were in darkness. From the city centre she could hear sporadic sounds of trouble, but round the Castle things were quiet. All in watching the big show, she thought. But then, before her very eyes, the lights of the town began to come on. Everywhere! What in the name of all that is holy was going on? She heard voices shouting. Close at hand and from far off. The streets were filling up and they were shouting to others to come out. She heard a snatch of the Lourdes hymn, faltering at first then stronger as more and more voices took it up. And from the direction of the Liberties a song she hadn't heard in years. 'A Nation Once Again!'

Feely! It had to be! He had pulled some stunt when her back was turned. She gathered her clothes round her and raced back into the kitchen. The audience, every man and woman of them, were on their knees, singing the Ave Maria. The guests, the visiting Yank among them, were kneeling on the sofa, their heads thrown back in praise. Noreen knelt weeping among the rushes of her humble cabin. Even the native speaker was miming the words with customary animation. And Father Frank was standing at his podium, arms outstretched and tears of joy pouring down his face.

The phone beside her, and every phone in the Castle (even the red one!) began to ring in ominous unison.

Ten

Frank took a couple more mouthfuls of air to clear his head. He needed time to think about what he, and half the country if the reports coming in were anything to go by, had witnessed. What exactly had gone on in the darkened studio earlier that night? Had Noreen's presence sparked off something supernatural? Had there really been a miracle of some sort? Had the Virgin of Ballychondom really walked among them? It would be easy in the days ahead to dismiss it as a mirage, a trick of the light, brought on by their collective exhaustion. Whatever the truth, he knew that his life had changed for ever. She had reappeared and her presence had given him strength.

He needed somehow to get through to the *cainteoir dúchais*, to have him slowly repeat what he had heard and what he had seen. Maybe then he could start to make some sense of it all. He picked his way through the lobby and sought out the old man's dressing-room.

Across the street, behind the lace curtains of the Step Inside Café, Sister Ellen watched the activity in the car park for the next hour. She had changed the notice on the door from OSCAILTE to DÚNTA and commandeered the premises for as long as was necessary. No one would dare disturb her vigil. She was working freelance now, avoiding Immaculata. Desperately she needed to atone for her mistake and work her way back into her superior's good books. The time had come to rid Ireland of this turbulent priest once and for all.

❖

The native speaker was sleeping soundly. Frank rearranged the blankets and smoothed the pillows under his ancient head. He had developed a soft spot for the old boy and his pessimistic predictions. He lowered the lights in the room. Since Fidelma had decamped, the native speaker had taken up residence here, wired up at night to a variety of bottles and machines to keep him alive. The Gaeltacht, as it was jokingly known. The old man started in his sleep and muttered something. Frank leaned forward hoping to catch a word, something of great import or beauty or wit, but the meaning was well beyond him. He slumped down in the armchair by the old man's bed and felt the need for sleep overpower him. He should shake a leg and make for home. But he closed his eyes and a moment later had drifted into a slumber.

Disturbing half-images of the past days rose to trouble him. Something was stalking him and he was struggling to flee. Then through his dreams he became aware of a voice calling to him.

'Father Feely! Is the Father round at all?' It was Major-domo MacBride from the corridor outside.

'*Tá mé anseo,*' he muttered, shaking the nightmare from his brain and trying to focus.

'There you are, Father,' said the major-domo, opening the door. 'I've been looking all over for you. I saw your car parked outside and reckoned you'd be here still.'

'Is everything all right?'

'Right as rain if you're talking about rioting in the streets to get to the chapels and the priests battering the people out of them. The landlady was telling me on the phone she tried to get into Holy Cross for the Stations but she didn't stand a chance with the crowds. Miss Noreen's wee turn, whatever it was, has set the cat among the pigeons.'

'Has everyone gone?' He tried to stand up but his legs had gone weak.

'All bar the Yank. He's still waiting to go on, no one's told him you've called it a day. I think I'll leave him where he is till morning. I've ordered O'Malley to send a squad car to run you home. The streets aren't safe on a night like this. Goodnight now, Father.'

Frank was halfway out of the chair when the bomb went off.

231

The force of the blast threw him across the floor and pinned him to the wall. For a moment there was silence. He thought he was dead; then with a suddenness that took his breath away the awful noise came flooding in, the ear-shattering crack of the Semtex and the low rumble of falling masonry. Part of the ceiling collapsed above him. Like a character in slow motion he felt his limbs in turn, a careful checklist till he was satisfied he was unscathed. He groped his way to the door and down the dust-filled corridor and out of the building through a gaping hole in the foyer. His car lay on its roof twenty yards from its parking spot, still burning fiercely. Round it lay the remnants of a thousand plaster virgins, reduced to dust.

O'Malley used his baton to force his way through the crowd and reach the safety of the Gardai station. On his desk he noticed the memos, one from Áras an Uachtaráin, the other from the Castle. He picked them up and tossed them unread into the wastepaper bin. He knew his orders. To secure the airport at whatever cost. Only Schnozzle's return would halt the anarchy that the country was sliding into. He made his way to the basement. In the yard stood the motorbike he had already earmarked. With a deft kick he started the engine, signalled to the sergeant to open the gate and gunned the heavy machine out into the backstreet.

The throng was heaviest as he approached O'Connell Street but he forced a way through them. Though it hadn't gone beyond a bit of stone-throwing so far, he knew how little it would take for things to turn nasty. The TV show had sparked off something close to hysteria. The clergy were to blame, he told himself. Building up expectations and then unable to deliver the goods. Half of them gone sick, he'd heard, the others too exhausted to carry on much longer. What had happened in Dundalk had been a lesson to him. Three dead and many injured after a mob had attacked the police station, according to reports. It seems a crowd had been doing the Nine First Fridays; the priest had come down with a septic throat on the last morning and they couldn't fill their run. You could see how they might be frustrated all right, having to start all over. All the same, three dead! And why take it out on the Guards?

The crowd thickened again near the Parnell monument. He kept the bike revved up. Like a frisky thoroughbred in the starting stalls, he felt. There was an aimlessness about them which worried him. Nowhere to go, half of them, up from the country hoping for the Pope's return. Nowhere to sleep and the churches that weren't closed already full to overflowing. The sooner our long-nosed friend returns and sorts this out the better. Once law and order start breaking down it's not so easy to put them back again. The priests were on the streets trying to keep them in check, leaving the pulpits empty. In places he heard they'd had to nail the confession boxes up and guard the church doors with clerical students. It won't be long before something gives, he thought. And when it did, O'Malley wanted to be as far away from dirty Dublin as it was possible to be.

The pike-filled lakes of the west were calling to him. He hadn't been to Sligo for years, or walked the roads he used to when he was a boy. He might take a trip to the quiet Protestant graveyard where your man was buried. His mother, God rest her, was always quoting him. 'I will arise and go now, and go to Innisfree.' He could do that rightly, live alone in the bee loud glade. But as he confronted the throng milling around the obelisk at the head of the street the words of a darker poem came to mind. He had learned it at school years ago and its ominous message had stayed with him ever since. 'What rough beast, its hour come round at last, slouches towards Bethlehem to be born . . .'

A queue had formed outside some abandoned shops on the north side of the square. Someone had set up business in the corner. He looked closer, professional curiosity getting the better of his caution. A freelance priest, or maybe an impostor? The young man had set up a mobile confessional and was busy hearing confessions at a fair rate of knots. A handwritten notice: LEGIT PRIEST! MODEST TERMS. ABSOLUTION GUARANTEED. O'Malley chuckled to himself. You had to hand it to the Dublin boys, they'd try anything to make a quick buck. Some jack-the-lad from the Liberties, couldn't bear the sight of so many country gobshites in town, he has to take their money. A fly boy, seeing

233

a gap in the market. Has been so often himself he knows the formula backwards. Doing nicely out of it, by the look of things. Old ones handing over fivers. Can hardly wait their turn. You wouldn't take a personal problem to a boyo like that! Quick return only. Bless me father for I have sinned. It would pay him to have a good lookout man, all the same. He'll be the one needing confession if the Christian Brothers catch him at it. They'll tear him a new arse or two for a stunt like that.

He kicked the bike into top gear and raced up the street, scattering the groups who barred his way. They leaped aside as he roared through. Minutes later he had left the slums behind and was heading for the airport, crouched low over the handlebars, the throttle opened full.

❖

Major-domo MacBride laboriously pushed the bicycle, its mysteriously wrapped cargo lashed to the saddle, up the steep hill towards Adam and Eve's, complaining to himself with every step of the way. A few effete parishioners, lounging outside the parochial house, tried to block him, but he explained the nature of his business curtly and they let them through. Poor Father Frank, he thought. If he seriously believed that these bodyguards of his were any match for the Sisters he was badly mistaken. He guessed rightly where he would find his old pupil, cowering in the cellar among the Camembert and the Châteauneuf du Pape.

'Good news and bad news, Father!' he shouted down the steps.

Frank checked that the coast was clear before emerging.

'The good news, and I have it from a reliable source, is that it was all a bit of a cock-up. You're not on the hit list after all! Word is that Sister Ellen, mad as a hatter, hails from Galway direction, was acting against orders. Something of a maverick. A freelancer. To cap it all, she went up with the motor, so you'll have no more trouble from that quarter.'

'Can you be sure of that?' Frank asked. He was pale with fear and exhaustion. 'What if another of them takes it into her frigging head to blow me to kingdom come?'

'They've enough on their plate searching for the Mad Canon and his tribe.'

Frank winced at the mention of Canon Tom. 'Is there any word . . . ?'

'They seek him here, they seek him there. He keeps popping up all over the place rallying the troops, but so far he's given them all the slip!'

'They'll not be long putting two and two together.'

'We'll cross that bridge when we come to it. But I have it from the horse's mouth that you're in no immediate danger. Which brings me to the bad news.'

'Those fucking statues . . .'

'Never worry about them, Father. She did us a favour when she blew their heads off. Every one a goner. The Corporation are down there at the minute, loading the remains into a dumper truck. But we've got another problem. It's the old fella. I'm afraid he's had a bit of an accident.'

The blood, what was left of it, drained from Frank's face.

'When did this happen?' he stammered.

'I'll tell you straight. I found him dead on the bed. He never felt a thing, God be praised. Sure I suppose we could say he had the priest with him at the end.'

'Dead?' Frank said faintly. 'You're sure?'

'As the proverbial dodo. Do you want to take a look at him, Father? He looks very peaceful. A lovely corpse.'

'In God's name! You haven't brought him with you?'

'What else could I do? The building is swarming with Sister Concepta's commandos. They'd have tumbled soon enough. He's outside on the back of the bike, sitting up and looking as pleased as punch.'

'Have you told anyone else?'

'Not a sinner, Father. If you take my advice, you'll be careful how you handle this one.'

'He needs to be given a proper burial. A Christian burial. He deserves a hero's send-off.'

'Maybe . . .' the major-domo said, dubiously.

'He should lie with the relics of his ancestors, back on the Yellow Meal Road.'

'Listen to me a minute, Father . . .'

'. . . or maybe we should bury him in Phoenix Park, in a mausoleum, the last of his breed.'

'Look at it this way, Father. What you're saying is all very well, but not just at the minute. There's too many hot-heads on the loose just now. The ordinary people may not have understood a lot of what he was saying, but the old boy had started to mean a lot to them. He was a link with their ancient past. A living fossil, so to speak, tying us to the glorious Gaelic tradition. To put the tin hat on it, he's the only one who could have interpreted the Dancing Madonna for us, should she ever turn up in person. Word gets round that he died in your custody and there might be all hell to pay . . .'

'What do you suggest?' Frank asked in mounting desperation.

'We don't say a word. Not to a soul! We'll put him in the parlour for the moment sitting up in his wheelchair and the pipe stuck in his mouth.'

'But won't he be a bit . . . ?' he wrinkled his nose.

'Devil the bit, Father. As fresh as a daisy. Sure if you'd drunk so much poteen as he did in his day you'd be rightly preserved for posterity too.'

'And then what?'

'That's the best part. Don't the pair of us know the very place where he'll be as welcome as the flowers in May?'

'The Patriot's?'

'Where better! A present to the lads from Baile Cliath?'

Despite himself, Snotters began to laugh at the audacity of his scheme.

'May his soul rest in peace,' Frank muttered, tracing the sign of the cross in the air.

'Leave it to me. When things have settled down I'll slip him back across the border on the bus. The Patriot will be over the moon when your man shows up in the snug. He'll have a permanent home there, mark my words!'

'You'll have to have him embalmed?'

'Isn't it the least we can do for the old language? I'll have a word with the landlady's brother and mark his card for afterwards. He's in the undertaking line at weekends. The poor man's run off his feet this weather. He tells me they're bringing them in by the truck load all week.'

Frank wanted to hear no more. The bomb that had shattered the studio had shattered his life. He welcomed it with relief. He knew how fickle and shallow it had all been, playing hail-fellow-well-met for the amusement of his masters. He had adopted cynicism as a carapace against the truth. But the time had come for him to come forth as his own man. What did he know of himself after all, except that he had been blessed as a child, called forth somehow like the children of Lir of old. He tore off the dog collar, symbol of all he had come to detest, and tossed it aside. He would never wear it again.

A ridge of high pressure, unseasonal for the time of year, settled uneasily off the west coast in the stillness before dawn. It was, the people agreed, an omen. By day the skies were blue and brittle; by night the stars twinkled brightly from the frosty blackness. Up and down the country they sniffed the air, noting its unexpected chilliness, commenting on its low humidity, cautiously exploring its unusual cocktail of aromas. Nostrils, dulled by years of mist and rain, savoured the smells of the country for the first time.

Tobias Sharkey the miser, on his deathbed in Annagery, twitched his nostrils for the last time to the sweet smells of dung and ditch from close at hand and the faint but unmistakable hogo of rotting tubers, harbinger of the next plague, seeping down the Yellow Meal Road.

In the townships round the capital the stink of unburied excrement seeped through the thin walls, mingling with the fetor of bacon and cabbage and cheap clothes.

Inspector O'Malley blew his nose between two fingers and flicked the gelatinous mucus in the direction of the airport station urinal, then stepped back and filled his lungs with the stenches of the building – farts and chalk and kerosene, and the diesel in the motorbikes from the basement and the sweat from the greaseband of his helmet.

Frank awoke refreshed, sampling the air of Adam and Eve's.

He flung open the casement windows. A light breeze was coming in off the Irish Sea, blowing gently over his parish, bearing its familiar aromas; incense, cigars and brandy, joss sticks and Jamaican sensemilla, chlorine from the swimming pools and jojoba nut fragrance from the whirlpool, all mixed together in a heady concoction. It was a smell you could only find here, in this small corner, this time warp of affluence. The unmistakable smell of new money. Then another, fainter aroma reached his nostrils, that of poteen and putrefaction, and he remembered with a sinking heart the events of the night before.

John Joe Sharkey, tossing alone (for once) in his bed, smelt the zoo. Across the green acres of Phoenix Park the undiluted smells of jungle and steppe and savannah assailed him. He could feel every fetid breath of the mangy lions, could sense every fold in the hide of the sweating antelopes. He knew every monkey dropping and every musk signal. They drove everything else from his nostrils, banishing from the apartment the subtler smells of his success. Though he had survived a thousand crises, John Joe knew that this time his number was up.

The elements are no respecters of puny, man-made boundaries. A finger of the same anticyclone crept over the Ulster mountains in the stilly night and settled four square over Main Street, Portadown.

❖

	s. d.	
Horfe-flefh fold for	*0 – 1 – 8*	*per pound*
A Quarter of a Dog	*0 – 5 – 6*	*fatned by eating the Bodies of the flain Irifh.*
A Dogs-Head	*0 – 2 – 6*	
A Cat	*0 – 4 – 6*	
A Rat	*0 – 1 – 0*	
A Moufe	*0 – 0 – 6*	

A fmall Flook taken in the River, not to be bought for Money, or purchafed under the rate of a quantity of Meal.

A pound of Greaves	*0 – 1 – 0*
A pound of Tallow	*0 – 4 – 0*

238

A pound of falted Hides	0 – 1 – 0
A quart of Horfe blood	0 – 1 – 0
A Horfe-pudding	0 – 0 – 6
An handful of Sea wreck	0 – 2
of Chick-weed	0 – 1
A quart of Meal, when found	1 – 0

The cardboard placard above the bed was Lily's handiwork, a meticulous replica in pokerwork of the notices that had hung in the butcher's during the siege of Derry. She had hung another in the window of the shop below, a talisman to ward off the attentions of the GPs. Their forefathers had endured great hardship then, holding out against the besieging papists and their allies against all the odds; they had been reduced to eating the rats from the sewers and the salted hides of the horses, but they had never surrendered.

But on this dreadful morning these sentiments gave Magee no comfort. He lay sweating on the bed in a rictus of fear, immune to the smell of socks and the odour of pig seeping through the floorboards. His mind was racing. Here was a crisis as great as that faced by the Apprentice Boys. His people were under mortal threat again, and only he could save them from the Lundies in their midst. Waves of terror passed over him and he cried out to the Lord for his burden to be lifted. Magee was party to a terrible secret, a secret that he had somehow to share with the unsuspecting townsfolk innocently sleeping all around him. Why him? Why had the Lord singled him out as His messenger in this moment of trial? Why had He chosen this moment to re-enter his life, after turning His back on him for so long?

But he knew he could not ignore the task before him. They had to be warned. They had to take action. He would have to risk all and speak out. For Magee had witnessed, only hours before, a foretaste of Armageddon!

Until the previous night, all his instincts told him to keep his head down. He didn't need Lily's constant nagging to remind him he was in deep trouble. With the collapse of the radio mast and the demise of the deejay the great evangelical crusade was finished. But the Belfast GPs who had put up the money were unsympathetic to these problems. Money was owed and they could not be kept waiting.

And yet Magee knew that he had no alternative. He had to go public on what he had seen and what he had heard. Furthermore he needed McCoy. Something was afoot that only the preacher could handle. Something bigger than anything they had ever handled before. Something that overrode both his loathing of McCoy and his fear of the GPs. He had seen the face of Chastity. And he had seen something else. A vision of the end days, with the harlot of Rome preparing to invade the very heart of the holy city. There was no time to lose! If the vision he had seen was true, the Pope would be on the Shambles before the day was done!

He had been in the Temperance Social Club the night before. A less sociable ambience was hard to imagine; the company was as quiet as the grave, the cue ball had gone missing from the pool table, and Lily had refused to cross the door, fearing a raid by the Committee. He had drunk tea and played a silent hand of cards. After the others had gone Magee had stayed behind. In the back room, hidden behind the rubble, was a television set. He plugged it in and watched the dancing dots fill the screen till his eyes grew tired. He had found the set in the gutted ruins of the Mater Hospital. Television, as a tool of the devil, was outlawed in the town, and there were those on the bench ready to hand down six months for possession. The few illicit sets still in Portadown offered no temptation to the citizenry to fall from the ways of righteousness, for the dampness of the lough and the hills to the north debilitated every signal. But every week Magee sullenly switched it on and listened to the static.

Until the night before, when he had suddenly found himself tuned in to the Free State!

He felt the hairs on his spine go stiff. He felt the blood drain from his head. He checked the windows and the army blanket that acted as a curtain. He double checked the door. He crept back to the set and stared at it in guilty anticipation. The screen was still filled with the dancing white dots, but if he stood back and half closed his eyes he found he could make out the silhouettes of shadowy figures on the screen. Gingerly he lifted the old coat

240

hanger he had rigged up as an aerial and moved it about the room. A picture suddenly appeared, broke into distortion and vanished again. He swore quietly and tried to relocate the position. The sound was sporadic, coming through in bursts of clarity. He tried to keep the volume down, but as he fiddled with the coat hanger the room was suddenly filled with a disputatious cacophony of southern accents. He dropped the metal and the voices disintegrated into a maddening hiss. But despite the danger of apprehension, Magee had persevered. He found a position that balanced a distorted picture with passable sound. And all evening he had sat transfixed in the dark room with the door locked. The strident bell summoning him to the Meeting House went unheeded. The hour of curfew came and went. Magee stayed put. Even after the generator went dead, blotting out once and for all the image of horror on the screen, he stayed immobile in the upright chair where he had sat all night, trembling at what he had seen and heard.

Though she was feigning sleep, Lily too was awake and terrified. She could feel him sweating. She could hear him groaning. In a minute he would start calling out again, maybe wakening the neighbours. God Almighty give me guidance this night, she prayed. She had put up with a lot during the years of their marriage, but she had never seen him as troubled as he was this night. She must help him sleep, help banish the nightmares that were wracking him. There was only one thing she knew that was strong enough to give him peace.

The room behind the shop was dark and smelled of pigs' flesh. She lit the tilly lamp and stepped back, waiting for the cockroaches to scurry away. The pig hung from the ceiling hook. She took a bench and climbed up to it. Its stiff snout brushed against her stomach, its ears flopped against her thigh. She hesitated. Then gingerly she put her fingers up its cold, stiff rectum. Dear God, let there be no rats, she prayed. He had told her that the rats would sometimes creep into the carcass and gorge themselves so full that they couldn't squeeze out. She groped further inside. Then her fingers touched something cold and smooth. The neck of a bottle. She tugged, but rigor mortis had sealed it in. She tugged again. It wouldn't budge. She climbed down and reached for one of the knives and cleaved the animal open between the legs. The neck of the bottle was hanging loose now and with a tug she freed it.

The remnants of a tattered label still adhered to the bottle, faded Celtic calligraphy framing a watercolour of the Yellow Meal Road. Lily could smell the stuff even before she uncorked it. If they were caught with hard liquor they could get the cat, but maybe it would help him sleep if only for a couple of hours. She knew it was her only hope.

In the Great Hall of Trinity College the Sisters of the True Faith were mustering. They stood to attention in the cloisters and court-yards, ten thousand veiled, black-clad figures, ten thousand arms punching the air in time to their hypnotic chanting. The noise was rising to a crescendo. On the dais, Immaculata McGillicuddy sat impassive, scanning the sea of eager, fanatical young faces. They had been at it since well before dawn. They would go on like this for another hour, till the crowds started to gather. Then she would let them loose on the streets.

On the shores of the Great Lake, by the great body of silver water lying motionless in the midnight silence, Alphonsus McLoughlin tossed and turned and could find no peace. Ringing in his ears he could hear the voice of the people calling him back to Ireland, refusing to be silenced. He went to the small window and peered out into the night. It was pitch black, and the stars shone with exaggerated brilliance in the brittle coldness. But then he heard the sound that the tribe had been waiting for all winter, the sudden crack of the pack ice melting on the lake and the dripping of the icicles from the trees on to the trailer roof, heralding the thaw.

He packed their few belongings into the aluminium canoe before sun-up and went back to waken Chastity. She said nothing as he lifted her carefully into the prow and pushed the boat over the sand bar into the slow-moving Negawnee River. He settled himself in the centre of the canoe and began to paddle methodically. It was a long hike upstream to the settlement, but the Greyhound bus would be coming through mid-morning on its way to Iron Mountain with connections for the world beyond.

❖

Frank stood for the last time in the tiled hallway of the mansion. A terminal silence had descended on the parish. Not a soul stirred. Even the ghosts of the place seemed to have deserted it. The native speaker had decamped earlier, to be sure of his place, the major-domo in attendance. Noreen too had slipped away discreetly in the small hours when the streets of Dublin were coming alive with people pouring in from every province, all heading towards the Phoenix Park. He had heard the crowds walking the highway below all night long, heard their laughter and excitement and heard their prayers too. They had been singing and chanting of their hopes for the future. Of their belief that somehow a poor broken statue, that his own father had once put his faith in, would mysteriously turn up to heal them, to solve their problems, to point them towards salvation.

It filled him with foreboding, this new mood of expectation. Surely there had been enough false dawns already. They had learned to take disappointments as their birthright. But what if this time it was different? What if she did turn up, confounding his scepticism, a harbinger of a new order that would unite them at last? What then? Who had prepared the people of Ireland for such a transition? Prepared them for the pain that such a new birth would entail? What could they know of the torment other nations had experienced, wrenching themselves away from the familiar gods of the past, forced to embrace those of a new millennium? He knew these people only too well, knew them north and south; knew them all, planters and dispossessed, rich and poor. Knew how set in their ways they were, how unshakeable in their prejudices. Happy to kill one another for another thousand years. As stubborn as a field full of mules in their resolution never to yield an inch.

He told himself suddenly that he no longer cared. His mind was made up. He wanted no part of it, whatever the future might hold. He would never return to the easy life of Adam and Eve's, fooling himself that he might be achieving some small measure of good by bringing solace and entertainment while all along he was propping up the conspiracy of oppression he had come to despise. He had been seduced too long by the easy life and its false popularity. And there was Noreen. He knew he had been unfair to her, trapping her in a relationship that was doomed to secrecy and deceit. He had no right to ask her to stay with him. No right to ask her to share a future with him, to live a lie.

He strode to the door for the last time and turned his face resolutely towards the north. In the distance, shimmering through the blue haze of the dawn, he could make out the foothills of the Ulster mountains. Back in the dark days in Derry, when he was fighting for his sanity against the horror that loomed over him like a great threatening bird, he had vowed that one day he would run from it and never return. Whatever the cost! That time had come. He would run for the boat, leaving the wreckage of his life behind him.

But escape was not to be so simple. Something more powerful, more immediate, closer at hand than the lure of the hills of home was calling to him. From far away, across the silent city, he could hear distantly but unmistakably the rhythm of a million voices raised in supplication. If he went now, running most of the way through the deserted streets, he could be among them. The crowds would be terrible once he reached the quays, but his face was known, he would get through. He looked back to the foothills of the north, but already the storm clouds had descended over them. He could hear, louder than before, the entreaties of the multitude in the distant park and knew that he was in the grip of a compulsion more powerful than he knew how to control. His place was with them. The hour of the rough beast was fast approaching.

In the privacy of the first-class compartment, in defiance of the sign that urged NO SMOKING, FASTEN SEAT BELTS, Pope

Patrick the First slipped off his ermine slippers and finished his cheroot. On the foldaway tray before him rested Immaculata's reports. He shuffled through them, pausing here and there to highlight a phrase or a name. Then he turned his attention once more to the activities of Father Frank. He noted the celebrity of the last native speaker, and saw it as an omen. He crossed himself as he read of Noreen's spectacular visitation. The time had come for the prophecies to be fulfilled. The time had come for a firm hand and a decisive mind. Ireland needed a man of destiny, and he had been called.

The papal aircraft landed at Dublin an hour later. His Holiness stood in triumph on the steps acknowledging the ecstatic greetings of the faithful on the terminal roof. He knelt to kiss the tarmac and they cheered. He accepted the supplications of the bishops and archbishops who made up the formal welcoming party. He greeted Sister Immaculata and inspected the guard of honour. He was driven across the runway to the waiting helicopter, where O'Malley saluted him and ushered him aboard. The flight to the Phoenix Park took only ten minutes. But even above the noise of the rotor blades he could hear the exultation of the multitude, a great paean of praise and expectation welling up from below. The helicopter landed and Sister Immaculata escorted him to the waiting Popemobile. They began their slow drive towards the altar which had been erected in the middle of the park. Surrounding him was the largest crowd ever witnessed in Ireland on any occasion, larger than any drawn by Dan O'Connell to the hill of Tara, or by Parnell or de Valera or any of the kings of old.

In the middle of things, under the jaundiced eye of Sister Goretta, were Noreen and the *cainteoir dúchais* and Snotters MacBride and Canon Tom and the parishioners of Adam and Eve's.

And in the thick of it, acting as mad as the best of them, was Father Frank himself.

Epilogue

For a week there'd been nothing but coaches through the Shambles, but at last the exodus was complete.

'If it wasn't for the shop I'd nearly go myself,' the vegetable man confided in Eugene, shouting above the engine of Doherty's Religious Rides, pulled up outside the Patriot's while the pilgrims had a pee and a pint under Bosco's eagle eye.

'I suppose there'll be a big demand for cabbage and spuds, with half the town down in Dublin,' Eugene said sarcastically.

'Maybe you're right. I'll have a word with the Derry bucko inside and arrange a lift. He would hardly have the neck to charge me full fare if I have to stand the whole way? Yourself and the Patriot aren't going? You'll be the only ones left on the Shambles!'

Eugene didn't answer. Though the Patriot hadn't been off the Shambles in living memory, it was still policy never to discuss his movements with an outsider.

'*Tiocfaidh ár lá*,' he said finally. Our day will come.

'Live horse and you'll get grass!' said Peadar, cautiously venturing into the bar to haggle with Bosco.

The Patriot was in a dilemma. Since the night he had caught a glimpse of the dear face of the Madonna (his Madonna!) on the TV screen, and heard for himself the rapture with which the native speaker greeted the apparition, he had been thrown into a rare flummox of indecision. For a man used to a lifetime of taking orders and obeying them, and for whom the problems of nationalism had always been crystal clear, these were suddenly muddy waters. He had gleaned enough from An Nuacht to know that the hunt was on for the Dancing Madonna. He had gleaned enough too to know that there was a plethora of prophecies doing

247

the rounds promising great results that would ensue if ever the Madonna and the Pope were to be united.

What if the foolish talk turned out to be true? What if her prophecy, as yet untranslated, were to foretell a united Ireland when the clans had gathered? The united Ireland he had dedicated his life to! He could die in peace at last. He alone knew the true whereabouts of the icon they were searching for. Had he the right to hold up the course of history? How would generations as yet unborn view him if it ever got out that he, the Patriot, had stood in the way of the republic!

The Derry ones had hardly cleared the town, with Peadar among them (full fare paid), than the Patriot made up his mind. He and Eugene would drive to Dublin proudly displaying the statue for all to see and take their chances with the rest.

He fetched the stepladder from the back and carried it up the stairs. Laboriously he prised open the trapdoor that led into the loft. He hauled himself up into the roofspace. He dusted the Madonna with his sleeve and carried her reverentially down the ladder.

'*Tá muid ag dul go mBaile Cliath*,' he told Eugene, who knew better than to question an order.

Inside the wreckage of the Martyrs Memorial it was cold despite the fire, but outside there was now the hint of heat in the sun. McCoy opened the Bible, a ritual he had observed unchanged since the station's collapse and let the pages of the decaying book flick through his fingers, searching for consolation.

The Lord would direct his hand. His finger lighted on a text; he opened his eyes and read it:

'Is thy servant a dog, that he should do great things?'

What did it mean? Who was the dog and what were the great things? There was a time he could have given an interpretation, when he still had that gift. He puzzled over its cryptic pithiness, examining it from every angle. He tried reading it backwards for hidden clues. Maybe the Lord in His own good time would vouchsafe an explanation. More than any man living, McCoy knew to be patient and not doubt or question His ways.

He held his hand once more above the sacred words, closed his eyes tightly and offered up a plea for heavenly guidance. His hand began to tremble. Then his whole body began to shake as the power of the Lord moved through him. His finger, poised above the page, stabbed violently downwards; once, twice, three times on to the sacred text. 'Thank you Lord for this sign!' he shouted. The force of the power holding his hand on the page was so great that he could hardly prise his fingers free. He read what was written, mouthing silent thanks for the familiar words. 'And the ravens brought him bread and flesh in the morning, and bread and flesh in the evening: and he drank of the brook.'

'Breakfast,' he thought, 'Praise the Lord!'

Out of the corner of his eye he had already seen the figure of Magee pedalling across the Shambles.

The butcher let him finish eating before he started talking. The Union Jack sausages were back, a desperate ploy on Magee's part to ingratiate himself with the Loyalist hardliners of the district. McCoy, who preferred his offal a uniform grey, dissected them carefully, separating out the red from the white and the blue, scrutinizing each bite suspiciously before sampling it. But hunger soon got the better of him and Magee watched with relief as he mopped up the technicolored juices with the last of Lily's soda farl and washed the lot down with a mouthful of tea. He belched and gave thanks. Only then did McCoy turn to him. He looked him over in silence for a minute or two before proclaiming, 'Like a dog returneth to its vomit, the fool returneth to his folly.'

Magee winced inwardly but didn't rise to the bait.

'Brother McCoy,' he began, 'there's something going on that you need to know about.'

He interrupted him. 'Will you not pray, Sammy Magee, and ask the Lord to cleanse you of your sins!'

'I will, surely.' He got to his feet and knelt down among the rusting rubble. McCoy prayed silently for a while, then springing to his feet took up the book and let it fall open at random.

'His fame was raised throughout all the country. Joshua, Chapter Six, Verse Twenty!'

'Your people need you like never before . . .'

McCoy started to interrupt him again but the Portadown man had heard enough.

'Jesus Christ!' he roared. 'I've already told you I'm sorry for the way things turned out. Do you want to rub my nose in it altogether? That's all in the past now. There is a new and terrible threat facing us! Even as the loyalist people sleep the wolf is closing in on them. If you had any idea of the risk I'm running coming here to tell you this, you'd know I'm serious.'

'Why me, Sammy Magee? What has this got to do with me?'

'What would you say if I told you that the Pope of Rome was about to set up his headquarters on this very spot? Right here on the Shambles! What would you say if I told you that at this very minute they are marching north, into Ulster, with the Harlot of Rome at their head? What would you say if I told you that they are searching high and low for their so-called Madonna, who's told them to take over the whole country, driving the Protestants into the sea?'

'I wonder why you're telling me all this. Aren't there enough hard men to be going on with in Portadown, or are you too scared to approach them?'

'There are traitors everywhere. Look at us now. Caught like rats in a trap, at the mercy of our enemies!'

'What are you asking me to do? Have I not borne enough burdens and suffered enough lashes for my people? And what thanks have I ever got?'

'This is our last chance! A chance to redeem ourselves in the eyes of the hard men. Ulster needs one man, only one man, brave enough and confident enough in his righteousness to put his life on the line.'

McCoy looked at him directly for the first time. 'Do you think I'm fucking mad altogether?'

'Not mad, Brother McCoy, but filled with the grace of the Lord. We'll go together! Like Daniel into the lion's den. Fearing

250

no man! Showing them what men are made of. Standing up for Ulster and shouting No Surrender in their faces.'

'You want me to go to Dublin?' McCoy said slowly as the enormity of Magee's plan began to unfold. 'You're the one who's mad!'

'No, brother! We'll defy them, throw their papist superstition back in their faces. We'll spoil their plans and fuddle their strat-agems. And we will prevail for the Lord will be on our side!'

'There's two or three million taigs gathered in Dublin . . .'

'And we'll take them all on, armed only with our Bible faith. Think of the look on Schnozzle Durante's face when you turn up to spoil his big day! Think of what he did to your daughter!'

McCoy's eye was drawn involuntarily to the postcards pinned to the wall above the remains of the dresser. Old King George and his stern-faced family still glared down at them through the grime. Magee fell silent, letting the other dwell on what he had said.

'Let us pray on this together, Brother Samuel,' McCoy said. 'Let us ask the Lord's advice.'

But even as he spoke his mind was already made up.

Eugene was moving awkwardly across the square under the weight of his precious cargo. If the Patriot had only spoken up a few hours earlier they could have found room on a bus or a van. Now nothing would do him but they'd set out for Dublin on their own, when every last sinner in Irish Street had gone.

Rust had eaten through the chassis of the ice-cream van and half its windows were broken. He hadn't seen McCoy drive it for months. There was no way this heap of scrap would make it to Hamiltonsbawn, much less Dublin. But the Patriot's wish was his command. He had left him in front of the bar room mirror, carefully donning his regimentals, black glasses, gloves and beret.

There was no sign of McCoy round the place; Eugene pre-sumed he'd be sleeping it off in the back somewhere. He noticed the bike abandoned in the porch. It wasn't like McCoy to have company, he thought. He climbed on to the roof of the van and

251

it lurched ominously under his weight with a muffled clang of chimes. He took the wrench from his pocket and began to unscrew the rusty bolts that held the shattered bakelite ice-cream cone in place. He slithered down, hoisted the Madonna up and clambered up after her. He had to rough-horse the bracket till it fitted round her bad ankle, then tighten the bolts till he was sure she would hold. He jiggled her but she was rock steady. The Dancing Madonna, lopsided but proud, now stood atop the ice-cream van like a masthead on a schooner.

Eugene slithered down once more, threw the cone with its faded Union Jack livery into the gutter, and hurried back over the Shambles to fetch the Patriot.

❖

'The Lord opened the mouth of the ass, and she said unto Balaam, what have I done unto thee?' McCoy bellowed suddenly.

'I don't quite follow you there, brother.'

'And thou shalt become an astonishment, a proverb, and a byword among all nations!'

'I still don't quite get your drift, but I like the sound of it.'

'At her feet he bowed, he fell, he lay down; at her feet he bowed, he fell; where he bowed there he fell down dead.'

'Them's fighting words all right!'

'And it came to pass when the people heard the sound of the trumpet, and the people shouted with a great shout, that the wall fell down flat, so that the people went up into the city.'

'Hallelujah,' shouted Magee. 'Praise the Lord!'

'Get the starting handle, Magee! We're going to Dublin!'

McCoy scampered into the box-room and furiously began to rummage among the garbage. He emerged holding high Chastity's old accordion. It was decrepit now, most of its reeds broken and out of tune. But as he strapped it on and opened the bellows, it blared again into life.

'Abide With Me! The anthem of our people! Sing along, Mister Magee! We'll beard the lion in its den, if it's the last thing we do!'

Without another look backwards, McCoy strode out of the

ruins of his chapel and into the Shambles, Magee stumbling after him, doing his best to join in.

The Patriot, resplendent in the uniform of the old brigade, emerged in time to see the ice-cream van, topped with the Madonna, disappear in a cloud of dirty diesel fumes in the direction of the hills of South Armagh. Eugene ran to the corner of the square after it, shouting pointless abuse. He heard the van splutter to a halt at the foot of Irish Street, then cough into life again as Magee crashed down through the gears. He turned back to the bar. They were abandoned, alone, impotent. They listened till the drone of the motor had faded over the far side of the Black Pig's Dyke.

A small figure emerged from the shadows at the far side of the Shambles. The figure of a girl, carrying a battered suitcase, walking awkwardly the length of English Street. Eugene and the Patriot watched as she stopped to reconnoitre the area, slowly scrutinizing the lowly houses, the hucksters' stalls, the deserted outhouses that ringed the Shambles. She turned her attention at last to the ruins of the Martyrs Memorial Chapel, standing forlornly in front of it without moving. She struggled over to the Temperance Tea Rooms and examined the notice that McGuffin had tacked above the door, offering refuge to fallen women. She stood for a long time as if undecided what to do. Then she pushed it open and stepped inside.

Chastity McCoy, heavy with child, had returned to the place of her birth.

From the helicopter above the deserted city, O'Malley spotted the van while it was still on the far side of Drumchondra. All his instincts told him it meant trouble. Why had it not been stopped? The Garda had their orders; nothing was to move on the streets within twenty miles of the Park. He lifted the field glasses and tried to steady them. Something odd was happening. The Guards on the checkpoints were waving it through. Odder still, he saw they were kneeling in the road, crossing themselves. The glasses focused and he saw for the first time clearly that it was a battered ice-cream van careening through the empty streets.

Unmolested, McCoy was speeding into Dublin in a pall of fumes. Magee had no need to ask directions; at every intersection the Guards were clearing the street and waving them through. O'Malley swooped lower. The Popemobile had finished its stately circuit of the Park and was heading for the gates, picking up speed. Schnozzle stood erect in the prow, acknowledging the hysterical homage of the faithful. The ice-cream van was racing through the city centre now, to the unmistakable sound of 'Papa Piccolino', straight on course for the Park. O'Malley lifted the radio and began to scream into it. No one was listening. They were all on their knees now as Magee, with a squeal of burning rubber swung through the gates of the Phoenix Park and put his boot flat to the floor.

On the roof the Madonna had begun to dance, a stately, one-legged pavane.